TIGHT WHITE COTTON

'The cane, please, if you would be so kind,' Ottershaw addressed me, and I handed it to him.

April began to whimper as the cane was laid across her bottom and tapped twice on the tender flesh, sending little ripples across it. Ottershaw lifted the thin stick, then paused, poised to strike.

'Is she noisy?' he asked me.

'Quite,' I answered. 'I usually beat her in my office.'

'Perhaps we should gag her?'

'Perhaps.'

'I find a girl's knickers usually make an effective gag.'

'Pull them off, then.'

Why not visit Penny's website at:
www.pennybirch.com

By the same author:

THE INDIGNITIES OF ISABELLE
THE INDISCRETIONS OF ISABELLE
(writing as Cruella)

A NEXUS CLASSIC

TIGHT WHITE COTTON

Penny Birch

This book is a work of fiction.
In real life, make sure you practise safe sex.

This Nexus Classic edition 2005

First published in 2000 by
Nexus
Thames Wharf Studios
Rainville Road
London W6 9HA

3

www.nexus-books.co.uk

ISBN 978 0 352 33970 6

Penguin Random House is committed to a sustainable future for
our business, our readers and our planet. This book is made from
Forest Stewardship Council® certified paper.

MIX
Paper | Supporting
responsible forestry
FSC® C018179

Printed and bound in Great Britain by Clays Ltd, Elcograf S.p.A.
Typeset by TW Typesetting, Plymouth, Devon

Contents

1

Taking the Cane

I never expected to end up having my bottom smacked – not me, not Patricia Laurdale. Certainly I didn't expect to be caned by a fat boy three years younger than me and not even out of school, let alone with my bare bottom showing!

Yet that is what he did. He made me bend right over and stick my bottom out. He pulled up my dress and he took down my knickers. He told me I had a pretty bottom, and then he beat me across it!

It started when Daddy was made headmaster of Fice's School in Yorkshire. Fice's was very different from the place where he had been deputy: remote, small and, above all, old-fashioned. The boys still wore uniforms with britches as well as gowns and mortar-boards. It was terribly smart, but would have seemed ridiculous in a modern town. In Wherndale it didn't seem ridiculous at all, but thoroughly in keeping with the surroundings.

As I was the headmaster's daughter the boys were all very respectful towards me, polite and helpful and even a bit afraid. I wondered why at first, because at St Mark's, where we had been before, the boys had been pretty cheeky. I'd been younger, it was true, but that wasn't the reason. St Mark's was really quite progressive and, while boys were given corporal punishment, it was rare, and only for the most serious offences. At

Fice's it seemed to be given for just about anything, and it was almost always the cane. A huge book was kept in Daddy's study to record all this, and I have to admit that reading it filled me with a certain horrid fascination. I wasn't supposed to look at it, of course, but with Daddy teaching so much of the time I had plenty of opportunity and not a lot else to do.

That was the main problem with Fice's: boredom. The nearest village was three miles away, and that was no more than a couple of dozen poky little houses clustered around a church. I kept house for Daddy, but that still left me with too much time on my hands. Eventually I asked if I might attend some of the senior boys' societies. Daddy didn't really approve but eventually permitted it as long as there was a master present. Unfortunately I wasn't allowed to join sports clubs, and most of the others were duller than anything. The literary society seemed the best and Father approved, so I joined in.

As always the boys were all terribly polite to me, but most were very formal and never saw me as anything other than the headmaster's daughter. None of them dared flirt with me, which I'd rather been looking forward to. What they did remind me of were the boys from the Billy Bunter stories, all manly and honourable, with no time for girls. We even had Bunter himself, a fat boy called Ottershaw. Daddy had actually banned the Bunter books at Fice's because he thought they undermined the dignity of the school, but all the confiscated copies were stacked in a corner of our library, so I'd read plenty.

Ottershaw was actually the one I got on best with, because he was less stuffy than the others, and plump and cheerful. All the formality was a bit intimidating, but he wasn't like that, and as time went by I found it increasingly easy to talk to him. There was something else as well, something that I found both puzzling and intriguing. The only other woman at the school even close to my age was the junior matron, Elaine McKeown. We got on well, but when I happened to mention that I thought Percy Ottershaw was one of the nicest of the boys she gave me a really funny look, then warned me to keep my distance because he was dirty. She wouldn't explain more than that and became very embarrassed when I pressed her.

There can be nothing like a mystery to make sure someone doesn't take the advice they've been given. I was desperate to know what Percy had done to make Elaine blush so. Certainly she didn't mean he was physically dirty, because he was one of the vainest boys in the school and absolutely fastidious about his personal appearance. Beyond that I couldn't imagine, unless he'd made a pass at her, and that didn't seem very likely at all. Boys did admire her and she sometimes received chocolates and flowers, being very pretty and not being the headmaster's daughter. She was engaged, though, to some terribly daring artist, and was obviously out of reach. I couldn't see Percy approaching her, especially when he was so much less attractive than most of his friends.

I was determined to find out, and I thought I knew how to do it. There was another reason for finding out the secret as well. After looking in the punishment book I really wanted to know how it felt to be caned. Not myself, of course, but from a boy's point of view. If I knew whatever dirty little secret was between Percy and Elaine, then I could ask him. Besides, he was so respectful to me that I was sure he would do just as I said. All I needed to do was find enough time to talk to him alone.

Wednesdays and Saturdays were half-days, and nearly all the boys were down on the playing fields. Percy wasn't in any teams and didn't like to watch, while he was senior enough not to do compulsory sports. In fact it was his last term at Fice's, so I only had a couple of weeks to catch him alone. Normally he would sit in his study and read all afternoon, which wasn't nearly private enough, but on one particularly hot Wednesday his housemaster decided to chivvy all the lazy boys outside and I happened to be passing as Percy came out of the main door. He was looking puzzled and a little cross, obviously unsure what to do with himself, then he began to walk slowly up the road towards the valley head.

I didn't want anyone to see us together, so I followed a little way behind, keeping out of sight. He walked really slowly, making it easy to follow him, but he kept going, out of the school grounds and on to the rough track that led to the open moor. When he got to the woods at the valley head he slowed down even more and began to look around, as if searching for something. We were well away from the school so I decided to approach him and managed to sneak up really close before he saw me. When he did he gave a start and for a moment looked really guilty, as if I had caught him up to no good.

'Hello, Percy. What are you up to?' I greeted him, and I'm sure he blushed.

'Just going for a walk,' he answered quickly. 'It's a beautiful day, don't you think?'

'Yes, beautiful,' I answered. 'May I walk with you?'

He agreed, although I was sure there was just a touch of reluctance, and we set off together. I had had it all planned: how I would tell him I knew about Elaine and threaten to tell my father if he didn't give me the full story. In practice it wasn't so easy, and I was still trying to get up the courage for it when we reached the old quarry at the head of the track. It was a lonely place, with rusting machinery, two old cars, and quite a few old beer cans and cigarette stubs lying around, which made me realise why Percy had looked so guilty when I caught up with him. Suddenly I had a reason to put my question.

'Were you coming up here to drink beer or smoke?' I demanded, trying to look really shocked.

Both were caning offences, with expulsion for persistent offenders, and from the colour of Percy's face I knew at once that I had found him out.

'Neither,' he stammered, but his face was red, just like a drawing I'd seen of Billy Bunter getting caught raiding another boy's tuck-box.

'Don't lie to me!' I snapped. 'I'll tell my father if you don't tell the truth.'

'And if I do?'

'I won't. I promise.'

He hesitated, obviously not trusting me, but he really didn't have much of a choice. Then he gave a shrug and reached inside his jacket to pull out a little bottle. Drinking was as forbidden for me as it was for the boys, Daddy being strictly teetotal, and just the sight of that dark bottle sent a wonderfully illicit thrill through me.

'What is it?' I demanded.

'Wine,' he said sullenly.

'Let's drink it, then,' I answered.

He brightened immediately and smiled, then nodded towards the old sheds at the back of the quarry. I followed him, feeling guilty and excited. The entrance to the shed he chose was choked with brambles, but he held them aside for me and let them swing back behind us, sealing us off. The inside was big and almost empty, with a great block of concrete that must once have had some machinery on it. A long window gave us a view out over the woods and the track, another faced towards the blank rock face of the quarry. It was perfect for illicit goings-on, expect that if anybody did come there was no obvious way out.

'If we see anybody we go out the back window and up a little gully in the cliff,' Percy told me as if reading

5

my thoughts. 'It's a bit tricky, but if I can do it you should be able to.'

'Open the wine, then.'

He took the bottle from his pocket, then a corkscrew. I watched, feeling nervous, guilty and wonderfully conspiratorial, as he carefully drew the cork. It popped open, and to my surprise he drew a small glass from another pocket, filled it half-full, sniffed the wine and then passed it to me.

'It's a 'forty-five,' he told me. 'A good year, but a bit young. Still, it should be all right in a half.'

I took a sip, then a swallow, finding a strange, earthy taste, then a hot feeling in the back of my throat. Nodding in what I hoped was a knowledgeable way I passed the glass back to Percy, who took a sip, frowned at the glass, then took another.

'Not bad,' he stated. 'Still, who'd believe me if I said I'd drunk it with the headmaster's daughter!'

I giggled, still thinking of Billy Bunter, but of an altogether more wicked Bunter, and a rude one, if Elaine McKeown was to be believed.

'You'd get the cane if we were caught,' I said. 'You know that, don't you?'

'It's absurd,' he answered. 'I'm eighteen. I bought this in a shop in Harrogate, quite legally. The school has no right to stop me.'

'You'd still get caned.'

'Not if they don't catch me.'

'You're very brave. Doesn't it hurt terribly?'

Percy didn't answer immediately, but took a sip of his wine, then passed the glass back to me and sat down on the concrete block.

'Yes, it does,' he admitted, 'but it's soon over.'

'But isn't it dreadfully shameful? I mean you have to take your britches down, don't you?'

'And our underpants. You just have to think about something else.'

6

'I couldn't stand it! I know I'd cry and everything.'

'It's worse if you make an exhibition of yourself – then you get teased. Anyway, you girls are lucky. You don't get beaten, do you?'

'No! That would be awful, not to mention indecent!'

'Why? I mean, why more so than for a boy?'

'Well, it's not the same! I mean, they couldn't – not to a girl!'

'They used to, knickers down and everything. I think they still do in some schools.'

I was blushing furiously and took a swallow of my wine to hide my confusion. Just the way he'd mentioned the girls having their knickers pulled down had set my stomach fluttering: it was just too much, too awful to think about. I mean a girl, having to pull her knickers down and show her bare bottom!

'I'm sure that's not true,' I said, trying to sound haughty.

Percy shrugged and took the glass back from me to refill it, then held it up to the bright sunlight to admire the colour, apparently indifferent to my blushes. He didn't seem bothered, but I desperately wanted to carry on talking about being beaten, even though it was doing strange things to me.

'It's worse for a girl,' I said defensively.

'I disagree,' he answered. 'You have bottoms, just like us boys, only better padded.'

'But . . . but . . .' I managed and then stopped.

I desperately wanted to explain that it was far ruder for a girl to show herself bare than for a boy, which I thought everybody understood. Apparently Percy didn't.

'What does it feel like?' I asked, keen to keep talking – but not about girls getting it.

'Let me do it to you and you'll find out.' He laughed.

'No! You couldn't!' I exclaimed, horrified by the proposal.

7

Suddenly he wasn't the safe, silly Billy Bunter any more, but a fat, wicked devil who liked the idea of a girl getting smacked across her bare bottom.

'I know about you and Elaine McKeown, you know,' I said quickly. 'You'd better not try anything funny!'

'You do, really?' he answered. 'And you came up here with me, alone?'

I couldn't answer him, because I didn't really know – but whatever it was, it was obviously pretty dirty, far worse than I'd imagined, and suddenly I was scared. Percy might have been fat and jolly and soft, but he was still a man and bigger than me, too.

'Don't worry!' He laughed. 'I've never made Elaine do anything she didn't want to, and I wouldn't to you.'

'Do you cane her?' I asked, trying to stop my jaw trembling.

'No,' he answered. 'You don't really know, do you? I'm sure she wouldn't tell you.'

'You tell me, then.'

'No, it wouldn't be fair. You might tell someone else.'

'I wouldn't. I promise.'

'How do I know? We haven't got a secret, so how could I be sure of you?'

'We do have a secret. We're drinking and we shouldn't be.'

'That won't do, because I'd get the worst of it if we were found out. Let me cane you and I'll tell.'

'You pig!'

'There's no need for a temper. The way you've been going on about it you obviously want it.'

'I do not!'

'Then I won't tell you about Elaine. I don't mind.'

I didn't answer, because I couldn't. The horrible little pig wanted to see my bare bottom, and then beat me. I now knew what Elaine meant about him being dirty; I guessed he had caught her out, just like he had caught me out. The difference was that I wasn't going to do it, even though my tummy was fluttering and part of me wanted nothing more than the dirty behaviour he was suggesting.

'Tell you what,' he said suddenly. 'Let me see your knickers and I'll tell you about Elaine.'

I just stood there with my mouth open, appalled by just how dirty he was being, but fascinated by the whole thing, by the thought of showing my bottom, by the thought of him making Elaine do rude things. Most of all I was fascinated by the thought of the caning he had the nerve to suggest I wanted.

'Come on,' he insisted. 'Just a peep.'

'You are a dirty pig, Ottershaw, and I ought to tell my father,' I answered, but I was already pulling up my dress.

'No,' he said. 'Don't. I want to do that.'

'Oh, all right,' I snapped.

'Turn around, then,' he said happily, 'and stick it out a bit.'

I stamped my foot as I turned and pushed out my bottom, utterly furious but unable to stop what I was doing. His hands went to the hem of my dress and he started to lift, slowly, revealing my legs, then my stocking tops and lastly the seat of my knickers. He didn't just take his peep but kept my skirt up – I could feel his eyes on my bottom, which felt very big and very prominent inside my knickers. I was just glad I'd put on plain white ones that morning.

'You're beautiful, Patty,' he whispered and kissed my bottom through the seat of my knickers.

A shiver went right through me, a lovely feeling, so that even though it all still felt dirty and improper, it didn't feel wrong.

'I'm going to take your knickers down, Patty,' he went on. 'They need to be down to show that lovely bottom, all bare and beautiful.'

I could have stopped him, but I didn't want to. He kissed my bottom again, and then, ever so slowly, he began to pull down my knickers. I felt every inch of it as my waistband slid down, revealing what I was supposed to keep secret, exposing me with his face just inches from my flesh. He took them right down, settling them upside down around my thighs, then kissed me on my bottom again, on my bare bottom.

'Can I cane you?' he asked softly. 'Please? Oh, you've such a pretty bottom, Patty, let me whack you.'

So that was how I ended up showing my bare bottom to the fattest boy in the school, and getting whacked on it. I said he could, although I could hardly believe it was me coming out with the words. Percy ran off immediately and I waited, bending over with my dress tucked up and my bare bottom showing. I could see him in the quarry, running to one of the old cars and snapping off the aerial, then running back, swishing it from side to side and grinning from ear to ear. I hung my head in shame for what I was doing, and then he was back behind me.

'I'm going to give you six,' he said, 'like we get. Then you'll know how it feels. And when it's over you'll thank me for it, because it's good for you, because it increases your sense of humility before God, or at least that's what your father always says.'

I gave a sob as I stuck my bottom out for it, looking back and waiting for the pain. He gave the aerial one last swish and then smacked me with it, right across my bum. I jumped and squealed as a fiery pain shot through my bottom, really stinging, like nettles, only worse.

'No, stop, stop!' I begged and covered my poor smarting bottom with my hands.

'Come on, Patty, push it out again,' he said, actually really kindly. 'It's what we have to do when your father beats us, so you must take it, for the sake of fairness, you see.'

'But I don't get caned!' I wailed. 'And I haven't been naughty anyway.'

10

'You've been drinking,' he answered. 'I'd get caned for that. Why shouldn't you? Now stick that pretty bottom out like a good girl.'

I sobbed again but didn't take my hands away from my bottom. Maybe he was right – maybe I did deserve to be punished – but it hurt so much. The first cut had begun to throb and my whole bottom felt warm, also heavy in my hands, the cheeks soft and sensitive, with the cane welt a fiery line of raised flesh running across both of them.

'Take your hands away, Patty,' he ordered, gently but firmly, 'and put them on your head. That's what we have to do, so it's only right you do the same.'

If he hadn't put that first stripe across me I don't think I'd have done it, but I did, despite knowing how painful it really was. With my hands on top of my head I pushed my bottom out and shut my eyes tight, waiting for the stroke with my whole body shaking. It came, hard, making me cry out again and jump up and down, then clutch my bottom.

'Hands on head,' Percy said. 'We get extra if we take them away. So should you, so now it's going to be seven.'

I could feel the tears starting from my eyes but I put my hands back on my head and stuck my bottom out again, simply unable to disobey him. My whole bottom was now throbbing and there was a big lump in my throat, but there was another feeling too: my fanny, strangely warm down between my thighs.

He gave me the third stroke and I jumped and squealed again, but managed to keep my hands on my head. I was shaking really hard, and the tears were threatening to spill from my eyes, but I pushed my bottom out again, beaten and obedient and needing more of the hot feeling that was building up between my legs. The fourth cut hit my bottom low and I really yelled and my knees buckled, making my bottom open behind before I quickly got back into position.

11

I swallowed hard, choking back my tears. He had seen my fanny from behind, I knew he had, and maybe my bottom-hole too, which was even worse. The fifth stroke caught me while I was still thinking about the dirty shame of letting a boy see down between my bottom cheeks and I jumped and cried out like before. As I closed my legs I felt my wetness, between my thighs. I was sure he would see and know I was excited, which had me shaking my head in shame.

'You see, it's no different for girls,' he said. 'You act just the same, shaking your head to dull the pain, swallowing to check your tears. A whacking is a whacking, boy or girl.'

I didn't answer, because it wasn't the pain that was making me shake my head but the awful fact that the beating was making me excited. In fact, the fifth stroke had hardly seemed to hurt at all, and my bottom just felt as if it was glowing. I pushed it out, not too far, then all the way, because I just couldn't stop it any more: I wanted my fanny showing, and my bottom-hole. I wanted him to see it all.

'Oh, you are pretty,' he said and my tears started to come.

The sixth stroke bit into my bottom and I cried aloud but quickly got back into my lewd pose, waiting for punishment with my bottom cheeks wide and my little hole showing.

'Just one more, darling,' he said and the seventh stroke came down hard across the fullest part of my cheeks, right over my bottom-hole.

I jerked and squealed again but relief was flooding through me, a great, wonderful wave of it. Percy was holding his arms out to me as I turned and I went to him. He had beaten me and should have been the last person I wanted comfort from, but it wasn't like that. It was because he had beaten me that I wanted to hold him, and hold him with my knickers still down and with the evidence of my punishment showing clearly behind me. I was sobbing and shaking as he held me close to him, crying freely into his neck as he stroked my hair and patted my inflamed bottom. I wanted to ask him to touch me, to feel my fanny, but I couldn't get the words out, and then he had taken my hand and was guiding it gently downwards.

'Oh God,' was all I managed, as he put my hand to the bulge in his britches.

'Do me in your hand, Patty,' he whispered. 'Come on, I'll take it out.'

I could feel his prick as he fiddled with his buttons, first a hard bar of flesh through his britches and underpants, then a hot, solid shaft, stiff and bare as he squeezed my fingers around it. He began to tug, making me toss him while he fondled my beaten bottom, squeezing the cheeks and running his fingers along the welts. His lips touched my cheek and then my mouth and we were kissing, our tongues touching as I jerked at his cock and held him tight against me. He took his hand off mine but I kept on tossing him as he began to fumble with the buttons of my dress, opening it and then pulling my breasts roughly out of my bra. As they came free his fingers went into the crack of my bottom, touching the hole, and then there was something wet and sticky all over my hand.

He moved back immediately, panting and red-faced with his prick sticking up out of his britches. I tried to give him a dirty look, but it didn't really work.

'That was great,' he puffed. 'Thanks, Patty.'

'It's all over my hand!'

'Just flick it off, or you can borrow my hankie.'

I took the hankie and did my best to clean myself up. He had sat down but his prick was still out and I was wondering if he was going to demand more.

'Do you want to do it?' he asked. 'I don't mind helping.'

'Do what?'

'Wank off, like you did for me.'

'Girls can't do that!'

'Yes they can. Just rub in your slit and you'll soon see.'

'No, I couldn't, I mean . . .'

At that instant the sound of the chapel bells rang out across the air, striking five o'clock. Percy's expression immediately changed to one of panic and he began to struggle with his britches buttons. I knew why, because we had walked a good hour to get to the quarry and supper was at six. As a senior he would have to tick the junior boys off a list as they came in, and if he wasn't there it was going to take a lot of explaining, at the least. Pausing only to drain the bottle of wine and give me a fleeting kiss, he left.

I was pulling up my knickers as I watched him run away down the track, then slow to a hurried walk as he reached the woods. My feelings were running wild: burning shame, high excitement and frustration all at once. I was wondering if I ought to try what he had suggested and rub myself, but I couldn't bring myself to do it and left, quickly tidying myself up and making for the school.

As I walked through the warm afternoon sun I tried to come to terms with my feelings. My bottom stung dreadfully, while my hand was still sticky from what he had done over it. I wanted to hate him for what he'd done, but I couldn't, because there was a tingly feeling between my legs and my knickers were wet over my fanny. It wouldn't go away, either, as it always had done on the few other occasions I'd let boys touch me. Instead, the hot throbbing of my bottom kept me excited and I knew that in the end I was just going to have to put my hand down my knickers and do it.

It happened when I reached the edge of the woods, the very spot where I'd caught up with Percy. I'd been so sure of myself then, so certain I'd get what I wanted. Now I had seven cane welts across my bottom and a wet fanny, while he had made me toss his cock and had then gone back for tea. He hadn't even told me about Elaine, although I could guess, because I was fairly sure I'd done it myself. I could even imagine her with his prick in her hand, tugging away with her uniform up at the back and her knickers pushed down, perhaps with a red bottom, just like mine. It was too much – I simply had to do it, and with a last guilty look around I sneaked in among the trees.

I quickly found a quiet spot and tucked my dress up, just as it had been while I was beaten. My knickers came down again, pushed slowly off to expose my whacked bottom to the wood. As I started to rub myself I thought of my beating – how he had pulled down my knickers and made me stick my bottom out, how he had punished me so hard, with stroke after stroke of the wicked aerial. Afterwards I'd taken his prick in my hand and tossed him off, a really dirty thing to make a girl do. Only now I was doing it to myself, rubbing at my fanny with my bottom bare because I'd been caned and I'd liked it ...

A really strange feeling started in my fanny and I thought I was going to wet myself, only for the most beautiful sensation to come over me, again and again, in waves as I rubbed and rubbed and thought of my poor beaten bottom sticking out behind me. It was lovely, like nothing I'd ever experienced before, but I felt awful afterwards, really guilty and dirty. I felt I ought to be punished, but then I had been, in a way, in advance.

Despite my pleasure, and what he had taught me, I felt that Percy had really taken advantage of me. The only crumb of comfort was that he had been caned himself and so at least he knew what he had put me through. In fact, thinking back on it, he seemed to have

15

been taking a sort of revenge, as if by whacking me he could get back at Daddy. The prick-tossing had come later, once he had become excited over my bare bottom. I determined that I would look at the punishment book as soon as I could and read all about how many strokes he had taken and what they had been for. That would make me feel better.

I didn't get a chance that day, but I did see Percy the day after and got a chance to demand the truth about Elaine. He admitted it was fair and that she did toss him off, then told me the outrageous and dirty lie that she liked to wet her knickers on purpose and then rub herself through them. I knew he was teasing because I couldn't believe Elaine would do such a thing, and I went home more determined than ever to read about his punishments.

In fact I was so determined that I waited until Daddy was asleep and then sneaked down to his study with a torch. The punishment book was on his desk as ever, and I was smiling to myself as I opened the thick green cover. Inside was line after line of Daddy's handwriting, with that of other masters as well, recording caning after caning, each set out to the same neat formula. I began to turn the pages, scanning each for the name Ottershaw. It wasn't in the first few pages, but that wasn't surprising as he was so senior, as well as careful, as I knew to my cost. I reached the start of Daddy's time as headmaster and his name still hadn't appeared. That put a lump in my throat because if he had had his revenge on me for a whacking from some other man, then it should have been that man's daughter who got it, not me!

I kept turning the pages, feeling more and more agitated, until at last I got to nineteen forty-seven, which had to be the year he came in. His name wasn't there. Percy Ottershaw had never been caned at all.

16

2

Wet Knickers for Elaine

I can remember when I started to like the idea of wetting my knickers, to the day. It was the second Sunday in December, nineteen forty-eight and I was in the choir at St Mary's, the church in my home village. We had been kept in to practise carols after the morning service, and the vicar was making us go over the same piece again and again. Betty Mills was next to me, a girl who had just recently moved to the village. She was very pretty, with curly black hair and large, dark eyes, shy and quiet. We'd been standing there for ages, and I was uncomfortable myself, so I wasn't surprised when she began to get fidgety. It was when she started to make little treading motions with her feet and wriggle her hips that I realised she needed to pee. She was blushing with embarrassment, too, and I felt really sorry for her.

Then it happened. Betty gave a little soft groan and I knew she'd done it. I looked down and could see her puddle spreading out around her shoes, while her face was scarlet with shame. I felt for her really strongly. There was a knot in my stomach and I was close to tears, just from thinking how awful she would feel with the pee running through her knickers and down her legs into her shoes before making the tell-tale puddle on the floor. She was bound to get caught, and the vicar wasn't going to be sympathetic, because he never was, about anything. He would probably tell her off in front of everybody, then make her clean it up with a mop and bucket while there were still other people around. It was dreadful, and I was wishing I could do something to help her, or at least comfort her, but I could do nothing.

It was the strength of my emotion when Betty had wet herself that made the idea exciting for me. If I had felt like that, then she must have experienced something ten times worse. The thought made me wet between the legs, although I didn't understand why. That night I touched myself over the thought of poor Betty struggling to hold her pee, then wetting herself, then her humiliation afterwards, when she had been made to scrub the floor while the vicar stood over her looking solemn and disapproving, as if it was her fault and not his. I felt awful afterwards, but the thought was there, and has stayed with me ever since.

It took ages before I plucked up the courage to do it myself. Living at home made it really difficult anyway, because there were always people around and I shared my room with my two sisters. I couldn't really do it out in the woods either, because it would mean coming home with wet knickers or no knickers and that was really risky. I didn't want it to be like poor Betty either, with everyone getting to know, but I did need to feel I had no choice. That was the real excitement – the awful helplessness of knowing it was going to happen but not being able to do anything about it. In the village I could always get to a loo. In the countryside I could nip behind a hedge and whip my knickers down. Several times I let myself get really desperate before giving in, but I never actually let it happen.

My chance didn't come for just over a year, by which time I was in training as a nurse. This was in Sheffield, and I was staying in a big Victorian accommodation block. I'd been home and came back on the train late at night. It was cold and I was feeling a bit miserable, and certainly not in the mood for being naughty with myself – not until I started to need to go. When I first felt it I was going to use the train loo, but there was this big, red-faced man in my compartment who kept leering at me and I was embarrassed because he would know what I was doing. That brought back the memory of Betty in the choir stalls. I began to feel bad and rather excited and wondered if the time hadn't come to wet my knickers. The man didn't get out at any of the smaller stations, and by the time we pulled into Sheffield I was wriggling quite badly. That was the crucial moment, because it was a good three-mile walk to my block and I couldn't afford a cab, so I knew I'd never make it. There was the station loo, and I could have used it. I didn't, and as I walked away I was telling myself I was bad, but I knew I was going to do it.

The first bit was the worst, because there were plenty of people about and the streets were brightly lit, so if I'd just let go I would have made a really obvious trail along the pavement. Just thinking about it made the tears start in my eyes and I pressed on, holding myself in tight and walking with hurried little steps. By the time I got out of the city centre I was really desperate. My bladder hurt and I was breathing in gasps. An odd swimming sensation had started in my head too and I was really regretting not having gone in the station. It wasn't as lonely as I'd thought it would be either, as Christmas was coming and everybody seemed to be out making merry. Two men coming out of a pub propositioned me and I told them to go to hell, which wasn't like me at all.

One of them laughed at me and I tried to run, but I couldn't, not properly, not with my bladder so full. I stumbled, tripping on a broken paving stone, and then it happened. My bladder just exploded and my knickers were filling with pee as I sank down on all fours. I did it in front of them, sobbing brokenly as the pee gushed from my fanny and into my knickers, running down my legs and into my stockings, splashing on to my petticoat and soaking into my dress, pooling between my knees and running out in a slow trickle behind me, right to their feet. They never said a word, but just watched me soil myself in front of them until I finally got control of my legs and jumped up and ran. It was still coming out, and it went into my boots and over my coat, but I didn't care. My head was swimming with emotion, awful guilt and embarrassment, but more excitement than I had ever known before and I knew exactly what I was going to do just as soon as I was alone. I didn't even make it back to my room, but masturbated in an alley with my coat open and my dress and petticoat pulled up at the front. I could feel the warm, wet pee in my boots and the damp coldness where my wet stockings had begun to chill. My knickers were soaking and plastered to my fanny, clinging to the lips and up tight between the cheeks of my bottom. I began to rub myself, first through the pee-sodden cotton of the knickers and then down the front, with my fingers in the wet mush of my fanny, twice wet, with my juices and my piddle mingled together. The climax was beautiful, really long and really sweet, while I thought of how I'd done it on the pavement in front of two strange men.

Rory was an artist I met in my second summer as a student nurse. He was full of passion and wild ideas, and I fell for him immediately. After the staid life I'd led he seemed wonderful, and he had my virginity within a week of us meeting. He told me that he loved me for my red hair and laughing eyes, and that he would be faithful to me for ever. I was not completely naïve and I knew why he really preferred me to the others. He had found out what I was like.

Men weren't allowed into our block and I had little free time, so it was quite hard to meet. We both liked the countryside and so would take the bus out of the city and picnic in some pretty spot. Rory would always bring plenty to drink and we would end up making love in the long grass. He would bring his sketch pad as well and used to like to draw me in a dishevelled state after we'd done it. I didn't mind, and it wasn't long before I was posing nude for him, in positions that got ruder and ruder. He gave me a lot of talk about being free with my body and not scared to show my beauty, which was very flattering, but really I'm sure it was just because he liked me to flaunt my naughtiest bits for him. My bottom was his favourite, and he loved to draw me crawling or bending down, with my fanny showing between my legs. He'd draw it in detail, too, every little fold and crease, along with my bottom-hole. That embarrassed me at first, especially when he let his friends see, but all my protests earned me was another long lecture on freedom of expression.

I hadn't told Rory about liking to wet myself, but he seemed to like my embarrassment at having my intimate details shown off, so I wondered if he would like the idea of me wetting my knickers. It seemed best if he thought it was an accident, at least the first time, so I waited until one of our picnics and made sure I drank plenty. I was in a pretty blue summer dress, with just knickers underneath as he had persuaded me to go without a bra. The thought of what I intended had me really excited, and I was giggling and tipsy, just dying to let it all out.

So I did, into my knickers and all over my dress as I sat splay-legged on the rug. I put my hands to my mouth in fake shock as it happened, pretending I'd lost control of my bladder because I'd been laughing so much. Rory watched as a big wet patch spread out across my dress and over the picnic rug, then abruptly reached forwards and pulled up the hem of my skirt so that he could see my knickers. I was in heaven as he watched the pee run out through the cotton. All I needed was his lovely cock inside me while I was still wet and it would be perfect. I asked him to do it and, after a moment of shock, he began to scrabble at his fly. He had me right there, lying in a pool of my pee with my legs kicked up high and my knickers pulled aside to let him into me. It was the most glorious experience I'd yet had, and after he had come over my belly and added his sperm to my mess I lay back and masturbated for him, coming and coming until I was too weak and dizzy to carry on.

By the end of the year Rory and I were engaged. Life should have been perfect, but neither of us had enough money to live on and he was too proud to take a job instead of trying to sell his work. I managed to secure a place as junior matron at Fice's public school, up in the dales. It was nice in some ways, with my own little flat and plenty of free time. It was lonely too, miles from anywhere, and very formal, so I had to take care to seem very proper and demure. The only other woman my age was Patty Laurdale, the headmaster's daughter, who was nice but very innocent and not really all that bright. Certainly I didn't feel I could talk about anything rude with her. The boys were friendly and a lot of them had crushes on me. They were all very naïve and gentlemanly and never tried anything, except for one, who was a dirty little pig.

His name was Percy Ottershaw and he was the fattest boy in the school and also the dirtiest, as I found out. I had a little routine every evening when I went to bed. I would strip right down to my knickers and sit down on the loo, then masturbate while I peed through them, always thinking of Rory and the nice things we'd done together, until I had a climax. My window was frosted and opened out on to the roofs, so I had thought I was safe. I wasn't, not from Ottershaw. He wasn't content

22

with just peeping at me, either, but came in through the window, bold as brass and presented me with his cock!

I had jumped up when I heard the window open and foolishly tried to cover myself, so I had pee all over my chest. He had really caught me, and I was very excited, so I pulled his cock off for him, all the while telling myself it was the best way to make sure he kept quiet about my dirty habits. He came all over my breasts, which was just too much, and I made him lick me as I sat on the loo, with my knickers off to let him get at my fanny and both breasts, filthy with his mess.

Three more times he visited me before the end of term, and each time it got a little worse. The first time he made me strip and get in my bath, then told me to pee. He watched as it came out, playing with his cock all the time, then had me pull him off over my chest again while I sat in my own puddle. The second was much the same, but he had me get in the bath with my uniform on, hat and all! He got himself hard while I wet myself, then told me to kneel in it so that he could see the wet patch over my bottom. I did it, but when he started to pull my skirt up I thought he was going to have me and that was going too far. He stopped, but put it in my mouth instead and made me swallow his stuff. The third time was the last and we both knew it because he was leaving that weekend. We did it in my bed, with an incontinence sheet under the cotton one. He was nude, while I was in knickers, a girdle and stockings, which he'd told me to wear. I wet the bed while he watched, rolled up on my back so that he could see every detail as it ran out through my knickers and over the bed. When I was done he had me get in rude poses, showing my bottom and rolling about in the pee until I was sodden from head to toe. All the while he'd been pulling at himself, and when he was ready he got on top of me from behind and put his cock in the crease of my bottom. My knickers were down by then and he could have had me, but he kept his word and didn't, coming instead up between my cheeks and over my bottom-hole while his balls slapped on my fanny.

Not surprisingly I felt guilty afterwards, and not a little cross. On the other hand, he never told, and he had licked my fanny for me every time.

I stayed at Fice's for three years and nothing like that happened again. I'd spent my holidays and as many weekends as I was able with Rory, and several times he had me pee for him before we made love. His art wasn't doing any better, but we were managing, so I didn't mind. The trouble was that his work was either too rude for public consumption, or just too strange. He was picking up a bit of a following, though, among those who liked his style and were looking for somebody to paint dirty pictures for them.

I had left Fice's because Mrs White, the senior matron, had taken a post at Highfield, a frightfully prestigious school in London, and a year later wrote to suggest that I should apply for the position of her deputy. They accepted me at nearly twice my previous salary and I moved into a cosy little flat off the Fulham Road. Rory was delighted at the chance to live in the capital and moved in with me as soon as he could. We had to pretend to be married to placate the landlady, who was a frightful old frump, but when I suggested to Rory that we do it for real he said he wanted to wait until he could provide for me. I accepted his choice because I knew it would hurt his pride to be kept by me, although that was more or less how things were anyway.

Two of the people who had commissioned rude drawings from him were a couple, the Bunchevs, who dealt in art and kept a shop in Ladbroke Grove. I had been the model for both drawings. One showed me in a meadow, on my knees with my dress lifted and my knickers down, showing everything and looking back over my shoulder with a cross expression. I thought it made me look as if I'd tripped over my knickers and landed in a cow-pat, but Rory had told me that I was supposed to be looking back at a farmer who was about to take a stick to my bottom for trespassing. The other had me kneeling on a chair with my hands holding up my dress behind and no knickers at all. Again I was looking back, only instead of looking cross, I just looked sorry for myself. They were supposed to be part of a series showing the sort of emotions girls went through before being punished. The first was called *Petulance*, the second *Contrition*.

The furthest I had ever gone towards making punishment a naughty thing was when Rory suggested that I ought to be spanked for enjoying wetting my knickers. He'd never given me more than a little pat, though. Percy Ottershaw had also given my bottom a couple of slaps, but considering how much corporal punishment was used at Fice's I wasn't surprised he wanted to do it to me. The pictures had just made me giggle, but when the Bunchevs came to collect them I actually found the couple quite scary. Both were tall and very stern, as well as being a lot older than me, and they treated me like a particularly stupid child. It was Mrs Bunchev who was really into smacking girls. He just liked to watch, but both were really frank about it. After they had left I'd felt strangely vulnerable, even though they hadn't done anything.

Now we were in London the Bunchevs were virtually neighbours, and Rory was keen to impress, seeing them as a route into the mainstream art world. Nothing would do but that we had to invite them to dinner and set up a little incident so that she could spank me. I was a bit scared but agreed, knowing that Rory would be there to stop it going too far. He had told them that I was going to be in a little ballerina dress and see-through knickers to show my bottom off, and then I deliberately dressed in my most demure skirt with a pair of big white knickers underneath. When I came down Rory asked what I thought I was doing and I answered him back. Mrs Bunchev actually suggested I ought to be spanked, then and there, so I called her a pervert and the next thing I knew I was down over her knee.

From there it got completely out of my control. My skirt was pulled up and my knickers taken down while I was held helpless across Mrs Bunchev's lap. I swore and cursed and tried to bite her, really playing it up, but it made no difference and I was given a really good spanking. It was hard and had me howling for real, with my legs kicking around and everything, but when she eventually decided I'd had enough my bum was all warm and glowing, and I felt as naughty as if I'd been allowed to wet my knickers in front of them. Once I had been spanked Rory drew me, still over her lap and with my legs apart so that they could see my holes. I had to suck and swallow for Mr Bunchev, who'd been playing with himself while he watched me being beaten. Then it was down on my knees to lick her to a climax, by which time I was ready for Rory. He mounted me from behind, like a dog, as he had promised to do, but instead of doing it in my fanny he put a buttery finger up my bottom and then had me in there. I had never been buggered before and could only pant and gasp and swear at him while he used me up my hole and came in it. I'd promised to keep up the pretence of being unwilling, and it wasn't hard, because by the time he had finished himself off up my bottom the tears were running down my cheeks. After pulling my knickers up I ran from the room snivelling, with their laughter following me, slammed the bedroom door behind me and threw myself down on the bed.

After a few hysterics to keep them happy I humped my bottom up and put my hand down the front of my knickers. My bottom was throbbing and the hole was really sore, with Rory's sperm running out and down over my fanny. As soon as I started to masturbate I knew I had to do it. I let some pee out, over my fingers and into my knickers, then more, so that it began to drip on to the bed. My clitoris was burning under my finger and I didn't care about anything other than my pleasure, so I just let go. It spurted out, hard, into my knickers, all down my legs, over the bed and on to the floor, and all the while I was biting the bedclothes so that they wouldn't hear the ecstasy in my screams.

Rory got plenty of commissions after that, as the Bunchevs started taking his work in their shop on a regular basis. It's a strange thing, art, because all those strange works he had been trying to sell for years suddenly had people fawning over them and saying how clever they were, just because in doing so they were agreeing with the right people.

Unfortunately Rory's success still depended on me being around to be punished. It wasn't the spankings I minded, because those were really quite sexy, if not so much of a turn-on as knicker-wetting. What I didn't like was the pretence of being unwilling, and I didn't actually like the Bunchevs very much either, although being punished by her really excited me. She wasn't content with spanking me, and soon started to use a hairbrush on me, then a cane. Both hurt a lot more than her hand and it was a nuisance going around with a bruised bottom half the time. On the other hand I had never needed to masturbate so often in my life, and if my bottom was often sore, then so was my fanny, from rubbing.

Whatever my misgivings, I had soon developed a taste for having my bottom smacked, especially by big, authoritative women. Mrs Bunchev wasn't perfect for me, though, because her authority wasn't real. But someone's was, and that was Mrs White. The senior matron was big and strapping and about fifty, and had

27

always been very protective and motherly to me, both at Fice's and Highfield. The idea of being put across her knee and spanked made me tremble right through, but she had never done more than tick me off verbally and a spanking was hardly something I could ask for.

What I could do was let her see my bruised bottom and see what she said. If she guessed I'd been spanked and was genuinely shocked then I could insist I'd fallen on my bottom or something – she would think it was Rory, but wouldn't be able to do anything. On the other hand if she liked the idea it was sure to show in her voice, whatever she said, so I'd know and I could ask if she would like to give me discipline now and then. It wasn't going to be easy for me, but I needed it badly and just had to give it a try.

I did it after Mrs Bunchev had given me a particularly hard session with her hairbrush. It had been just me and her, me over her knee in the back of the shop, which was becoming commoner and which I liked less than having it done in front of an audience. For one thing it meant going home with wet knickers because I wasn't supposed to like it and so couldn't very well masturbate when she'd finished, even though I always had to kiss her bottom cheeks and lick her fanny. It did give me a wonderfully colourful bottom, though, with both cheeks black and blue.

Letting Mrs White see wasn't too hard, because we only wore knickers and bras under our uniforms and I often changed in her sitting room. So it was just a question of wearing rather skimpier knickers than usual and keeping them well up my bottom so that my spanked cheeks showed. I made sure to lift up my dress just at the moment she was coming into the room, and there it was, my smacked bottom, plain to see. I felt really nervous standing there, knowing she could see I had been punished, but I finished taking my dress off calmly, all the while waiting for her to say something.

What Mrs White did was to take me in her arms and hug me, all the while saying how awful men were and how sorry for me she was, and asking if it had hurt very much. She thought it was Rory who had spanked me, as I had expected her to. She was cross, but sympathetic too, and being in her arms was making me so excited that I wanted my punishment from her even more. Only I didn't dare ask her, because there was nothing in her voice that suggested she found the idea of me having been physically punished exciting at all. So I thanked her for her sympathy and finished changing, all the while seething with frustration.

I quickly came to regret showing her my bottom that day. She became more protective than ever, and almost every morning would want to check that I hadn't been spanked again. It was incredibly frustrating, because I would have to stand there in just my underwear with my knickers pushed down at the back while my bottom was inspected. I would get really excited, but she never made a sexual move and the only chance I had to relieve myself was by sneaking a quick one while I sat on the loo with my hand down my knickers.

The worst part of it was that Mrs Bunchev was getting keener and keener on me, demanding to punish me more and more often – and harder. No sooner had my bottom returned to a nice even pink than it would be back over her knee for another good hard spanking and more bruises. Then in the morning I'd have to show my bottom to Mrs White and she would get indignant and start threatening to do something about it. She never said exactly what, but it obviously involved calling the police in on Rory, which was the last thing I wanted.

Eventually I had to tell her the whole story, about the Bunchevs and Rory's art deals and the spankings. Mrs White was outraged, really furious, especially with Mrs Bunchev, who I blamed, while I painted Rory as the innocent. I never admitted to liking it, but begged Mrs

White not to make a fuss. She wouldn't have it, and declared her intention of paying the Bunchevs a visit as soon as possible, with me in tow.

It was Saturday before she managed this, with both of us briefly off duty. I hate rows and was worried about the effect it would have on Rory's sales, but I could do nothing as Mrs White marched me to the Bunchev's shop and pushed me inside. Mrs Bunchev was there, alone, seated behind the counter, looking very elegant and severe as she always did. Just the look of haughty disapproval on her face when she saw us would have had me stammering and apologising. Not so Mrs White, who launched straight into her opinion of Mrs Bunchev's character and behaviour, finishing with the information that if she saw so much as a pink mark on my bottom again she would know what to do about it.

Mrs Bunchev answered with a sneer and told Mrs White to mind her own business. That started the argument off with a vengeance, and all I could do was stand back and watch in horror. Mrs White really lost her temper but Mrs Bunchev stayed very cold and stiff, which only made it worse. I could see exactly what was going to happen. Eventually they would run out of steam and Mrs White would leave, thinking she had done the trick. Only she wouldn't have, and the next time Mrs Bunchev got hold of me I would really be for it. At the very least I would be made to strip and then caned in the nude, maybe made to kiss her bottom-hole to apologise, maybe whipped across my breasts. She had threatened to do both before.

It didn't happen that way. After what seemed an age of arguing, Mrs Bunchev tried to push Mrs White out of the shop. That was a mistake, because Mrs White must have weighed more than twice as much and was really strong. Mrs White resisted the push and they grappled for a moment, really spitting at each other. The stalemate only lasted a few seconds, and then Mrs

White had Mrs Bunchev firmly by the arm and was telling her that she was going to get a dose of her own medicine. Mrs Bunchev went wild, but there was nothing she could do. She was pushed down over her desk and held there, kicking and swearing and making all sorts of threats but unable to break Mrs White's grip.

Mrs Bunchev got spanked, which was wonderful to see. She had a smart, expensive dress on, which was hauled unceremoniously up on to her back, exposing her long, stocking clad legs, the taut straps of her suspenders and the seat of her silk knickers, tight over the small, firm bottom I had been made to kiss so often. Now it was going to be spanked, just like mine was, with no more dignity or modesty either, because Mrs White had begun to pull her victim's knickers down. Mrs Bunchev really fought to stop the wispy silk knickers coming off her bottom, kicking out viciously and threatening murder. It didn't make any difference: Mrs White pulled them down and Mrs Bunchev's bottom was bare, with her fanny showing between her thighs. She kept struggling once they were down, but not so badly, as if having her bare bottom shown was the worst of it and she was already chastened.

If the fight started to go out of Mrs Bunchev when her knickers were pulled down, the same was true of her coolness, because she started to squeal as soon as the spanking began. Mrs White laid in with a will, making the little buttocks bounce and wobble. Because she was so slim Mrs Bunchev's cheeks kept coming apart, too, and showing off her bottom-hole, which I found even more satisfying because of the way she had made me show off mine so often. Her thighs got slapped, too, which produced even louder squeals than the smacks on her bottom. By the end Mrs Bunchev was snivelling as badly as I ever had, and her fanny was wet and open, just like mine got when I was punished. She had given in completely, too, lying limp over her desk with her legs cocked apart at the knee. Her knickers had come off completely and were draped over a painting by the window, while her rear view was so open that I could see the glistening white juice at the mouth of her fanny and every wrinkle of her little brown bottom-hole. She didn't seem to care and stayed put for a bit even when Mrs White let go of her. When she did get up her jaw was trembling and her eyes were big and moist, while her hair had come loose during the spanking, making her look much younger and very vulnerable. Rubbing at her red bottom cheeks, she ran into the back room.

Mrs White didn't bother to follow, doubtless considering the lesson well taught, but stormed out, ignoring the three goggling men who had watched Mrs Bunchev get her spanking through the window. I followed, although what I would really have liked to do was join Mrs Bunchev and gloat over her while she masturbated – because I knew full well that that was what she would be doing.

It had been good to watch Mrs Bunchev being spanked, and the incident made me feel a lot happier about myself. She stopped demanding to punish me, but never mentioned it to Rory, or, I think, even her husband. What he thought, I don't know, but he always followed her lead in any case.

Rory's work was now selling well enough on its own anyway, and my thoughts began to turn to marriage again. Rory agreed, but said we ought to wait a couple more years, so we set a provisional date for the summer of nineteen fifty-seven. I was happy, and everything should have been perfect, but after a couple of months I was feeling bored. There was no excitement in my life any more. I missed the tension of being sent for spankings, and the glorious sexy feeling that came afterwards, and even the pain and humiliation of being put over Mrs Bunchev's knee and having my bottom stripped and beaten. It had been so emotionally power-ful, and while Rory would occasionally smack my bottom for me, his heart wasn't really in it and the very fact that we were in love somehow made it less intense. Even peeing in front of him became less fun, because most of the feeling of dirtiness had gone out of it and I couldn't get the wonderful sense of helpless embarrass-ment that had first excited me at all.

By the summer I was ripe for trouble and kept thinking of the way it had happened in Sheffield the first time, right in front of two men with me totally out of control as I wet myself all over the pavement. I wanted the same thrill, so strong that I just had to masturbate. Most of all I wanted to wet myself and then get spanked for it, for real.

In July somebody came back into my life: Percy Ottershaw. He had just finished his National Service and was working as delivery boy for the wine merchants who supplied Highfield, which was how I met him one day: I was coming into work while he was unloading their van.

Percy had developed a lot since leaving school. He was as big as ever, but his stint abroad had hardened him and a lot of it was now muscle. His personality had changed, too – he was more careful and more confident, and very much the young gentleman, but I was sure he was the same dirty little boy underneath. As we talked I remembered how rude he had been with me and it made me blush. He saw and smiled and from that moment I was lost.

He hardly knew anybody in London and wanted to take me to dinner, to which I agreed, telling myself it was only fair to be friendly to a fellow exile from Yorkshire. Underneath I knew full well what he was hoping for and the prospect was making me tremble, although I felt terribly guilty about Rory at the same time. It was easy, though, because as his art had become more popular Rory was forever off with the new friends he'd made and often didn't get back until the early hours.

I agreed to let Percy take me to dinner on a Friday night when I knew Rory was going to some frightfully intense debate on modern art. There was the lovely thrill of being bad as I bathed and dressed and I didn't find it that hard to overcome my guilt at all. Percy had always had a thing about my underwear and I was sure I would at least be letting him have a feel, so I put on tight white knickers that made my bottom bulge a little at the sides, a girdle and my best stockings. Over that went a lacy petticoat and a pretty blue dress, along with smart black shoes, topped off with a little hat and matching gloves.

Percy picked me up from the end of my road in his company van and drove across the river to a restaurant on Putney Hill. He was very polite and self-assured, even correcting the wine waiter, which I would never have dared to do. It was quite expensive, too, and I don't suppose he was earning much, but he didn't stint me at all, and I was soon tipsy and giggling over his stories of things that had happened at Fice's and while he was abroad. I had been prepared to give in, but by the end of the meal I was sure I would. He had to take control, though, and he did, in the same bold way he had when he first accosted me, simply parking the van in a quiet alley down by the river and getting his cock and balls out of his trousers.

I began to stroke him and he began to talk, intimately now, of how often he thought of me and of what we'd done together at Fice's. His cock was soon hard in my hand, while my bladder was straining from all the wine I had drunk, and I was ready for anything he suggested. He seemed happy to simply talk while I tossed him off, and in the end it was me who asked if he would like to watch me pee again, preferably in my knickers. He smiled, took my hand off his cock which he pushed back inside his trousers, and opened the van door.

My heart had already been beating fast, but on discovering I was going to be made to do it outside it went faster still. The van had a metal floor, so I'd been thinking of just pulling up my dress and letting him watch while I tossed him, but this was better, much better. He took me by the hand and led me down to the edge of the river. The tide was out and a big expanse of mud showed in the dull orange glow of a distant street light. I couldn't see anybody, but I felt really exposed, and my heart was really hammering when he told me to pull up my dress and do it in the mud.

I was already standing in it, with my nice shoes all dirty, and that, and the smell of the river and Percy's beaming, lecherous face, all brought back those wonderfully rude, helpless feelings that had given me so much pleasure. My bladder felt fit to burst, so there was no pretence as I quickly glanced around and then began to pull up my dress. I took my petticoat with it, showing him my belly and the front of my knickers beneath the ruffles and bows of my raised clothes. With my legs set a little apart and my front pushed forward I tensed, let go and then I was in heaven as the warm pee began to trickle into my knickers and run down my legs.

Percy watched me do it, squeezing his cock through his trousers as I wet myself for him. I wanted to show him more, perhaps the view from behind, with the wet patch spreading out on the seat of my knickers. He liked my bottom, and I thought he might be tempted to spank it, so I began to turn, only to tread on a stone under the mud. I went down, face first, right in it. I tried to catch myself but it was really deep and my face went in. My hair was plastered with it, my dress ruined, and all the while my pee was still gushing out into my petticoat while my wet bottom was stuck up with my knickers showing to the air.

I pulled my face out, gasping and spluttering, unable to open my eyes and slipping and sliding in the filthy muck as I tried to rise. Percy was laughing behind me and I suppose I must have looked pretty ridiculous, but rude too, very rude and very helpless. I asked him to help and he said he would, but not until he'd had his fun with me. It wasn't surprising he was getting a thrill from the state I was in, especially with my bottom showing and the pee still dribbling through my knickers, but I felt more than a little resentful as I waited for him to do whatever he intended.

He had always made me feel like that, and it had always been part of the thrill, but as I heard the rasp of his zip coming down I was hoping that he would at least hurry. The wet had soaked through my dress and I could feel it on my breasts. I was cold and a bit dizzy from the drink, feeling rude and naughty but also used. In due course I knew I'd be masturbating over it, but just then I only wanted him to hurry and come, which I was sure he was going to do. I waited for the slapping sound of his cock being pulled, but it didn't come – and then he started to urinate over me.

It was done really thoroughly, his hot stream splashing out over my bottom, on my dress, in my hair and down my legs, until I was dripping with it. All I could do was kneel there, soiled and filthy, with my mouth wide and his pee mingling with my own as he emptied the full contents of his bladder over my body. Not even Mrs Bunchev had urinated on me, and I didn't know whether to laugh with joy or cry with shame and anguish. It seemed to go on for ever, and most of his pee went over my bottom, until my knickers were sodden and must have been pretty well see-through at the back. They had come well up my crease when I fell over, too, and a lot of my cheeks was showing bare anyway, with the tight, wet cotton cutting across them to make them bulge and swell.

Percy had me in the back of his work van, naked and eager, and we pawed and licked at each other's bodies without restraint. He made to spank me and I let him, feeling him warm my bottom while I sucked on his cock. I took his balls in my mouth and let him finger my fanny and my bottom-hole too. He wanted to fuck me and I let him take me from the rear as I felt my breasts and he held my bottom cheeks wide. The taste of my fanny was strong on his cock when it went back in my mouth and he came like that, down my throat, with me swallowing his stuff while his fingers worked in the wet mush of my fanny. I came with his cock still in my mouth, a long, glorious climax beneath his fingers as my mind swam with thoughts of sodden, pee-soaked knickers, see-through in the dull orange of a London street light.

Before, when I had let Percy do rude things to me at Fice's, I had felt unfaithful to Rory. Now it was much worse, because Percy was grown up and he didn't just want a quick thrill from me, but regular, dirty sex, and more. I let him, because it was so much more thrilling than my home sex life with Rory. It began to get more and more serious, and after one particularly good session he even joked that we ought to get married. Rory was away, as was more and more often the case, and Percy had come to the flat. I had shown him the picture of me getting my first spanking across Mrs Bunchev's knee.

I wanted Percy to punish me really hard, maybe with a cane, but of course he couldn't because of the marks it would have left. Instead he gave me a good hand-spanking. It was done really skilfully, with my legs cocked open across his thigh so that I could rub my fanny while I was beaten. I was only in my knickers, but he took them down and hooked them around his leg, so that I was pulled really tight against him. He then gave me the most expert spanking I'd ever had. First it was with the tips of his fingers, slapping the cheeks of my bottom to make them sting and tingle until they were warm all over and I was moaning in pleasure. I started to rub my fanny on his leg and the spanking got harder, with his hand cupped so that it was really noisy and the sounds of my punishment rang out around the room, the slaps of a firm male hand on soft female buttocks and my cries and moans. As I started to wriggle and pout my bottom up for more he began to slap it harder, across my seat to send shock after shock through my fanny as I rubbed myself on him. I came on his leg, crying in absolute ecstasy, and when my climax was over I got down on my knees and sucked his cock for him with my bare red bottom stuck out behind.

It was the best spanking I'd had, and I told him so, which was when he suggested that we were made for each other and ought to get married. I couldn't, though, because I was still in love with Rory, and that night, after Percy had gone, I cried myself to sleep for the first time since the night I'd left home.

Rory wasn't back in the morning, and nor had he returned by the time I came home from work, and I began to get worried. I would have felt silly calling the police and didn't really have anyone to turn to, so I called Percy and he offered to drive me to where Rory might be. This was a sort of artists' colony in Stepney where several of his friends lived, and which he had been visiting more and more often. I never really felt welcome there, and we had argued about it once or twice, but that didn't stop him going.

When we got there it was obvious that there was a party going on, with loud music blaring out and all the windows open and bright with light. Percy was in his work suit and I was in my uniform, so we got a funny look from the leather-jacketed young man who opened the door to us, but he let us in anyway. I asked if Rory was around and he jerked his thumb towards the stairs. We went up, looking into each room as we passed. Everyone seemed to be having a great time, drinking and smoking and dancing, with several couples kissing quite openly in front of others. One girl even had her breasts out for her boyfriend to feel, and by the time we got to the top of the house I had a big lump in my throat and was dreading what I might find.

Sure enough, Rory was with a girl, and he wasn't just kissing her either. She was a petite blonde, very pretty and heavily made up, and she was naked, and she was down on her knees with my fiancé's cock in her mouth. I could see right between the cheeks of her bottom, and I spent an instant just staring at the round, wrinkled hole in the middle before what was happening really sank in. Then I just ran.

I know I was just as bad myself and I had no right to preach, but that didn't make it any better. All the way back to Fulham I was crying and cursing him. Percy never said a word, but stayed with me, and after I'd hurriedly packed my things and put them into his van we went back to his flat. He didn't try to touch me all night, but let me have his bed and hugged me before I went off to work in the morning.

The following winter, on the second Sunday in December, nineteen fifty-eight, ten years to the day after I'd watched Betty Mills wet herself, I married Percy Ottershaw.

3

Tar Baby

I had taken money to suck old Manolis's cock and now I was going to be made to regret it. It was stupid of me, because big Carla had been wanting to make an example of me for a long time and now I had sucked her husband's penis, so she had all the excuse she needed. That he had been asking me to do it for months didn't matter. That she hadn't touched him for years didn't matter. That I needed the money to eat didn't matter. I had done it, and now I was Gabriella the whore, and I was to be punished. I should have stuck to soldiers.

When I went to apologise and ask for forgiveness big Carla would not listen to me, but called me wicked and the daughter of the devil, and chased me out with a besom. I even went to the Father and asked for his protection, but he told me I was guilty and should accept my penance with a meek and contrite heart. Whoring was a sin and they all knew I was a whore, so if big Carla had decided that it was time for me to be punished, then doubtless it was God's will, and right, and just. He did say he would come to watch and would pray for me, but he knew they would strip me and I think he just wanted to see me bare so that he could pull his skinny old cock in the sanctum.

For two days I waited, expecting them to come and take me down into the square. When they had me there

I knew what they would do. They would strip me bare, not just with my top pulled down as Maria Costanza had been stripped for stealing, but naked, without even my shoes. They would tie my hands and fix the rope to the back of Manolis's donkey cart. They would lead me through the streets and Carla and Carla's sisters and Carla's daughter would whip me, whip me on the back and on the buttocks and on the legs, and all the while they would call out what I had done. Up in the olive groves they would tie my arms around a tree and finish my beating and spit on me and rub dirt in my face and on my breasts. If they were still angry they would tie me under the donkey, just for spite.

On the third day I found out that they didn't dare, because Maria told me. If they beat me they would leave bruises, and if they left bruises the British soldiers would see when they came to my house. Then the British soldiers would come for them, and that was why they did not dare. So they dared not beat me, but they would not let me go unpunished and each evening they would talk and try to decide what to do with me. I was hoping that they would choose to take me up into the olive groves and tie me under the donkey, bare, and so disgrace me. It would not have been so bad, not so bad at all.

They chose not to, and after a week I was thinking I was not to be punished at all. I began to walk through the square again and wear my prettiest dresses, which I hadn't dared to wear in case they were spoiled when they stripped me. Big Carla would call after me, and tell me I was a little whore and ask how I dared to show my face, but I would not answer her. I even tossed off Andros's cock for him when he asked, and they knew and I didn't care. Again it was stupid of me, because in my pride I made them more angry than ever.

A gang had been working on the road to the coast, laying the new smooth black surface for the soldier's cars and trucks. When they reached the village they said they would do the square and the large road, and they brought their machines and barriers and great barrels of tar, so that the air was full of the thick, hot smell of it. Everybody went to watch, and big Carla was there, with three of her sisters and her daughter, talking together by the pump and watching the men work.

That evening Maria came to me and said I should go away, at least until the road was finished. I laughed at her and asked what was so important about the road, when I heard Carla's voice at the door. Maria hid, but I stayed, wondering if they had found the courage to whip me or if it was to be the donkey. Carla came in and I stood. She had her sisters and her daughter behind her and each had a stick, not the sort that might be used to beat a girl but thick lengths of olive and chestnut. I knew I could not fight, but if they were to have me then I would go with pride and not like a brat to a spanking. To save my dress I let it slip to the floor. There was nothing beneath, and as Carla saw my bare body she nodded and her mouth turned up at the edges.

'Come into the square, Gabriella Angela,' she said to me. 'Your sins have found you out.'

They took me by the arms and led me out of my house. I said nothing because I did not want to plead, and when we came to the square I saw what was to happen. The work gang had left and in the middle of the square stood their machines, and by the machines was an open barrel of tar, still liquid but cooling in the evening sun. Manolis and his son Costas were there, each with a sack. I was to be made a tar baby.

They fixed my wrists together with straps from a cart, bands of leather thick enough to take my weight several times and far too strong for me to break. To these a rope was tied and I was led to the very middle of the square. All of the village had come out to see me spoiled, and the gaze of each man was on my body, feasting on the fullness of my breasts and bottom, the shape of my legs and the narrowness of my waist. Each wanted me punished, and each would enjoy the sight.

'You are going in the tar, Gabriella,' Carla told me. 'And when it is smeared on every part of your body you may come out. We will tie you to the lowest bough of the cedar, by your wrists, so that you can be seen all around. A plaque will be fixed around your neck, naming you a whore. All night you will hang there, and in the morning all the village will see you. Doubtless when the work gang arrive they will take you down and clean you, so when you tell your friends there will be no marks to show and they will think you nothing more than a spiteful whore.'

I said nothing, but she smiled at me and her daughter laughed, then dipped her finger into the tar.

'No warmer than the road on a hot day,' she said. 'Why be so kind to the little bitch?'

She envied me, because she was a virgin but had a hot cunt.

'You may push her face in the barrel, little one,' her mother answered. 'But she is to be shamed and disgraced, nothing more.'

So Carla's daughter took me by the hair and pushed my face in the barrel and held my head under until I began to kick and struggle. It was hot and stung, and when she pulled my head out I dared not open my eyes. Then I was taken by the arms and lifted and put in the tar barrel. I felt my feet break the crust and the hot filth slid up my calves and my thighs, soiling my cunt and covering the fat of my bottom until it came to my hips. With their sticks the women daubed my breasts and my belly, my back and my arms, until every part of me was filthy with tar. Even my breasts had been lifted to smear the undersides and a stick had been pushed between the cheeks of my bottom to dirty the cleft. With that it was done.

43

'You may climb from the barrel, Gabriella Angela,' Carla's voice came to me.

I tried, but with my wrists bound it was hard and I fell, landing on my knees with my behind spread to the square. Carla's daughter laughed, exclaiming on the pinkness of my cunt and anal hole against the blackness of the tar, but her mother told her to mind her words. I got to my feet and stood, feeling the warm tar run down my body. My hair hung heavy with it down my back and it was wadded beneath my arms and in my cunt hair. My skin stung as if it had been scrubbed or like a bottom does after a smacking. My eyes were closed tight and I was helpless, but I put my chin up to show that they had not broken me.

'Put the thorns on her, Manilos,' Carla ordered. 'In the morning we will see if she still has her pride.'

I heard the men step towards me and the shake of the sacks as I was covered with thorns, wild thyme, and the stems of dog rose and sea holly. With the tar coating me I felt no more than faint prickles, but I could picture myself: first black with tar but still beautiful, now ragged with sticks and leaves and looking ridiculous. Still I kept my chin high.

My lead was grasped and I stumbled as I was pulled into a walk. They led me to the cedar and threw the rope over the low bough. I was pulled up on to my toes and the rope was tied off, leaving me hanging for my public shame.

Some had laughed while it was done; others had remarked on my wickedness, saying justice had at last been done. I was spoiled and shamed, hanging in my misery, made the target of a public mockery that would break my spirit and leave me cowed and obedient, as Carla intended. She was wrong. That night many a hard cock would be pushed into many a wide cunt, but it would not be their wives the cocks' owners thought of but me, naked and soiled. The young men would take pleasure in their hands, or in the mouths of the girls, and it would be me they thought of. The Father, too, would think of me, and be torn two ways, because although he would relish my torment, he would be wishing he could visit me and sheathe his cock in my bottom, as he did each holy day.

With the thought of so many cocks hard for me, my nipples had gone stiff under the tar and long drips hung heavy from each. They saw and decided I was excited, and Carla's daughter said I must truly be the devil's child to take pleasure in such a thing. Her mother told her that my nipples had merely come out in response to my pain, and she laughed, but she was wrong.

'Hang there for the night, Gabriella Angela,' she said, 'In the morning, when they have cut you down and cleaned you, you may come to beg my forgiveness.'

Others murmured approval for her mercy. I heard too the murmur of prayers and knew the Father had come forward to speak to me.

'Think hard on your sins as you suffer, my child,' he said. 'Suffering is given that we may cleanse ourselves, and in the morning you will no doubt be a purer and better person.'

With that he walked away, leaving me hanging in my straps with the tar congealing on my body and the smell of it thick in my nose. A heavy chain was hung around my neck, the attached plaque branding me a whore hanging down below my breasts to leave them showing. My humiliation was complete and they began to celebrate, dancing and drinking in the square, taunting me and poking my breasts and bottom with sticks. Their lust and envy was plain and I would have laughed had I not feared worse, but I held my peace. At last they began to tire of baiting me and as the bell of the monastery chimed midnight Maria came to give me water, then quickly ran off for fear of being put up beside me. Only the Father stayed, saying he wished no lewd acts to be performed on me during the night. When all were gone he felt my breasts and buttocks through the thorns and tar, pressing prickles into my flesh, and left me.

I was faint with pain and exhaustion when I heard the next voice, a British voice, coming from in front of me.

'Fuck me, will you look at this!'

'Jesus, it's little Gabby. Come on, boys, let's get her down.'

I could neither see nor open my mouth, but there were tears of gratitude welling behind my eyelids as my straps were cut and I was lowered to the ground. My lips were opened and water put to my mouth. I swallowed and managed to thank them, but was told to lie quiet and that they would help me. A blanket was put around me and I was put over a shoulder and carried away. At their camp I was taken to the bathhouse and stood while the thorns were picked from me. I was put in a tub. I was given brandy and scrubbed with turpentine and spirit, each soldier eager to help, and as they washed me they told me who they were.

There was the Corporal, who was never called by his name. There was Billy, who knew me and always paid in cigarettes. There was fat Percy, who also came to me and liked to smack my bottom. There was Settle John and Red John, who said he was a communist. There was Hartles, and there was the Tyke, whose voice was different from the others'.

When the tar was gone from my face I managed to open my eyes. All seven soldiers were looking down at me, little more than boys, with their faces full of concern and sympathy, or stern and serious, but always with the glint of lust, because they had a naked girl and they could expect her to be grateful. Another woman would have been resentful, or scared, but I knew men: once their cocks were getting hard they didn't think with their heads.

46

Their cocks *were* hard, because I was naked and they had to touch me to get the tar off. My breasts were lifted to get underneath and my bottom cheeks were held apart to clean my crease. My nipples were done really carefully so as not to hurt me, but still they were left sore and hard. My hair was spoiled and they took razors and shaved my head and they shaved my cunt, fat Percy and the Tyke, who said he had been a barber in England. When I was clean I was pink and without a hair on my body. My skin tingled and my nipples wouldn't go down. My cunt was open and wet from all the feeling and rubbing.

They knew they could have me and I wouldn't try to stop them. So they soaped off the turpentine and sprayed me with scent Hartles had bought for his girlfriend in England. They took me into a room and they pulled out their cocks, all but fat Percy, who was told to keep watch. They took turns, one by one, while the others looked on, the Corporal first and then all five of the men.

I was fucked by the Corporal, on my back on the bed, and he spunked on my belly. Settle John had me standing, holding me up by my bum to show how strong he was. I bounced on his cock till he came, deep in me, without thought for what might come of it. Red John had me kneeling, but put his spunk on my breasts. Hartles had me lick up his mate's come and did his in my mouth when my breasts were clean. The Tyke was the joker and thought it fun to wank on my bald head and rub in the spunk, saying it would make my hair grow back the sooner. Only fat Percy held back, and was ordered to return with me to my house.

He gave me a shirt so long it covered my bottom, and together we set off back for the village. When he came to me he would always smack my bare bottom and spunk across the reddened cheeks. So as we started back I asked him why he had not taken his pleasure when it was to be had for free.

'After what was done to you?' he answered. 'It wouldn't have been right.'

'Then visit me soon,' I promised him, 'and you may have me for a full afternoon. I will serve you wine, and olives, and bread, and you will pay nothing.'

'Thank you, very kind,' he answered. 'But after what they did, do you still mean to take men?'

'What else may I do?' I answered. 'How else will I live? Big Carla would take me as a servant were I to beg meekly enough. I would scrub floors and clean the cess. I would work in the hot sun and be an old woman before I was twenty years. I would rather whore.'

'But won't they punish you again?'

'Yes.'

'Then let me tell you something, and maybe it will help. At my school, the boys were beaten, with a cane. It could be for anything – for swearing, for lateness, for slovenliness, for not doffing your mortarboard to the Victor Ludorum in Blood's Passage.'

'What is . . .?'

'Never mind, I wouldn't expect you to understand. I'm not sure I do, actually. What matters is that the fear of punishment always hung over our heads, much as it does over yours. I made it my fantasy. Not to *be* caned, you understand, at least not by a man, because I couldn't take that. No, to *give* the cane. And so, because I wanted it so much, I felt I could have taken it, if I'd had to.'

'And that is why you like to smack my bottom? Because you were beaten yourself?'

'No, I was never caned. For five years I avoided it. But, for me, sex is a girl's red bottom.'

'When they had tarred me, and hung me from the tree, and the men wanted me, I could have laughed. Is that what you mean?'

'Something like that. You're very strong, but if you could make their punishment your pleasure they could not touch you at all.'

48

'I think I already understand what you mean. Now come inside. You are going to spank me, fuck me, and put your cock in my bottom, and make me scream with pleasure.'

'Well, er, if you insist.'

We had arrived at my house. The village was quiet, without a sound. I wanted Percy to have me, and I wanted the people to hear me in my pleasure, so they would know, and know I was not hanging in the square in my disgrace, and know I was not broken. He took me across his knee and he made my bottom warm. He had me squat and he watched me do my piddle on the floor. He made me kneel in the pool and put his cock in my cunt from behind. He took olive oil and put a finger in my bottom. He put his cock in after that and did his spunk up my hole, and I came while he did it and I screamed and they knew.

I took fat Percy's words to heart and put my mind to the pleasure of punishment. I practised, too, with spankings and canings and whippings from the men who came to me. I learned proper English as well, and how to speak to a man to make my punishment more pleasurable to him, what to say and when to cry and when to moan. As my knowledge grew, so did my wealth, for officers were coming to me now and other men of importance, and they did not pay in cigarettes. The Chief of Police from the coast liked to beat me with his baton and put it in my rear while I sucked him: big Carla no longer spoke badly of me. The Bishop himself came to put candles in my bottom and pray as they burned, and the Father no longer took his pleasure for nothing. Panigari the Judge liked to whip me for his friends to see, and he made me his mistress and put me in a villa on Agrotiki, with blue tiles on the roof, a houseboy for a servant, a great dog for a guard and a beautiful carpet in red and gold. When my master came with his family I was the maid. When he came alone or with his friends I was the whore.

I was happy on Agrotiki, for the life was easy and my houseboy's cock was long and seemed to be forever hard. Panigari would come out with his friends and I would dance for them and strip and perform the lewd tricks I had learned. I would climb in the fountain and pee like the statues whose cunts flowed with water. Andros would come on my breasts and I would lick up the spunk and show as it ran down my chin. Chiron would mount me and they would laugh and clap at his antics. When I was done they would tie me and whip me and play with their cocks, until each was ready. Their cocks would go in my cunt and in my bottom, in my mouth and between my breasts, until I was sodden with spunk and purple with bruises. But I was bored also, for it was seldom more than once a month that the men came to the villa.

Beneath the villa was a beach, to which I would go to be alone. To the north a cliff rose, with smooth, sun-baked stones at its foot and little gullies and bays to which no one ever came, save me. Often I would think of how I had been taken and tarred, and then I would masturbate, with my bottom in a prickle bush and my thighs spread to the sea. Or I would think of fat Percy and wish he could be there to spank me, or the Tyke and how he had come on my head when I was bald.

A freighter emptied its tanks in the bay and Panigari was furious, for the sand of his beach was thick with tar and the thick scent of it filled the villa. He cursed and roared and said he would see the crew in jail, but I could only draw in my breath and close my eyes as I thought of my body, filthy and black, with my breasts dripping tar and the olive stick pressing into the crease of my bottom. The orgy that evening was poor, and even the sight of me sucking on Chiron's penis and licking his sperm from the marble beneath him failed to rouse the men to their normal passion.

I went out the next day, down to the beach, with the smell of tar thick in the air. Andros was to clean the house and I was alone. With men a girl must show that her pleasure comes from them, or make believe that she is shy and unwilling. Alone, she may take her pleasure as she pleases.

Out of sight of the villa I found a lump of tar, fat and soft, the size of my fist. I pulled off my bikini top and took the tar, moulding it in my hand as I thought of the tar sticks slapping on my bare body. For a moment I held back, then put the lump to my chest, rubbing stripes of dirt on to my breasts, squeezing it between them and feeling them with my hands. With my breasts brown and filthy I was in rapture. I walked, enjoying having them bare and dirty, thinking sexy thoughts and playing with the tar lump. I reached a place where the brush came down to the edge and stopped and chose a large sun-baked boulder. For a while I collected tar, with my dirty breasts dangling and slapping, alternately sticking together and peeling apart as I moved. When I was ready my bikini pants came off, leaving me bare. Pushing my bottom out towards the sea I began to soil myself, smearing filth over both heavy cheeks until my rear was as filthy as my breasts. My belly came next, my dirty hands cupping the little bulge and holding my waist, feeling how tight it was and how my hips flared beneath, my round, soiled breasts above. I coaxed each nipple to erection beneath a coating of dirty tar, then again began to walk and collect tar, filthy and brown and maybe happier than I had ever been.

With a big pile of tar on my boulder I sat in it, feeling the lumps squash and spread beneath my bottom and ooze in the crease. One was pressed tight to my bottom-hole and I thought of how I'd fallen when I climbed from the tar barrel and shown the pink of my anus, of my cunt too. I had meant to save that, but I couldn't. Taking up a big lump, I held it over my pubic

51

curls, savouring the moment of holding back but knowing I was going to do it. My will broke and I squashed the tar to my cunt, sighing with pleasure as I fouled my pretty mound and wiggled my bottom in the filth beneath it.

I needed to come and could hold back no more. All I had meant to do was tits and bum, as the English say, perhaps my belly as well. Now my cunt was dirty, and my feet and legs. I turned over, crawling on the boulder and lying face down with my breasts and belly in the tar, squirming in the hot dirt. My hands went behind me, spreading my bum cheeks to the sun and opening my cunt as if in the hope of entry. Some of my hair had dipped in the mess and I gave in to the last indignity and did it, rubbing the tar in to spoil it. My face was last and again I paused before slapping two wads to my cheeks and smearing it over my forehead, nose and chin.

I was filthy from head to toe, soiled and befouled with tar, my hair ruined and my cunt wadded with it. Only one more thing remained, and as I scrambled up the beach I was searching for a suitable thorn bush. I found one, a clump of wild thyme as fat and round as a pillow, rich green with a thousand tiny spikes piercing the surface. My bottom went into it, wiggling down with the thorns pricking my tar-fouled skin, until I sat sprawled in the bush with my bottom hot and stinging and my thighs spread to the sea. I began to masturbate, slapping my cunt to get at my clitoris and revelling in what I had done to myself and how I would look. I was feeling my breasts and squirming my bottom into the thorns, rubbing my face and belly and thighs, smearing the tar over myself, smacking my cunt and dipping into my hole. My breasts and bottom felt huge, my nipples like taut points of fire. My clitoris seemed to grow and my cunt seemed to burst. My whole body was burning when I came and the screams echoed from the rocks to send the startled gulls soaring into the air.

It took Andros three full hours to get me clean, while Chiron sat and watched. Both had me afterwards, one in my mouth, the other in my sore cunt. By then I was bald, and when Andros wanted to come I made him do it on my head and had him lick me as I rubbed it in. He said I was crazy and put me to bed with a bottle of brandy. But as I slipped towards sleep with my fingers in my cunt I was smiling and thinking of what it meant to be made a tar baby.

When Panigari began to hurt me I left Agrotiki, along with a boat and his daughter's papers. I travelled to Patra and so to Athens, and on from Athens to England, to London, where I used Panigari's money to buy a shop. I was alone, because I dared not mingle with the community, but I did hope to contact those who had known me when they were soldiers, most of all fat Percy. He had been the kindest and the most thoughtful, and I missed the feel of his cock in my belly and the smack of his hand on my bottom.

I knew his name, because I had his shirt, which I wore at night if it was cold. He was not from London, but he had once told me he wanted to live there and make his living from selling wines, so I was hopeful. When a year had passed a new directory of telephone numbers arrived, and in it a P. Ottershaw was listed. He was living in a tiny flat beside a bomb-site, but he was dining on fine food and drinking a wine finer even than those I used to steal from Panigari.

He was as pleased to see me as I was to find him, and we quickly became drunk together, sharing his wine bottle by bottle as we talked of our lives. I told him how I had done as he said and about Panigari and of making myself a tar baby again on the beach at Agrotiki. He spoke of how he had come to London, and of a girl named Elaine who liked to wear white pants and do her toilet into them while he watched. She was going to marry another, which made him sad, but his cock was hard in his trousers and my cunt was wet in my pants.

I wanted to be beaten and I wanted to be fucked, but most of all I wanted to be made a tar baby again, as I had the first time, naked and hung up by my wrists, writhing in a coating of tar and prickles. With an audience to watch me in my shame and watch me in my ecstasy. Percy thought it funny and promised to help, mentioning a place where a bomb-site was being laid with tar to make a place for the people to park their cars. We walked there together, laughing and leaning on each other for support, Percy's hands on my bottom and breasts and mine on his crotch. Twice he stopped to press me down over the front of a car and both times my dress came up and my pants came down, and both times my bottom was spanked. We got to the site and my bottom was tingling, while the juice from my cunt was wet on my legs. A high wall of iron boards cut us off from the street, and we pushed through a gap. Beyond it was dim, with only a glimmer of light from two high windows at either side. The smell of tar was strong in the air and as my eyes changed I saw the barrel, squat and black in the dim light, with a thick length of wood thrust into it.

'Take my hair and push my face in, as Carla's daughter did,' I begged him. 'Then put me in and soil me and ruin my hair and the hair on my cunt. Tie me and use me, really use me. Put me in the tar, then fuck me in my bottom.'

Percy's hand caught in my hair and I was being dragged to the barrel. I cried as his hand twisted hard and my head was thrust at the tar, stopping an inch from the surface. He tore off my dress and pulled down my pants, all the while with my face an inch from being utterly soiled. I kicked off my pants and also my shoes and I was nude, as nude as I had been that night, naked and helpless, for spoiling and disgrace. In went my head, deep in the tar, held down then pulled up, only to be thrust in once more until I was kicking out behind as my breasts squashed and squirmed at the side of the barrel. He lifted me up and I went into the tar, feeling the same hot, sticky joy as the filth rose up my body to dirty my feet and my calves and my thighs. My cunt hair was ruined and my bottom immersed, my cheeks floating and big on the surface, then slimy and hot beneath.

With the tar to my hips I was soiled with the stick, Percy slapping my breasts and smearing my belly, caking my hair and delving deep in the crease of my bottom. My nipples went hard and were hung with drips, which he tweaked away and rubbed in my face. Both breasts were lifted and soiled underneath, and my armpits and bum crease, again and again. He took out his cock and said it was hard, so I climbed from the barrel but tripped and went down, with the barrel tipping over behind me to make a pool on the ground. I squealed as I landed with my breasts hanging down, my bottom up high and my cunt pink and wide. A voice came from above me and I knew we were being watched. Then Percy's cock touched my bumhole.

I was buggered in the filth, really hard, with my tits swinging and scattering droplets of tar beneath me. My eyes were tight shut and I could see nothing, only hear Percy grunting and feel his cock in my back passage, while all the while somebody was screaming from above, calling us perverts and filth and threatening to call the law. Percy went faster but I was in heaven, with the envy and shock of my audience to add to my pleasure and his prick rammed up my filthy bum again and again as the tar oozed over my body and dripped from my hair and tits. He came up my arse and I stayed down, kneeling in tar as his come ran from my anus down over my cunt.

The woman was shouting and calling out threats, but I began to smear the mixture of spunk and tar on to my cunt, slapping and snatching at myself. Percy started to beat me, using the tar stick to wallop my buttocks again and again, calling me his Gabriella and his little whore. As my orgasm rose I began to scream, crying and begging as my mouth filled with tar. My climax broke and my cunt seemed to explode. The stick hit my buttocks again and my knees gave way, landing me face down in the filthy pool beneath me where I lay, clawing and clawing at my cunt as Percy beat me and beat me. I screamed and swore and spluttered in the tar, until at last my orgasm began to fade. As my breath came out in a long, deep moan, a strange thought came to me. How would it have been if they had tied me under the donkey?

4

Matron

The hospital was quiet, so quiet that I could hear the soft gurgle of the heating system and the distant background hum of the generators. With the clock just creeping towards four the time was ideal, dark and quiet, with two full hours before the shift changed – two full hours for April.

She was half bent across my desk, looking at me, freckled and so pretty, with her little snub nose twitching ever so slightly in her nervousness. Her hands were flat on the desk and her bottom was pushed out, making an enticing ball beneath the white cloth of her uniform skirt. I picked up the cane I was going to use on her and saw her lower lip tremble. Her eyes followed me as I lifted it and flexed the three-foot length of brown rattan. April bit her lip.

'Come on, get it out, there's no point in delaying this,' I ordered.

'Yes, Matron,' she answered.

I loved watching her strip her bottom for beating. She always got so embarrassed about it, hesitating and fidgeting, until by the time her little round arse was bare her face and neck would be red with humiliation. It was the same now: hesitantly putting her hands to the hem of the skirt while her eyes pleaded for mercy. I just sneered at her, not even bothering to speak. She gave me a look of pure misery as she lifted the skirt, showing her stocking-clad thighs, then the bare skin between stocking tops and pants, with her suspender straps cutting in to make her soft flesh bulge. Her lower lip came out further as her pants came on show, with the cheeks of her behind stretching out the tight white cotton into two sweet mounds. With her skirt tucked high into her belt and the full expanse of her panty-seat on view she stopped and once again gave me her pleading look.

'Don't be pathetic,' I told her. 'You look like a hurt spaniel. You've got a beating coming to you and you'll take it on the bare. Now get those pants down.'

April's response was truly beautiful to see. She nodded dumbly and, as she put her thumbs into the waistband of the big pants, her eyes glazed with tears. One heavy, clear drop rolled out as the twin dimples of her lower back were revealed, then another from the other eye as the top of her crease came on show. The two tears ran down her cheeks in time with her pants sliding down over her bottom, until she was bare behind, with the pants still covering her fanny in front and stretched taut down around her thighs.

She was ready: the little round orbs of her bottom bare for punishment, bare for me to put a dozen or more scarlet welts across. It was stuck out, and quivering slightly from the all-over trembling of her body. I gave the cane a cut through the air and saw her wince, then went to check the door although we both knew full well it was locked. Her eyes followed my every move, round and wet with her tears, full of apprehension for what was about to be done to her. The tea she had brought me when she came was still on the desk, now cold, but I took a sip anyway. It helped to leave them bare-bottomed for a while, just to make them more aware of what it meant to have their pants down for a beating. Certainly it had worked with April, because in the four months since I'd first thrashed her she had become haunted by the exposure of her bottom.

Only when I'd finished the tea did I take mercy on April, putting the cup down and lifting the cane high over her bum cheeks. I held it there, letting her tension rise, watching the anxiety in her face. Her muscles began to twitch, first in her buttocks, then down the full length of her legs. Unable to hold herself still, she began to wiggle her toes, her eyes flicking from my face to the cane and back.

'Control yourself,' I told her. 'You look like you need the lavatory.'

'Do it, then. Beat me!' she gasped.

I obliged, bringing the cane down hard to make her bottom bounce. April yelled out and I knew she was immediately regretting having asked for it as her feet and legs danced in her pain. I waited, allowing her to recover her pose while the thin white welt that crossed her bottom turned to an angry red as the blood flowed back. Once she had managed to hold herself still and stuck her bottom back out I sank down to inspect my work. My stroke had landed well. The welt ran across both cheeks, ending in a drop-shaped blemish where the cane tip had caught her. She was marked, the cane line showing my authority over her, betraying her low status and the huge gulf between her, the one with the whipped bottom, and me, the one who had done the whipping.

April knew it, too, because she was trembling hard and the tears were running down her cheeks as I rose to my feet. I put the second stroke lower than the first, full across the fat of her cheeks. Again she did her silly little dance before getting her bottom back in position. I put the third stroke lower still, along the sensitive groove where her bottom cheeks met her thighs. She squealed louder than before, but recovered more quickly, sticking her bottom out just that little bit further and settling with her feet a little apart. I could already see the tuft of hair that hid her fanny lips from the rear, but stepped behind her to get a better view. She was moistening, as

59

beaten girls always do, with her lips beginning to swell and white fluid beading at the mouth of her vagina.

'You are disgusting, April,' I told her and she responded with a sob.

I went back to beating her, laying stroke after stroke across her nude bottom in a slow rhythm that still allowed her only a second or so to recover between each cut of the cane. After the inspection of her sex she had set up a low, miserable whimpering noise. This turned to open snivelling after the sixth stroke and I thought she was going to start blubbering, only for the sounds to take on a broken, choking quality. She got noisier as I went on, and with each stroke her feet slid a little further apart and her bottom stuck out more. By the twelfth she looked more like she was expecting a man to take her from behind than as if she was in the middle of a punishment. She had begun to moan, too, which was distracting me from my task. By the fifteenth her legs were as far apart as her lowered pants would allow and her noises had turned to openly lewd groans and a sluttish giggling. It was obvious what she needed.

'Stop giggling, you stupid little girl,' I snapped, 'or I'll have to do it harder.'

April pushed her hand down the front of her pants, touching herself. The make-believe was over. She was masturbating and it was no longer any good pretending she didn't like what I was doing to her. That was good, because I could really thrash her while she was coming up to orgasm, hard, so that she writhed and kicked and squirmed and farted, just so long as I kept telling her what she wanted.

'So what's it to be? Your usual filth, I suppose?'

'Yes, that, please.'

'Disgusting tart! I'll make you do it for real one day, you know, not just so that you can rub your dirty little twat over it.'

She gave a choking sob and began to rub at herself harder, waiting for me to start telling her dirty fantasy.

I gave her another stroke, laid right across the crest of her cheeks to make her flesh flatten out like a burst medicine ball. It was hard, and right over earlier welts, but she just groaned.

'Very well, April, if you can really stand to be so dirty,' I began as I continued to beat her. 'If you think just having your bottom bare is humiliating. It's only me watching now, but think if it was a whole crowd. Perhaps one day I'll beat you in a ward, perhaps Beatrice Ward with all the old ladies, with sister and two or three of your colleagues watching. Think how they'd whisper together, wondering what you had done as you bent over the desk. Think of all those eyes on you as you pulled up your uniform and took down your pants. Think how they'd gloat over you with your bottom bare. Think how the juniors would giggle at your blushes with your fanny showing from the rear. Think how the old dears would cluck with approval as I beat you. Think how they'd discuss your delinquency as your bottom went red and you danced and wriggled in your pain. Then, just when you thought it could not possibly get any worse, you'd lose control of your bladder. You'd wet yourself, into your pants and over the floor. Imagine how disgusted they'd all be as the pee ran out. Imagine what they'd say. How dirty you were, how revolting your behaviour was, how you couldn't even control your bladder under a little necessary discipline . . .'

'I can do it,' she gasped. 'I'm going to do it! I am! It's coming out!'

'Not on my floor, you little bitch!' I spat, but it was too late.

I saw the yellow liquid spurt out in front of her, then more was running back into her pants and dripping from beneath them.

'I've done it!' she cried. 'I've wet myself. I've really wet myself! It's all coming out! Beat me, June, hurt me!'

I didn't need asking. As I brought the cane around hard across April's bottom the pee was really coming, gushing out around her fingers and down her legs, then spraying out over the desk as the thin rod smacked down on her bottom. She gave a thick, choking cry and I knew she was going to come, masturbating in her own pee while I thrashed her naked bottom. I went on whacking her as the piddle ran out. It pooled in her lowered pants and dribbled out through the gusset, splashing on the floor and over her shoes. Some was coming out at the sides of her pants as well, running down her thighs and into her stockings. With each stroke of the cane she would cry out and drops of pee would shake from the taut, wet material of her pants, spattering the desk and floor. Soon she was standing in a big puddle. Her shoes were full of piddle, her pants and stockings were soaked and her bottom was a mess of violet welts, but she held off, right on the edge of orgasm, utterly soiled but in complete ecstasy.

'Do it, you little whore,' I yelled, 'or I'll make you do something worse, in your pants, in front of everybody!'

She came, sticking her bottom out and squirming it about, making little treading motions in her puddle and whimpering to herself. I kept beating her, thrashing away at her purple bottom while her legs danced and her cheeks wobbled, the pee spraying everywhere as she cried and gasped her way through the climax.

Then April was sinking to her knees, spent and filthy, going down to kneel in her own pee puddle. I pulled the stroke I had been about to give her and watched as she sank down to the floor, hanging her head so that her hair dangled in the pee.

'I'm done,' she sobbed. 'Thank you, June, thank you so much.'

'You're filthy, April, do you know that? A really disgusting little tart.'

'Yes, Matron.'

She turned to me, made a wry face and looked back down at the disgusting mess she had made on the floor. There was a huge puddle of pee, which she was kneeling in, with the hem of her skirt in it too. Her pants were dripping piddle and her stockings were ruined, while even her suspender belt had got wet. In a way it was just what I wanted, but it was awkward too, because there was always a chance that somebody would want to see me in my office. Fortunately I had anticipated that one day April would actually do what she liked to masturbate over and so I always kept a bucket and cloths in one corner. I nodded towards it as I sat down in my chair. As she crawled to get it I parted my thighs and slid a hand down the front of my pants, finding my fanny wet and ripe.

April gave me a shy little smile as she started to mop the urine up, then turned so that I could have the best view of her well-beaten bottom. She looked glorious, kneeling in pee with her caned buttocks naked between pants and skirt, a chastened, humiliated girl crawling in her own piddle. I could see her sex, wet from her excitement. Even her bottom-hole was puffy. As she scrubbed her bottom wobbled and her anus seemed to wink at me. It was too much, and I pushed my pants down over my thighs. She giggled and turned, burying her face between my legs. I was in heaven as her tongue found my clitoris, then I was coming almost before she had started to lick. My eyes were closed as I went through my orgasm, but my mind was full of the sight of her bottom – bare, welted from the cane and wet with her own piddle, shown off for me to masturbate over with the tight hole winking and her sex wet, wet for me.

I didn't normally let them lick me, because it eroded my authority. April was special, though, and what she had done made it impossible to resist. It took me a moment to recover myself after my orgasm, and when I opened my eyes she was kneeling in front of me with her hands folded in her lap and her mouth set in a knowing smile, also with her bottom planted firmly in her pee puddle. Our intimacy had crossed a new boundary and we both knew it. I was going to have to punish her, but first I needed to discomfit her to wipe the smugness off her face.

'Come along, clean the rest of your mess up,' I ordered, 'and put those filthy clothes in the wash. Oh, and you're to go without pants today, bare under your skirt. Don't think I won't check.'

'But, June, they'll see my marks!'

'Good, then they'll know you've been disciplined.'

'Not in the male wards, at least. Not that!'

'Yes, and maybe we'll find one to give you your next beating.'

'No, June, not that, not a man!'

I just laughed at her.

That was the fantasy April feared most: being beaten by a man. Deep down she wanted it, and to be fucked afterwards by the man who had punished her. On duty she was the sternest and most formal of my nurses, especially with the male patients, to whom she allowed no latitude whatever. They showed her a great deal of respect, and never seemed to guess that underneath her strict demeanour she was frightened of them. Brought up by a divorced mother to regard men as beasts and her virginity as sacred, the idea of a cock in her pretty little fanny filled her at once with terror and a strong feeling of arousal.

We both knew that her uniform skirt was much too long to reveal her whacked bottom around the wards, although it would be a while before she could risk wearing a short skirt in public. Certainly neither of us was going to chance the possible consequences of our relationship becoming public. Having a man cane her was a different matter. She thought I was teasing, but I wasn't. There was a man in Baldwin Ward who liked caning girls. He caned his wife, anyway: I had seen the marks. She had come in to visit him and had pulled the curtain around the bed. I knew what that meant – dirty behaviour – and I wasn't having any of it. Usually they got their wives to jerk their cocks, although I've known some who were brazen enough to try and have full sex.

I had already got Ottershaw down as the dirty type and had no doubt what they'd be up to. Sure enough, when I tugged the curtain open there he was, with his wife's hand bobbing up and down under the bedcovers. I've known wives to show their tits and even their fannies, but Mrs Ottershaw had her back to him and her skirt up to show her bottom. She had tight white pants on, half down to let him see it bare. He was feeling her and it took them a moment to make themselves decent. In that moment I caught a glimpse of her bare bottom, which was marked with long, dark welts that could only have been made with a cane.

I couldn't see Ottershaw turning down the chance to put a stick across April's bottom. Since I'd caught them his wife hadn't dared to do anything dirty, and with a week of convalescence to go I knew he'd be getting frustrated. By then April would just about be ready for another dose of the cane.

For the whole week I kept her warm, making her go without any pants and lifting her skirt to inspect her cane marks every night. Twice she asked to be allowed to come but I refused her, telling her to do it in her room if she couldn't contain herself. On the Thursday I moved Ottershaw into a private room, which I had April tidy while his wife was visiting. It was approaching eight in the evening and we had just come on duty, while visiting hours were about to end. April was arranging some flowers when I came in, and Mrs Ottershaw was just about to leave, doubtless leaving her husband frustrated at the missed opportunity to have his dirty little cock pulled.

When Mrs Ottershaw had gone I ordered April to tidy the blankets on the lowest shelf of the wardrobe. She bent to do as she was told and, not surprisingly, Ottershaw's eyes went to her bottom. As I passed I took the hem of her skirt and tweaked it up, revealing April's bare rear view, just for an instant. She squeaked and he gave me a look of deepest astonishment. But it had been done, and I knew her bruises were still dark enough to make the fact that she had been beaten unmistakable.

'April is to be punished, Mr Ottershaw,' I said, 'and as I am aware that you cane your wife I have decided that you should administer a similar beating to her. I trust that meets with your approval?'

It took him a moment to recover himself, and even then he only managed to nod. April had risen and was staring open-mouthed at the man who had just been offered the chance to take a cane to her naked bottom. As we watched his expression changed from astonishment to a self-satisfied grin, and he thanked me as April and I left the room.

Ottershaw was due to go out on the Sunday morning, and for the next two days I took every opportunity to rub April's face in her predicament. I had her attend to him as often as possible, and he never wasted a chance to remark on how pretty she was and on the fine shape of her bottom. By Friday afternoon she was in a lather of expectation, simultaneously terrified and in desperate need of her beating. She knew she was in trouble, because I'd told her she could put her pants back on. I'd done it for the pleasure of having them come back down again, and she knew it.

I took her to him at three in the morning. He was awake, sitting in the dim orange glow of the night light with a smug expression on his round face.

'Good evening, Matron, good evening, April,' he greeted us, his dirty lust showing in every word. 'May I ask, Matron, why she is being beaten?'

'For amusement,' I answered honestly.

I had judged him to be a libertine rather than a genuine disciplinarian and was proved right as he answered with a pleased nod. It made no difference to me either way, but I knew it would make it worse for April to know that he was getting excited by the sight of her naked rear-end and her reaction as she was caned.

'May I position her?' he asked.

'Very well,' I answered as I turned the key in the door, sealing us in until April's punishment was done.

'Thank you,' he said, and turned to her. 'Now, my dear, I'm going to smack your bottom. I'm sure you understand the importance of obedience for a girl in your position, so it will be easier for you if you do just as I say.'

April glanced sideways at me out of her big, moist eyes, then nodded. Ottershaw had climbed out of bed and was pulling on a red silk dressing gown over his pyjamas.

'Good,' he went on as he fastened the cord over his ample paunch. 'Now, if you could kneel on the bed, please, with your delightful derrière towards us.'

April hesitated but then obeyed, climbing on to his bed and adopting a kneeling position. He took his pillows and plumped each of them, then laid them in front of her.

'Skirt up, my dear,' he instructed. 'We don't want it in the way, do we?'

She gave me a last, miserable look and eased her skirt up, exposing taut white pants that covered her bottom and the lower part of her back, making her cheeks seem to hang in them like two balls in a cloth bag.

'Good girl,' he told her. 'Now pop your knickers down and it'll soon be over.'

April took hold of the back of her pants and started to lower them, all the while looking back at us with a sulky pout. Ottershaw's gaze was glued on her bottom as she exposed it, following the stretched waistband as it glided down over her little fleshy cheeks until they were quite bare.

'Very pretty,' he remarked. 'Now bend down with your tummy on the pillows.'

She did it, slowly, with every sign of reluctance, ending up nonetheless with her face in the sheets and her bottom the highest part of her body. Despite her display of distaste for being made to adopt so vulgar a pose, I noticed that she had not kept her knees together. The rear of her fanny showed, with the hairy lips poking out in a little dark-lump, while the cleft of her bottom was slightly open with only a dark shadow to hide her anus.

'The cane, please, if you would be so kind,' Ottershaw addressed me, and I handed it to him.

April began to whimper as the cane was laid across her bottom and tapped twice on the tender flesh, sending little ripples across it. Ottershaw lifted the thin stick, then paused, poised to strike.

'Is she noisy?' he asked me.

'Quite,' I answered. 'I usually beat her in my office.'

'Perhaps we should gag her?'

'Perhaps.'

'I find a girl's knickers usually make an effective gag.'

'Pull them off, then.'

Ottershaw put the cane down and April expelled her breath in a long sigh. With quick, obviously practised motions he pulled her pants down her legs and off, then balled them and offered them to April's mouth. She gaped obediently and he pushed them in, stuffing her mouth until only a little tag of white cotton was left hanging out. Once more he lifted the cane and tapped her upturned bottom. Her buttocks tensed, only for him to suddenly put the cane down again.

'What about restraint?' he asked. 'Does she kick about much?'

'Not too much,' I answered. 'But tie her up if you think it necessary.'

'Oh, I do,' he answered. 'And as she had the good taste to wear stockings we can do both her ankles and her wrists. I often think a girl in big knickers and stockings is just made for gagging and tying, don't you?'

'I suppose so,' I answered, although his remark had made my stomach flutter as I myself was in stockings and big pants.

He bound April with the same calm efficiency he had used to gag her, peeling her stockings off one by one and then securing her wrists in the small of her back and lashing her ankles tightly together. With her legs closed her fanny was barely visible, but with her arms and legs tied and her mouth full of her pants she made a charming sight anyway.

'Now, my dear, I shall beat you,' Ottershaw announced and once more took up the cane. 'How many strokes, Matron?'

'A dozen,' I answered, 'and she is used to it, so take no notice if she thrashes about.'

'A dozen it is,' he answered gleefully and brought the cane down hard on April's bare bottom.

She jerked as the cane hit her, but managed no more than a muffled grunt. He lifted it again as her bottom wobbled back into shape, then brought it back down, again making her buck and grunt.

I watched every stroke as he beat her, enjoying her pained reaction and the gradual change as she came on heat. Ottershaw was very calm and very methodical, laying the strokes on hard and even until a dozen welts decorated the skin of her bottom. By then she had cocked her legs apart to show us her fanny and I knew she was fully aroused, perhaps aroused enough to have her virginity taken by the man who had just beaten her. He, however, had other ideas.

'How will you come, little April, with your hands tied?' he taunted. 'I can see it is what you want, but with Matron's agreement I think a further punishment might be in order before you are allowed your relief.'

'What did you have in mind?' I asked as April managed a choking sob.

'An enema,' he said cheerfully. 'After all, you must have the equipment to hand, and it's quiet. Doubtless she has given them, so what could be better than that she should take one? I am sure that you will concede that it would be a quite deliciously humiliating experience for her.'

'Yes,' I admitted, thinking of how she had come before.

I had given my girls enemas before but had not planned to take matters on this occasion so far, yet April was squirming her bottom at the suggestion and had not closed her knees. Obviously the little tart was game – or else she was willing to accept it in order to postpone her fucking.

'Perhaps if you would be so kind?' Ottershaw asked, and gestured at the door.

'Lock it behind me,' I answered, keeping my voice level and authoritative but aware that by conceding to the enema I had allowed my control over April's punishment to slip to a degree.

I hurried to collect the equipment, aware that there was nothing to stop Ottershaw from mounting April's bottom and taking her while I was gone. Only his gentlemanly manners suggested he wouldn't, and men's manners were something I'd long ago learned not to rely on. Nevertheless, when I got back he was doing nothing worse than stroking her buttocks. He had also turned the light up and moved it, illuminating her bottom in a circle of pale light. April gave me one of her pleading looks but I knew her too well to be fooled and responded by putting down the enema equipment on a chair in her plain view.

'Bottom up, my dear,' Ottershaw declared. 'We need your little hole showing for this, as I'm sure you will appreciate.'

April meekly lifted her bottom and the cheeks parted, revealing the tight brown dimple of her anus. I knew how humiliating she would find the position, even after her caning, and let her stay like that, with her fanny and bottom-hole on show as I prepared her enema. I let her see it all, pulling on my gloves and opening the big tub of grease right in front of her face as she looked on in horrified fascination. As I dipped a finger into the pot and drew it out, glistening with a thick coating of grease, she swallowed hard. She knew exactly where it was going: up her tight little bottom-hole.

Ottershaw watched with a dirty grin as I moved behind April and spread her bottom cheeks further apart with two fingers, stretching her anus. I touched it, smearing the grease on to the little hole, then pressed at the centre and watched my finger slide up her bottom as she gave a moan of pure shame. For a while I kept it in, wriggling it about in her rectum so that she really got to know how it felt to have her anus lubricated. Only when she began to sigh and was obviously enjoying it too much did I pull my finger out. Her bottom-hole closed and squeezed out a fat worm of grease, at which Ottershaw chuckled.

I went back to where she could see me and greased the bulb that was going up her bottom. The nozzle was a big one, which could be inflated to hold it in, allowing the nurse to attend to other matters while the enema went in. April swallowed once more at the sight of it, then closed her eyes and lifted her bottom. Ottershaw was still behind her, admiring his handiwork and the greasy hole of her anus. As I lifted the nozzle he gave me a big grin and stood back a pace, allowing me room.

'Relax, my dear,' he instructed as I spread April's bottom cheeks once more.

Her anus pouted and I pressed the nozzle to it. It slid in, her hole gaping to take it then closing on the narrow part. Holding the tube, I squeezed the attached bulb, inflating the nozzle in her rectum to lodge it firmly inside her. Ottershaw was by the sink, holding the rubber bottle that would shortly be filling April's bowels.

'A pint, do you think? Two?' he asked.

'One,' I instructed.

He turned the tap on and I watched the rubber bulge as the water ran in, doubtless in just the way April's rectum would shortly be bulging inside her. There was a stand nearby, from which he hung the bottle before passing me the tube that ran from it. I took it and joined it to the one protruding from April's bottom, held it up so that she could see it and turned the tap.

Her eyes went wide almost immediately and I knew it was happening, her bottom filling up with water as she wriggled helpless in her bonds. Soon she was writhing her buttocks from side to side, then frantically wiggling her toes as her rectum filled and her tummy swelled with water. I had judged the amount carefully, enough to be severely uncomfortable but not too much to hold in. Sure enough, when the last of it had run in and I had deflated the nozzle and eased it from her anus April was squirming in desperation but not leaking at all, despite her well-greased hole. She was clamping her bottom, though, really tight, and Ottershaw and I shared a chuckle at the sight.

'I am sure this has excited you,' I addressed him. 'Perhaps you would enjoy it if she were to relieve you in her hand?'

'I would,' he answered. 'Very much.'

He untied her and she spat the pants from her mouth. Rising, she sat up straight on the bed as he lay down. She was uncomfortable, I could see it, wiggling her bottom from side to side on the bed and looked around with nervous little glances. I could tell she was excited too, as she gave the same shy giggle she always did when she needed to masturbate. I sat down in the visitor's chair, feeling very warm and very excited by the thought of watching her touch his cock.

'Now, April,' Ottershaw said as he opened his dressing gown. 'Have you done this before?'

She shook her head dumbly and I saw her give a little shiver as the cord of his pyjamas gave way and his cock and balls came on show. Rather than touch them she gave me a nervous glance, seeking help.

'Take a little grease,' I told her, 'and rub it well in.'

She reached for the grease pot and took some out, rubbing it between her hands before reaching tentatively for his genitals. In the course of her work she had touched men but, I was sure, never for pleasure and she hesitated for a long moment before taking a sudden grip on him and starting to rub. Feeling extremely pleased with myself I sat and watched the slimy mess of his penis and scrotum moving about in her hand and the discomfort on her face, enjoying both. Ottershaw had already been half stiff and quickly came to erection. I don't think April had ever even seen a hard cock before, because her hand was trembling as she masturbated him and she was being very clumsy about it, rubbing him rather than tugging up and down on his shaft.

'You must learn to do that properly, my dear,' he said. 'Curl your hand around the shaft and move it slowly up and down so that the foreskin peels back and forth over the glans. Yes, that is better. Good girl, ah yes, beautiful.'

She gave him a little smile as if to thank him for showing her how to do such a disgusting thing, then began to pull at him more firmly as her confidence grew. I was enjoying the sight and starting to feel the need to come myself. It wasn't dirty enough, though, not just in her hand. I wanted him mounted on her, with his fat belly rubbing on her bottom as he took her from the rear with her load of water sloshing in her belly. She was ready, I could see – or, at least, I was sure that in her state she would not dare to disobey me.

73

'Now you may have her, Mr Ottershaw,' I said. 'That's if you want the little tart.'

'Indeed I do,' he answered, 'so long as she's willing. But I think it would be kind to allow her to expel her enema first, or we might have a rather messy accident.'

'I would, I would,' April pleaded, kicking her feet on the ground in her urgency. 'Please let me go!'

'I think you had better,' he said. 'But put your knickers back on first, just in case.'

She jumped up from the bed and hastily wiped her hands on a towel. Suddenly it was getting out of my control. I wanted to watch April as he had her, but it was clearly impractical with a pint of water in her rectum. Also, Ottershaw was starting to take control of the situation. This was not what I wanted. April was supposed to see him as the wicked, dirty old pervert, allowed to do disgusting things to her only because I ordered it. I had expected him to be coarse and demanding, not polite, and nor had I expected him to handle her with such skill. She was shaking hard, her jaw trembling from the feel of the water in her bowel and her fingers unsteady as she fumbled for her pants and tugged them back up and over her bottom. Ottershaw gave a chuckle at the sight, doubtless enjoying her sense of panic as she struggled not to disgrace herself. I expected her to look hurt, but instead she gave him one of her dirty little smiles and I knew I had to take back my control.

'Stop, April,' I ordered. 'I think it might be more amusing to have you do it in your pants.'

She stopped, staring gape-mouthed at me, her thumbs still in her waistband.

'I . . . I don't . . .' she began, with her face showing more worry and consternation than ever before.

It was so beautiful, so exquisite, and I had to come while she did it. I couldn't hold myself any longer and my hand edged up my skirt to the front of my pants.

April was still standing there, holding her pants up in the most ridiculous stance, with her bottom stuck out a little and the taut seat towards me, hesitating.

'Do it, you little tart!' I ordered.

'I think that would be a little hard,' Ottershaw broke in. 'Come on, April, run along – and no playing with yourself in the loo, mind.'

She went immediately, running for the loo in a flurry of dishevelled skirt and jiggling bottom, fumbling with the key before bursting out into the passage with the back of her pants still on show. Ottershaw gave his dirty little chuckle and turned to me as the door closed.

'Wonderful!' he exclaimed. 'Her face when she thought she would have to fill her knickers, what a picture! She is such a sweetie, and to think I thought her cold and aloof! I must thank you for allowing me this opportunity, but I see you are ready yourself. May I help in any way?'

I could find no answer. On the one hand I was furious, but I desperately, urgently needed to come. It was all slipping away, all my careful control, all my resistance as my thighs slid apart and my hand went down the front of my pants. My fanny was warm and moist, my clitoris urgent for my finger. All my thoughts of making girls do rude things with coarse, vulgar men came crowding into my head. There were girls with cocks in their hands and in their mouths. Pretty girls with men's come on their faces and over their breasts. Pretty young nurses with their uniforms off and their nervous expressions betraying consternation as they offered themselves to some dirty old man on my orders. Only it wasn't April bent down with her bottom vulnerable, or any of my other girls, but me.

My thighs had come up and open as I slid down the chair, revealing the front of my pants with my fingers working down them. I was open, really open wide, spread in a way no man had ever seen me before. My fingers were rubbing hard on my clitoris and I was pulling my panty gusset aside, exposing myself to Ottershaw and unable to stop myself. He was between my legs, grabbing my thighs and rolling them high on to my chest. His cock nudged my fanny and I cried out as I started to come, then again as my hymen tore and my precious, precious virginity was gone – not little April's, but mine.

5

The Ottershaw Diet

Ever since I'd left school I had been putting on weight, and I didn't know what to do about it. Not that the boys didn't like me: it was the girls who were so nasty. In fact the boys loved it, even if they would never have admitted it, and I think that's what made the girls so unpleasant.

Slim was in, with Twiggy and the Shrimp everywhere you looked and busts and hips very firmly out. I had plenty of both, even at twenty, more than I could hide, with a round, wobbly bottom to match. I was the fattest girl in the typing pool and I got teased all the time, and the worse the teasing got the more I wanted to eat, just to keep myself happy.

It was Tina Jones who started to call me Piggy instead of Joanna, making a joke on the name Twiggy. The nickname stuck and I became more miserable than ever, but now I was determined that I was going to diet. Unfortunately, nothing I tried seemed to work, and I kept putting on weight and Tina kept teasing me. I even knew why she was doing it, but it didn't help. There was a boy in the post room, Mark, whom she really fancied but who just wasn't interested in her. He was interested in *me* and, while he was far too cool to actually ask a fat girl out, he took every chance to snog me and feel my breasts. Tina knew, and it really made her mad.

When it came to a head it was because of Mark. He had to come up to us two or three times a day, and would always do his best to catch me alone for a quick feel. I didn't mind, and even used to make it easier for him. My favourite was to go for stationery when I knew he'd be coming, so he could nip into the storeroom and we could have a good snog and a cuddle. This time it was after lunch, and he'd been drinking, so he got really bold. He pretended to stroke my back, then suddenly snapped my bra open and before I knew it my top was up and my breasts were out. I tried to protest but it was really too nice, and I let him feel them, only to be told that now I'd let my breasts out I was going to have to suck his cock.

I really didn't know what to do, but he took it out and put my hand on it, then told me to sit down on a chair. He wasn't the first boy to get his cock out on me, because there was something about me that made boys bold. I'd even sucked before, but this was different, because the door wasn't even locked and I was terrified someone was going to come in. Mark didn't care, but pushed his cock at my mouth, told me to get sucking and said he was going to make me swallow and not to whine about it. He took hold of my tits and felt them while I sucked him. My nipples were really hard and his cock tasted lovely, and I was half-wishing he'd fuck me, but he didn't, just contenting himself with telling me how beautiful I was and how lovely my tits were while I sucked on his erection.

He was going to spunk in my mouth, he'd said so, but instead he pulled it out at the last second and did it in my face and over my tits. I got spunk everywhere, in my hair and in one eye, over my blouse and over my bra, but most of it went on my breasts, and as he finished off he rubbed his cock in between them and over my nipples, making a real mess. Despite the state I was in I was really turned on and would have let him do anything. He was finished, though, and just took a handkerchief out of his pocket for me to wipe myself with.

That was when Tina came in. She really got an eyeful as well. Mark's cock was still out and pretty well hard, sticking out of his fly and looking really big. My breasts were bare and splattered with his spunk. So was my face. I tried to cover myself and was stammering out apologies and excuses. Not Mark.

'Hi, skinny. Wish you'd got a pair like that?' he said happily. Then he put his cock away and just walked out, leaving me to face Tina.

I was sure she was going to report me, and that would have meant the sack, without any doubt at all. She was looking at me, really angry and red in the face, so I kept on apologising and begging her not to say anything when she suddenly told me to shut up.

'You make me sick!' she spat. 'A fat pig like you going for someone like him! How dare you! I mean, how dare you think he could possibly fancy you! It's not because he likes you, you know, it's because you're easy!'

'He . . .' I started, only to be told to shut up again.

'Listen,' Tina hissed. 'Mark's not for the likes of you, but you're getting in the way of a good friend of mine, and I don't like that. See?'

I nodded.

'She's not a tart like you,' she went on. 'She doesn't throw herself at every boy who comes along. He wants her, but he'd have to play it slow, because she's got class, and she could do without you sticking your fat tits in his face!'

Tina was furious, red in the face and shouting so loudly I was sure someone would hear. I was still cleaning myself up and had my hands on my bra catch when she came forward and slapped my face, really hard.

'That'll teach you, you fat, greedy bitch!' she spat. 'Keep your hands off him! Stick to your own type, fat and ugly!'

Tina turned on her heel and left. I was almost in tears and could only sit there, feeling really bad. Even though I was telling myself I should be grateful she hadn't reported me, it didn't make me feel better. She'd only done it to save Mark, anyway. It was also obvious that there was no 'friend'. It was she who wanted Mark, and she hated the fact that he preferred me.

It wasn't surprising, though, because everyone knew how Tina treated men, and Mark was no fool. She liked to be taken out to expensive restaurants and be given fancy presents, and if her boyfriend was lucky he might be allowed to peck her cheek on her front step. Certainly she was never going to suck him off, much less let him fuck her. So she hated me and I'm sure she really believed Mark preferred her and would have asked her out if I hadn't been there and been willing.

After that Tina got worse and worse, teasing me all the time, putting me down and spoiling my work to get me in trouble. She'd flick ink on my letters or press an odd key on my typewriter as she walked past, so I'd have to start the job again, and soon the supervisors were starting to call me lazy. I didn't dare do anything to hit back, either, because all she had to do was tell them about Mark and I'd be out. It made me want to eat more, too, so in the end I decided I *had* to do something.

The other girls in the pool were either on Tina's side or didn't like to speak out, so I decided to go and see my aunt Elaine, who was the only relative I had in London. She had married a man in the wine trade and lived in a flat in Chelsea. He was a fat, jolly type, and it was so obvious that he didn't care about his weight or what other people thought that I started to feel better straight away. We got on so well that I told them both. Elaine said I ought to rise above it and ignore her. Percy was a bit more practical.

'How much do you weigh, my dear?' he asked.

'Twelve stone,' I lied. I weighed nearer fourteen.

'And this Tina?'

'Oh, no more than seven, I suppose. She's really slim.'

'Good. Then waylay her on the way home, sit on her head, pull up her skirt, take her knickers down and spank her bottom. If you can, take a photo and tell her it'll appear on the company noticeboard if she doesn't leave you alone. In any case the humiliation and the threat of a repeat performance is likely to be enough to keep her in check.'

'I couldn't!'

'Fortune favours the bold, my dear.'

'Don't be silly, Percy,' Elaine put in. 'Poor Joanna would be bound to get the sack if anything came out, and Tina would be sure to report her – maybe to the police, as well! Besides, you're always saying how a spanking should never . . .'

She stopped and I'm sure she blushed.

'I spoke in jest,' Percy answered her. 'A more practical suggestion might be to leave and take a job elsewhere. We can always use another typist at Carew's.'

'Really?'

'Certainly, my dear. I have just been made buyer, and only need give personnel the word. Consider the job yours. As to your other problem, I do have a suggestion – two, in fact.'

'Tell me, please.'

'The first is not to be so damn' silly. You have a beautiful figure, take it from me as a man. You should be proud of it, not worry over what some jealous little snip thinks. However, I know how you girls will worry over such things, so my second suggestion is this. You will visit us for dinner every second Sunday, and when you do we will weigh you. If you have lost weight I personally shall present you with a ten-shilling note for each pound lost. That would be fifty of these beastly new pence.'

'That's a great idea!'

'But, my dear, there is a "but". Should you *gain* weight, then you must expect a stroke of the cane for each pound put on. A stroke on your bottom, that is, not on your hand, so it won't show, and it will be delivered by your aunt for the sake of modesty.'

'Percy!' Elaine cut in.

'No, it's all right, honestly,' I said. 'I think that might really make me try.'

My head was buzzing with ideas as I walked home. I was much happier for a start, and I thought Percy's idea might really work. The idea of being beaten scared me, maybe enough to make me actually lose weight. I was glad it would be done by Aunt Elaine if I did fail, though, because the thought of bending over for Percy to whack my bum gave me odd feelings, uncomfortably like the ones I got when I gave Mark a chance to grope me. I was also determined not to rise to Tina's tauntings. I actually preferred Percy's suggestion, but knew I could never dare go along with it. What was funny was the way Elaine had broken off when telling Percy not to be silly. She had been going to say something about spanking, how it should never some-thing. She had stopped, and the only thing I could think of was that it should never be done in anger, or maybe haste, but that it ought to be done as a punishment, calmly and formally. Somehow that didn't seem right.

Two weeks later I received thirty shillings – or one pound and fifty new pence – from Percy. I was really pleased with myself, as not only had I lost three pounds but things were getting better at work. I had ignored Tina and she was starting to get bored of tormenting me, while a new man had taken her eye. This was Anthony Croom, who was actually a Director and a major shareholder. He had spoken to her at a firm do, and she was really gone over him, although he was married and had a baby son. She claimed he'd taken her out and tried to seduce her, but nobody really believed it. It kept her away from me, though, so I was happy.

I was a bit too happy as it turned out, because with Tina off my back I forgot all about my diet. When I visited Elaine and climbed on the weighing scale I was up a full five pounds. They were sorry for me but they wouldn't let me off. Percy went to sit in the living room with a glass of brandy while I followed Aunt Elaine into their bedroom. I was really shaking, and it got worse when I saw what was on the bed: a long, dark brown cane with a crooked handle.

'I suppose you had better bend over the bed, dear,' she said, picking the wicked-looking thing up.

I went over, feeling thoroughly sorry for myself. There was a mirror behind me and I could see my bottom in it, looking big and round under my dress. I was about to be beaten on it, and all I could think of was that it was right because it was so big.

'Pull up your dress, then, dear,' Elaine said, her voice kindly but strict.

'My dress?'

'Certainly your dress. Come now, I must be able to see what I'm doing, mustn't I? Besides, it's not as if I haven't seen you in your knickers before, and less.'

I couldn't really argue with her, so I reached back and pulled up my dress. It was quite short anyway, and left as much thigh as I dared showing, but there was a huge difference between showing my legs and displaying the seat of my knickers for a caning. I had guessed it might come to showing them, though, and had chosen an old school pair, large and white and demure, if rather tight because my bottom had got fatter since my schooldays.

'Thank you,' Elaine said. 'And now your knickers, please.'

'My knickers? Why?'

'So that your bottom is bare, Joanna: that is how it's done. Now come on, don't be silly, pop them down.'

I reached back, hardly knowing what I was doing as I eased my knickers down over my bottom. I had accepted that I was to be whacked, but not like this, not with my bare bottom showing. My aunt obviously didn't mind, so I felt a bit silly, but it was just so shameful having to show off the size of my bottom as well as have it beaten. I could see it in the mirror, big and bare and wobbly, with a bit of hair showing between my thighs.

'Right down, Joanna dear. Do behave yourself,' Elaine chided.

I swallowed hard but did as I was told, taking my knickers right down to my knees. Now it was all showing, my whole big, fat bum, naked in the mirror with the lips of my fanny showing between my thighs. I was so glad it was only my aunt watching as I was making a really disgraceful exhibition of myself.

'This may be painful but it has to be done, Joanna,' Elaine told me. 'Besides, you may find that afterwards you are less resentful than you might have imagined.'

Actually I was already thanking her, although I was burning with humiliation. If this was how it felt just getting ready for a beating, then . . .

I squealed aloud as the cane came down across my bottom. It stung crazily and I was immediately clutching at my bottom and dancing up and down on my toes.

'Don't make such a scene, dear,' Elaine said calmly. 'It's not so very bad.'

That was what *she* thought, because my bottom was on fire. I could see it in the mirror, a long red double line running across my cheeks with a blotch at one end.

'Come, come, Joanna, in position,' Elaine ordered.

Once more I stuck my bum out and again she brought the cane down, even harder and lower, leaving another scarlet line and sending me dancing up and down again until I managed to recover myself. Three more times she did it, and each time I had to get back in position, with

my bare bottom stuck out so that my fanny showed.
Then she would whack me and I'd jump about until I
could control myself again. By the end my poor bottom
was decorated with five red lines and was really burning
hot. My knickers had fallen right down and I was bent
over so far my bumhole showed behind, but the pain
and the heat were so strong that I didn't care, and
Elaine didn't comment.

'If there's anything you need to do, just go ahead,' she
told me, and left.

She had said it in a really friendly, confidential way,
like my mother when I'd started my periods and needed
to know how to cope. I knew what she meant, too,
because my fanny was really warm and for all the pain
I felt excited. I couldn't do it, though, not masturbate
myself, not in their bedroom. I got guilty enough doing
it in my own room, thinking of Mark, let alone now,
when they'd know and when it was because my aunt
had had to cane me!

Instead I pulled up my knickers and followed her.
Percy gave me a knowing smile but didn't say a word
about my beating, and nor did Elaine. Instead they
asked how it was going at work. I told them about Tina
and the Director, and Percy immediately perked up.

'Croom, you say? Anthony Croom?' he asked.

'Yes, that's right.'

'You don't say. He's a customer of my firm, one of
the best. The fellow drinks Richebourg and d'Yquem
the way most of us take Beaujolais. So this Tina girl's
after him, eh?'

'She says she's been out with him, and that he tried
to seduce her.'

'Not impossible, though I'd think he'd have better
taste if she's as skinny and obnoxious as you say. If he
did try I bet he succeeded, in any case.'

'She says not. She wants to marry him and says she'll
be a virgin until their wedding night.'

'Ah, now that's not sporting. I mean, the Crooms have just had a little one, so I don't suppose there's much going at home. So Anthony would be up for an affair, maybe, but no more.'

'Percy!' Elaine cut in.

'Sorry, dear, but you know how it is.'

'No, I don't,' she answered. 'I thought you were quite happy when Alice was little.'

'You're different,' he answered. 'But you'll admit we've had more time since she's been at school. Anyway, we're embarrassing poor Joanna.'

How he thought anything could have been more embarrassing than him knowing I'd just been caned I wasn't sure, but he said he'd have a word with Mr Croom, which pleased me immensely.

Sure enough, the very next week Tina let it be known that she had decided Anthony Croom wasn't good enough for her and had ditched him. It was so obviously phoney I could have laughed, but I kept quiet. That lunchtime I found Mark and took him into a quiet corner of the loading bay. He had my breasts out again and I sucked him and swallowed his spunk, which was great and I was really pleased with myself afterwards.

I tried really hard at my diet, remembering how awful the caning had been. I also remembered the warm, needful feeling in my fanny afterwards, and the way Aunt Elaine had expected me to want to masturbate. It suggested she did the same, in which case she got whacked herself or she wouldn't have known. I guessed that Percy disciplined her now and then, just like I'd been done, knickers down and bare-bottomed, over the bed. It seemed likely that was what they'd brought the cane for, and the idea of her getting it like I had made my feelings even stronger.

Despite the odd urge to get caned again I was good and lost weight for my next two visits. Percy paid up with a smile but I was sure he'd rather been hoping I'd fail and get a good whacking, so that he could listen through the wall and know what was going on. He never said anything, though, nor tried anything.

It was coming up to Christmas and, as usual, the firm was giving a big party with turkey and Christmas pudding for everyone. This would be a week after my next appointment with Elaine and Percy, and they were going away after the New Year, so I knew I would have a full month to lose any weight I gained over the festive season. I was already a stone lighter, and most of it had come off my hips and tummy, so Mark began to be more open in his attentions to me. Tina didn't like it at all, but didn't want to be seen chasing after Mark when she had said Mr Croom wasn't good enough for her. The way she went on you'd have thought she was waiting for a prince at the very least. She began to tease me again, though, just out of spite.

The day I was due at Aunt Elaine's it was snowing hard, and I was shivering by the time I arrived. Elaine wasn't there, and Percy explained that she had gone to collect my cousin Alice from school in Wales and had chosen not to drive back in the snow. I could see why, with at least a foot on the pavements outside and more in the drifts. Percy offered me a glass of some special brandy he'd opened and I accepted gratefully. It was rich and strong, warming me deep inside, and as he began to chat happily of this and that I relaxed, content just to listen and sip my drink and occasionally put in a polite remark. Only when I'd finished my second glass did he suggest weighing me, and I gladly accepted, eager for however much I had earned in the last two weeks.

To my horror I was a pound up on the previous fortnight. I could have lied, or quickly reset the scales, but I suppose I was just too honest for my own good, because I told Percy. I didn't think it mattered, anyway, because it was only a pound and Elaine wasn't there.

'Oh dear,' he said, 'that is awkward. You won't be too embarrassed, I trust?'

'You're not going to cane me, are you?'

'Why, certainly. I would have paid you, after all.'

It was true, and I couldn't really think what to say, except that it was indecent and rude and it would make my fanny wet. I didn't say it, though – especially the last part. Every time I'd escaped punishment I'd had that odd regret, and with the brandy inside me and the flat so warm and cosy after the freezing night I was suddenly determined to go through with it. Percy was right, anyway. I'd have taken the money, so it was only right that he should take the cane to my bottom.

He went to fetch it, humming a carol to himself as he walked to the bedroom. I didn't follow but kneeled on his settee with my bottom towards the fire. If my backside had felt big when Elaine made me take my knickers down, it felt huge now, a great ball of wobbling flesh sticking out behind me. My knickers felt tight across the seat and my fanny was already warm, while my lower lip wouldn't stop trembling.

'I think you know what to do, Joanna, dear,' Percy said as he came back.

'Not like Elaine did it. Not bare!'

'Well, I don't know,' he answered. 'Elaine did say that you were a little prissy about taking your knickers down for her, but don't you think you should?'

'*Why?*'

'Because, my dear, you are being punished. Besides, I am effectively your uncle, so it's not even improper. Look, you may keep them up if you wish, and even retain your tights and skirt if you really insist, but I shall be very disappointed in you. Physical punishment is a serious thing for a girl to take, and it should be done properly, with the bottom bare, otherwise you won't really understand that you've been punished.'

'I will!'

'No, no, Joanna. You see, for you to be bare while I am clothed creates the necessary inequality between the one who wields the cane and the one who accepts it. Baring your bottom shows an admission of your guilt, an acceptance that you deserve punishment. Keeping it covered suggests a defiance of the punishment you have accepted as just.'

'Oh all right, I'll do it.'

I did, all of it. First it was a skirt, a thick woollen one I'd chosen to keep out the cold. I felt really vulnerable with it up, partly because my tights were showing and my knickers through them, and partly because Percy was watching my every move. My tights went next, eased down to leave my bottom feeling simply enormous. Last it was my knickers, which took a real effort, but I managed it and bent down, bare-bottomed, waiting for the cane and knowing he could see the whole plump ball of my naked bum and the lips of my fanny too.

Percy was right, though. On my skirt the stroke would have been just pain, nothing more. With my knickers down to show my bare bottom it was so much more. He brought the cane down across my buttocks, just once, but it was enough. I squealed and jumped and rubbed myself a bit, like before, then covered myself again. It wasn't much, I suppose, but I felt really, truly punished. I'd been bad, and my uncle had made me take my knickers down and had whacked me for it. Just knowing that he had seen my bare bottom was what mattered: six or twelve strokes might have hurt more but I wouldn't have felt any more contrite afterwards.

Percy was in a strange mood over lunch and said he had to visit an old friend afterwards, so when I was dropped off near my lodgings it was still the middle of the afternoon. I didn't go in, though. I really didn't want to. All I could think of was how it had felt to be made to take down my knickers and show my bottom.

Aunt Elaine had hinted that I might want to masturbate myself after a caning, but that wasn't what I needed. For one thing, I always felt so guilty afterwards, and confused, because although it feels nice it's supposed to be wrong.

It had stopped snowing but it was still cold, with hardly anyone about. I began to walk, pushing through the snow in the vague direction of the park. Because it was so cold I could really feel the heat of my fanny, and of the cane mark, too. It kept running through my head, all the time: I'd been made to take my knickers down and I'd been beaten on my bare bottom, a thought that went round and round in my mind until I knew that I just had to do it. Not in my lodgings, though: it just wasn't private enough. The landlady, Mrs Toller, was a busybody at the best of times and always keen to pounce on anything she thought of as improper. That meant almost everything, and just knowing she was in the house would have ruined it for me. Besides, there were no locks on the doors and the idea of her catching me masturbating myself was truly unbearable.

I felt really guilty as I decided to do it under the railway arches. There were some where the railway cut across the end of the park, and I could see them, cold black mouths half hidden behind some trees. They didn't look inviting, but they did look lonely, and I felt so dirty that they seemed the right place for me – a dirty place for a dirty girl. I walked over, feeling bad but determined too. There were only two other people I could see, both walking dogs, but I was sure they were staring at me and knew just what was going through my mind.

The arches looked more forbidding the closer I got, but also more private. The last two were completely shielded by trees and I couldn't imagine anyone going there at all. I pushed in quickly, sure that nobody had seen. Underneath it was dark and gloomy and smelled of earth and damp, with water dripping from the brick arch above my head. I chose a dry place were I was sure I couldn't be seen and stopped to listen, my heart pounding at what I was going to do. All it needed was a hand down the front of my knickers, a few quick rubs and I'd be there. But it wasn't so easy. I knew I was alone, but I didn't feel it. I felt as if everyone was watching me and thinking what a tart I was. I could almost see Tina's face, sneering down at me because I was dirty while she was so clean and perfect. That almost stopped me, but it also brought out my stubborn streak and I decided that I had to do it. Otherwise I'd be behaving how she wanted. I'd be the fat girl who knew her place.

Swallowing the lump in my throat, I undid the lower buttons of my coat and pulled up my skirt at the front. My hand went down my tights and into my knickers, finding my fanny, plump, warm and wet. I was in heaven immediately and I closed my eyes, stroking the soft fur of my mound and thinking rude thoughts of bare bottoms and breasts, of Mark's hard cock and hot sperm, of showing my fanny to Uncle Percy. I was sighing as I began to rub, and it didn't matter where I was any more. In my head I was on a soft bed with Mark between my thighs and his lovely big cock inside me, telling me how nice my big breasts were, how he loved the fullness of my hips and my round, fat bottom . . .

It hit me and as I came I was thinking of how lovely it was to have big breasts and a plump, wobbly bum, a bum with a cane mark across it to show I'd been beaten. A mark to show people cared about me, to show that people wanted to take my knickers down. For one moment it was lovely, perfect, and I wanted to strip, to expose myself and jiggle my fat bottom and breasts about in the sheer ecstasy of being a girl, showing what I'd got to the world. Then it was fading and I was cold, and guilty, and scared, but triumphant too. I'd done it, and damn to Tina and Mrs Toller and all the other prudes.

All week I felt funny about what I'd done, but at the same time guilty and pleased with myself. Something must have showed, because Mark was all over me and he asked me to go to the pictures with him on Saturday night. I said yes, although I could hardly believe it, as normally he just wanted a grope. I sucked him behind some packing cases anyway and swallowed his spunk again, but afterwards, when one of his mates pinched my bum, he said I was his girlfriend and to leave me alone.

It got round in no time, and all the girls were looking at me and whispering. Some of them even congratulated me – and then Tina came over. I'd been typing a letter, a really long one with lots of fancy words, and had almost finished. She came to stand over me, holding a cup of tea in one hand and a sticky bun in the other. I tried to ignore her, but everyone had gone quiet and was looking at us.

'What did I say the other week, Piggy?' she said.

'My name's Joanna,' I answered, 'and you might have said all sorts of things. I don't remember.'

'What I said, Piggy,' she went on, 'was to stick to your own type, fat and ugly.'

'So?' I managed.

'So you haven't, have you?' Tina snapped. 'You've been pestering Mark again, haven't you? Whining round him, asking him to take you out! Well, I don't warn people twice, Piggy!'

Before I could react she had pushed the bun in my face and, as I pushed her hand away, she poured the tea out, right over my head, then over my typewriter and my letter. Someone laughed as I struggled to get the icing and hot tea out of my eyes and I hit out. But Tina had gone and the next thing I knew Mrs Tench, the supervisor, was looking down at me.

'What is this?' she demanded. 'What are you doing, Joanna?'

'Piggy had an accident,' Tina put in. 'She was trying to eat her cake too fast, as usual.'

'Well, clear yourself up!' Mrs Tench snapped at me. 'This will go on your record, which is very poor already.'

I couldn't find anything to say, because I knew they'd all stick up for Tina and I'd be called a liar, which would go on my report as well. Mrs Tench always sided with Tina anyway, because that way she had the most popular girl in the pool on her side, which made it easier to keep order. As I cleaned myself up in the Ladies I was in tears, and I was thinking of what Percy had suggested and how nice it would be to do it, if only I had the courage. Of course I didn't, so I went meekly back to my desk to start the letter again, then got into trouble for being slow.

That was on the Thursday, and Friday was the Christmas party, so we all came in with our best dresses on and plenty of make-up. Not much work got done and there were people coming in and out of our room all day, mainly men. Tina had hung a piece of mistletoe over the door and made a big thing of it, saying it was just for the pretty girls and I had better keep away. I ignored her, but she wouldn't let it go and kept calling me Piggy all day and telling one man after another about how she had taught me my place the day before.

The party was in the big hall, which was set out with tables and decorated, with a big tree and tinsel and holly and everything. Our typing-pool table was right at the end, between the one for the post room and the one for the janitors. Tina was showing off, saying who should sit where and trying to make out there wasn't room for me so I would have to go on the janitors' table.

I was still standing there, trying to work out what to do and feeling miserable, when the directors came in. It was really embarrassing, with everyone looking at me, and I was just about to surrender and go to the janitors when Anthony Croom came in, saw me and smiled. He excused himself to the Chairman and started towards us, which put Tina in an immediate flutter, adjusting her hair and trying to look cool and uninterested at the same time. He didn't go to her, though, but to me.

'Joanna, isn't it?' he asked. 'Percy's niece?'

'Yes, sir,' I answered.

'I knew from the description,' he went on. 'There couldn't be two such lovely girls among the firm's typists. Are you looking forward to our Christmas do?'

'Yes, sir, only I don't have a seat.'

'Nonsense, there's plenty of room at my table, and you'll brighten things up no end. Load of old fuddy-duddies up there, you know – frightfully boring.'

The last bit was said in a whisper, and he took my arm. I wouldn't have dared go, but he led me, right up the middle of the room. We went past the typists and the secretaries, past the supervisors and the room heads, even past the managers, right to the top table, where he sat me at the end, between himself and Mr Greaves, the Managing Director. I could see the whole room, with Mrs Tench looking at me in outrage and Tina staring in utter, furious hatred.

'What ho, Greavsie,' Mr Croom addressed Mr Greaves. 'This is Joanna, the niece of an old friend. Don't mind if she joins us, do you? I'd thought she'd add a splash of colour.'

'Not at all, not at all,' Mr Greaves answered, giving me a broad grin with his gaze fixed firmly on my chest. 'Pleased to meet you, Joanna.'

The others were the same, the men anyway. Their wives didn't look too happy, except for Mrs Croom, who patted my shoulder and winked at me. At that I guessed it was all Uncle Percy's doing. If so, then I was sure he had meant well but I wasn't certain it was really such a good idea. After all, I would be back in the typing pool on Monday.

I didn't really know what to say, either, but the Crooms and Mr Greaves, who wasn't married, and even the Chairman, who was, all paid me plenty of attention. After a while and a few glasses of a really delicious wine I began to feel a bit more at ease, and even began to flirt a bit with Mr Greaves, because I knew that Tina was staring at me.

We had devils on horseback, and turkey with all the trimmings, and Christmas pudding, and all the time Mr Croom kept my glass filled up, first with the nice white wine, then with a strong red one, then a sweet white one I liked best of all. By then I was giggling and Mr Greaves had his hand on my knee under the table. I didn't care, but I did need the loo.

I wasn't too steady as I walked back down the aisle between the tables. Tina watched me all the way, but I just stuck my tongue out at her and walked on, deliberately wiggling. In the Ladies I had a pee and splashed some water on my face, then started to adjust my make-up. I was just doing the lipstick when the door opened. It was Tina, along with Debbie, Mandy and Judy, three of her friends, and she had a really nasty look on her face.

'Well, look who it is, Piggy herself, painting her snout. Don't bother, Piggy, you don't look human anyway, so there's no point.'

I didn't answer, but quickly put my lipstick away and started for the door. Tina stepped in my way and pushed me back, her friends lining up behind her.

'Now I'm going to tell you what's going to happen,' she sneered. 'That way you'll really understand why you should do as you're told and stick to your own. First you're going to stand here like a good little pig while I do my business. Then your head is going down the toilet. Yeah, that's right, the one I've just used, because that's all you're fit for: my shit. I'm going to flush it, Piggy, right over your fat face, and then we'll see if you want to run back to Mr Croom. Take her arms, girls.'

The three of them came forward and I backed away. I could tell they weren't really sure about it, but Tina was. When they weren't quick enough for her liking, she grabbed my arm and tried to twist it, then smacked my face.

I hit her back, not because I thought I could beat her or even to try and get away, but because I was scared. Even before my hand touched her I was thinking what a stupid thing it was to do and how I was really going to get it now. Then my palm caught her across the cheek.

For one moment nothing happened. Tina stood there, staring at me with a big red hand mark on her face and her mouth open in amazement. Her friends had stood back, and two of them had their hands over their mouths, hardly able to believe I'd done it.

'You hit me!' Tina exclaimed. 'You, Piggy, you actually hit me!'

She couldn't believe it. She couldn't believe that someone as low as me had had the sheer cheek to slap her face just because she was going to teach me my place, and at that I just completely lost my temper, and so did she. She snatched at me, raking for my face with her nails, but I caught her arm and then we were really fighting as her friends screamed at her to really punish me.

It was a completely unfair fight. I was fat, frightened and alone, while Tina was slim, confident and had her friends. Percy had been right: it was like handling a doll. All her tough ways and hard words were nothing, just air. She tried to scratch me and pull my hair, but I didn't even feel it. My first proper punch sent her to the ground and then I was on top of her, with my full weight on her chest as I slapped her face and pulled her hair and tore her frock. Her breasts popped out as I ripped her bra off them and she screamed in outrage. She tried to cover herself and I grabbed her wrists, forcing them over her head to pin her down, helpless underneath my weight with her hair everywhere and her dress torn open and her naked tits rising and falling in the yellow toilet light.

Tina's friends were yelling at me to get off and calling me a bully, but not one of them tried to help her. I didn't care, anyway. All I wanted was revenge – revenge for all the horrid things she'd called me and all the nasty things she'd done. She'd been going to push my head in the toilet bowl, too, and flush it, and all because I had a fuller figure than her, because I was fat, as she said, and at that moment I decided she was going to find out how it felt.

I was too furious to think straight, but pulled Tina towards the door by her hair. She thought I was going to flush her and she really struggled, getting to her feet even though I never let go of her hair. She was screaming and clawing, trying to keep away from the cubicle doors, only to lose her balance as I jerked her the other way. We crashed against the door together and out into the hall, to land on the floor and roll over, right by a trolley with a huge Christmas cake on top of it.

I heard the hall go quiet suddenly, but only in the background. I was already snatching at the cake and ramming it into Tina's face as she tried to get up. She went down again and I jumped on her, straddling her stomach. The cake had got on to her chest and her little breasts were covered in it. A good deal had gone on her tummy, too, and I sat right in it, feeling it squeeze up around my fanny. I didn't care. I had her where I wanted her and I was going to feed her, feed her until she was as fat as a balloon, feed her until she was too fat to walk, feed her until she burst.

Tina tried to fight me off but I got hold of her wrists and kneeled on them. Then I put a handful of cake right in her face, smearing it over her mouth. I took hold of her nose and pinched it, hard, grabbed more cake and slapped it in her face just as she opened her mouth to breathe. She tried to stop it going in, spluttering and spitting out bits of cake as I crammed it into her mouth. More went in and she started to choke, coughing and gagging as she writhed under me. Then hands were gripping my shoulders and arms and pulling me back. I swore at them and for a moment broke free, to stuff another good handful in Tina's face and tear her frock open right down to her belt.

Someone caught me around the waist, pinning my arms, and I was lifted off Tina, leaving her half naked on the floor with her breasts bare and smeared with cake and broken icing, her face a caky mess and her pretty party frock ruined. I was still screaming and calling her everything I could think of, trying to kick her and break free. The place was in uproar, with people shouting and screaming – and clapping, too. Tina's friends had come out of the Ladies and were yelling that I'd attacked her. Everyone was asking questions and no one knew what was going on at all.

I got the sack, not surprisingly, because Tina and her friends said I had attacked her and I had nobody to back me up. Mr Croom pointed out that I had had no reason to attack her and that it was I who had gone into the Ladies first. It was no good, though, because plenty of people knew about what she'd done to me on the Thursday and they decided I'd been trying to get my own back. I didn't even bother to tell anyone what she had threatened me with, because I was sure they'd just say I was making it up and being spiteful and disgusting as well as a liar. So I got the blame and I got thrown out, and only Mr Croom's intervention stopped the police from being called.

Fortunately, Aunt Elaine believed me and Percy made good his offer of employment, so the next Monday I started as the junior typist at Carew, Ungoed and Phelps, the wine merchant's where he worked. I was still furious, though, because Tina was such a liar and I *knew* she would have put my head down the lavatory if she'd been able. I hadn't kept my date with Mark, either, because I'd been so upset, and I blamed her for that as well.

Christmas was the busy time for the wine trade, and I worked so hard at first that I didn't really have time to brood. There were endless invoices to type and I even helped with loading and unloading the vans, so when I got home at night I'd be too tired to do more than crawl into my bed. In fact, Tina would have become just a nasty memory in time, only she wasn't content to let it lie.

New Year was almost as busy as Christmas, but then it all stopped, and suddenly where once I'd been worked off my feet I now had hardly anything to do at all. Percy went off to France to sample the 'sixty-nine vintage and Aunt Elaine went with him. I was bored and in need of some male company. All the men at Carew's were terribly polite to me because I was Percy's niece, so not one of them had even pinched my bottom. Two had asked me out, but they were both really weedy types whom I didn't fancy at all. I wanted Mark and the way he just asked for what he wanted and expected me to give it.

So I wrote to him at the firm and apologised for standing him up, implying that I would be willing if he wanted another date. He wrote back, but only to say Tina had met him that Saturday and they were now going out together. I was a bit upset but tried to be grown-up about it and expected nothing more to happen. What I didn't realise was that he had shown Tina my letter and so she knew were I lived.

Even then it might have been all right, but Mark had to come round to see me. I knew what he wanted from the start – sex – because all he was getting from Tina was a kiss and a cuddle. Mrs Toller wouldn't let him in, of course, so we took the bus to his parents' house. They were out and we had a great afternoon. My tits were out almost before we were through the door, and he was kissing them and feeling them and saying how lovely and big they were. We went on the sofa and he got his cock out, demanding that I suck it. I did, while he felt my tits and bottom, and by the time he was really hard he had a finger up my fanny and I was game for anything he fancied.

What he fancied was my virginity, and he took it on the floor, with my legs spread for him and my clothing pulled up and down to let him get at me. He was good, and came all over my tummy the first time. His next climax was in my mouth, after he'd talked me into letting him have me doggy-style. The third was over my tits and then he had to go, because he had a date with Tina and was already late.

I was in a great mood on the bus home, thinking of her waiting outside some cinema in the cold while he was rubbing his erection between my breasts in the warmth of his bedroom. Mrs Toller gave me a filthy look when I got back, doubtless guessing what I'd been up to, but I didn't care. I masturbated that night, when it was quiet and safe, and had the best climax ever, better even than my first, when a friend had shown me how to do it.

For the next two days I was so happy. I'd always liked sex, but having a cock inside me was something else. I wanted Mark, too, and although he was with Tina I was sure it wouldn't last. After all, with her he was lucky if he got to squeeze her tits. With me he got it all. I wasn't going looking for trouble, though, not after what had happened at the Christmas party. But, unfortunately, trouble came to me.

I don't know how Tina found out – perhaps from the smell of my perfume – but on the Wednesday night following the loss of my virginity she and her friends caught me on the way back from work. Carew's was in Bloomsbury, and the best way to get home was by Tube and then across a little park. I'd walked it at night a hundred times, and always hurried a little, but when Tina and Judy stepped out from behind some bushes I very nearly wet my knickers.

Tina was smiling and carrying a long wooden clothes brush, which she smacked against the palm of her hand as she looked at me. Judy had a stick, and I was sure they really meant to hurt me. I stepped back, but there was a rustle behind me and I turned to find Mandy and Debbie there. All I could do was walk back towards the bushes as they closed in on me, right into a little dark piece of lawn, almost completely out of sight.

'Don't try anything, Piggy, because this time we're ready for you,' Tina spat.

'What do you want?' I managed, trying to sound brave even though there were four of them.

'We're going to teach you a lesson,' Tina answered. 'I told you to stick to your own kind, but you wouldn't listen, would you?'

'What do you mean?' I tried.

'You know, Piggy. You've been sniffing round Mark again, you dirty, fat tart . . .'

She ran at me and grabbed my arm. I pulled away but the others were closing in. I just couldn't fight properly. I mean, I'd done it – I'd let Mark fuck me. There wasn't the anger that had helped me before. And besides, I guessed what the brush was for. It was to spank my bottom. Deep inside me I wanted it.

It was no good, anyway, not with four of them. They got me on the ground face down and held me. I was still struggling but one of them wrenched up my skirt and the next thing I knew my tights and knickers were down and my bottom was bare. Tina laughed and they were pulling at my clothes, lifting my top and wrenching my tights off. Then it was up with my jumper and bra, and my tits fell out as my tights and knickers left my ankles, along with my boots. The buttons on my skirt gave in and it was ripped off. My coat was pulled off and then my jumper. Last of all my bra went and I'd been stripped naked. I had one girl on each limb and my bare bum uppermost. They were laughing, saying how fat my bottom was and slapping it. I'd really given in, expecting my bottom to be beaten with the brush, and to my horror I found that the idea was sexy.

They did me as I was held nude on the grass, laughing and taking turns with the brush, spanking my bottom and sniggering about the way my big bum cheeks wobbled and shook. It really stung and I squealed and begged for mercy, but it only made them worse, until my whole bottom was a ball of burning flesh and they were crowing with joy over my pain and humiliation. I had given in completely by the end, and was just blubbering into the grass, with my bottom on fire and my fanny hot and wet. I was praying they wouldn't find out I was wet between my legs, but I wanted it at the same time. I couldn't help myself, and as I lay there sobbing a terrible thought came into my head. I ought to be finished off by being made to kiss Tina's fanny.

'That's not all, Piggy,' Tina laughed.

I didn't answer but just lay there, waiting to be rolled over, feeling miserable and beaten but hoping she'd be rude with me. She let go of my leg and Debbie took it and I was sure it was going to happen: fanny kissing after my punishment, maybe even licking. Tina sat on my back and pulled my head up by the hair, then bent down to my ear.

'You're going to take this like a good little pig, aren't you?' she hissed.

All I could do was nod.

'Who's got the foam?' she demanded.

One of them gave her a canister and I realised that it wasn't going to be the bitter-sweet humiliation I had expected. Far from it: I was going to have my head shaved. That was too much. I'm not a very brave girl and I *had* fucked with Mark: maybe the spanking was fair. But they weren't having my hair, not for anything. I burst into tears and just went crazy, screaming and writhing in their grip, crying and begging and then swearing at them, promising to be good if they'd just not do it, then calling them bitches and whores and every other word I could think of. Tina laughed, a really cruel, smug laugh.

'Keep her still, will you?' she ordered and at that moment one of my frantically kicking legs came free.

I really kicked, as hard as I could, then twisted over with all my strength. Tina went down with a squeal of surprise and rolled off my back. I saw Mandy's face right above me and I hit her, then kicked again and caught someone really hard. All the time I was screaming and shouting, terrified of what they were going to do to me, with the tears streaming down my face even as I punched and kicked and scratched. Someone grabbed my hair and I bit her hand, then it was all just feet and fists and nails and fear and anger . . .

And then they ran, Judy first, the others after her – except Tina, who was half under me. She screamed to her friends to come back but they took no notice. And then I was on top of her. I was crazy, as crazy as when I'd tried to feed her the Christmas cake. All I could think of was her and what she'd done to me as I wrenched up her coat. Then it was her skirt, pulled high, and down with her tights and knickers to leave her little round bum showing in the dim light. She was screaming and struggling, just like me when I'd been about to be spanked, helpless and bare. I groped for the brush and found it, then laid in, spanking Tina in a frenzy, smack after smack, making her bottom dance and turning her angry demands to squeals of pain. I didn't stop: I wanted her to know how it felt, what it was like to have your bottom stripped and beaten. I wanted to take it all out on her, every nasty remark, every time she'd called me Piggy, for the lavatory – but most of all for trying to shave my head.

Tina had given in long before I'd finished with her and was lying there, her bottom dark and blotchy where it had been pale, mumbling that she was sorry over and over again. My anger was fading and I stopped. But I needed one last thing. Still keeping her on her back I turned and went up on my knees, then twisted her around beneath me. Tina looked up at me, her delicate face stained with tears, her eyes round and wet. I edged forward, kneeling on her arms, my naked fanny over her face, and told her to kiss me. Her mouth fell open and she looked up, her face showing a whole range of feelings. Then she was leaning up, puckering her lips, and she kissed me, right over the hole, once, twice, and then she was licking my cunt.

6

Nude in Chelsea

It started as a joke, no more than that, just one of those silly things students do without meaning anybody any harm. I can't even remember who brought up the idea of streaking, but it was a great hit and soon there were five of us giggling and making excuses for why we wanted to do it. With the boys it was simple bravado – not from the really cool ones but from their hangers-on, wanting to show off in order to be in. It was different for us girls, or at least it was for me. Pippa was a little flirt and more of a show-off than any of the boys. She was still in hot pants and minis when the rest of us had switched to bell-bottoms and maxis. Bobbie always did what Pippa did, anyway. Me, Lauren, I got bullied into it by Angel.

She just told me that I was going to do it, then announced it to everybody else. They all started calling for me to do it, and the men all looked really excited at the prospect of me stripping off. I suppose I was flattered, but I was much too timid to back out, anyway, so I said I would. Of course, it was Carl who took over from there, planning the whole thing with Angel adding suggestions here and there.

He said it had to be down the King's Road, which was the other side of the block. A little way towards World's End there was a church, with an alley running alongside it. We were to run down this and to a dead end, where he and Angel would be waiting in his beat-up old van. It sounded simple and pretty safe, so we all agreed and piled down to the hall to get ready.

I was drunk and giggly and really looking forward to it, but I still felt a bit shy and so didn't start to strip off until Pippa and Bobbie were down to their pants and bras. My fingers were really shaking as I undid my blouse and unfastened the button of my trousers. I shrugged the blouse off and immediately started to feel self-conscious with my bra showing. The material of the cups was thin and showed my nipples, which was actually more embarrassing than having them bare. So I let my titties out next and for the first time in my life I was topless in front of more than one man. I had begun to feel really nervous, but everyone was looking and laughing and saying how brave we were, so it was far too late to back out. Besides, Pippa was starkers by now and really showing off, jumping up and down to make her titties bounce and screaming with excitement.

Getting my trousers off was awful. They were tight yellow bell-bottoms and really tight on my thighs and hips. I had to wriggle to get my bum out of them and my pants came down at the same time, so that my bare bottom was sticking out for everyone to see while I tugged the trousers down to my knees. It was only then that I realised I should have taken my boots off first. They were knee-length with big heels, and it was impossible to get the narrow part of my trousers off them. By then Bobbie was naked too, and all the men were watching me strip. I got into some really silly poses before I managed to sort myself out, sticking out my bum and hopping on one leg and showing simply everything. I was red with blushes by the time I was nude, and wondering if the men behind me had seen my pussy from the back. Nobody seemed to notice, as they were all too busy eyeing up our bums and tits. I put my boots back on just in case there was anything nasty in the streets, at which one of the men called me kinky. But Pippa was already opening the door and there was no time to find a reply.

We were screaming with laughter as we dashed out into the street, and all my misgivings were swept away at the sheer fun of running nude in public. At first there was nobody much about, but it was still thrilling just to be naked when it wasn't allowed. Then we came out into the King's Road and suddenly we had an audience – a *big* audience. The pubs were just coming out and the road was crowded: students like ourselves, groups of men out for an evening drink, couples walking together, and all of them staring at us. Some just gaped, others seemed shocked, others delighted, some simply amazed. One man in a cheering group made a grab for Pippa's bum but she wriggled away and ran on, laughing. I dodged as I reached him, stumbled and nearly went headlong. With my big heels I'd already been at the back, but now I was well behind, with Bobbie's jiggling bottom vanishing around the corner of a pub.

I saw her hesitate, then stop and I knew something was wrong. Someone called out and I came up to her shoulder to find one of the boys being held by one policeman and the other struggling with two more. They had Bobbie, too, but not Pippa and we both turned and ran. A shrill whistle sounded behind me, then Pippa's laugh, but it wasn't fun any more, not for me. I was thinking of my dad, with his face red and angry and his dog collar cutting into his neck as he lectured me.

The group of men who'd tried to grope us earlier were blocking the pavement, grinning and with their arms spread to catch us. Pippa tried to break through and they caught her, laughing and imitating the police. One of them caught my arm but I threw myself right out into the road and he let go. There was a screech of tyres and for a horrible moment I thought I was going to be hit, but the car stopped and I was across. I saw an alley, no more than a black opening between two shops, and dashed into it. The whistle sounded again and my bare arm grazed the rough brick as I ran for the light at the far end.

I came out into a mews, one of those little tangles of red-brick buildings and short roads that always seem so quiet and respectable. Now it wasn't, it was a terrifying place, with the police behind me and nowhere to hide. I should have given up, but I just couldn't bear the thought of being caught, so I ran on, even though I knew I could never get away. There was a big van by me, and I went behind it with some silly idea of hiding, only to find that the next car was a big Rover with the boot wide open. The driver was there, too, a short, fat man with a big wooden box in his hands and his mouth wide open in astonishment at my nudity. I didn't even stop to think, but had climbed in and slammed the boot down behind me before I realised what a stupid thing I'd done.

Completely trapped, all I could do was hug my knees and wait for the hideous embarrassment of the boot being opened and having the police, and the driver, looking down at my naked body. Just a moment before I'd been revelling in being nude, feeling free and uninhibited, naughty and sexy all at once. Now I was scared and vulnerable, and being bare made it so much worse. I heard the policemen's footsteps and then a voice, speaking in such calm, authoritative tones that tears of shame began to well up in my eyes. At any moment that respectable, proper man was going to be looking down at my naked body, stern and disapproving, just like my father. Another voice answered the first, female, sounding tired and a little angry, as if to imply that I was not only a delinquent but a thorough little nuisance as well. Their footsteps approached my hiding place and I began to shiver, with the tears running freely down my cheeks.

'Good evening, sir,' the male voice said, obviously addressing the driver of the car.

'Good evening, officer,' he answered, his voice public school but tinged with a Yorkshire edge.

'Have you seen a young woman run past, sir? Naked?' the policeman asked.

'Naked?' the man echoed.

'Yes, sir, one of these streakers, about five and half foot, long blonde hair . . .'

'My dear Sergeant,' the man interrupted, 'the back streets of Chelsea are, sadly, not so rich in naked girls that a description is needed to pick out an individual. I have seen no naked girls, blonde or otherwise. Believe me, I am sincerely sorry not to be able to help you.'

'Are you sure, sir?' the policeman persisted. 'She ran down the alley, must have passed right by you.'

'No doubt, yet I must have missed the spectacle while in my garden. As you see, I am unloading claret.'

'Right, well, keep an eye out.'

'For naked blondes? You may rely on it, Sergeant. Now, if you will excuse me? This case is heavy.'

That was it. The police left and I'd been saved. All I could feel was gratitude, with the awful prospect of confronting the police and my father fading. My heart was pounding and I was mumbling the words 'Thank you' to myself over and over. I didn't even really care that I was naked, just so long as I didn't have to face that awful disapproval and listen to the inevitable lecture while I was told I was silly, and immature, and immodest and all the things I'd been brought up not to be.

I lay still, with my legs curled up and my hands over my breasts, expecting the boot to open at any moment. There were noises outside: the man going into his garden, the police returning and searching nearby, all the while discussing how I had vanished so completely. One even tried the back of the van, but not the car boot

109

and at last I was left in silence. I was still nervous, and trying to think of what to say, but when the man finally came to get me out it was as much as I could do to smile.

He smiled back and threw a bathrobe in to me, which I took gratefully and wrapped around myself as I climbed out. There was a high wall beside us, with an open door in it through which he hustled me, across a tiny walled garden and up a staircase. Only when the door of his flat had shut behind us did I feel secure, and as I sank down in a chair I managed to thank him.

'Think nothing of it, my dear,' he answered. 'You have enlivened my evening, both from a sense of adventure and with the unexpected display of your beauty. To betray you to the police would have been the act of a churl.'

'It was sweet of you, anyway,' I answered. 'I'd have thought you would have disapproved and turned me in.'

'Disapproved?' he echoed. 'My dear girl, you must think me frightfully priggish.'

'But I thought ... Well, you're older, and you seem so ... so respectable.'

'I am not yet forty, and as to my respectability, must that make me a prude, or an authoritarian?'

'Oh I'm sorry, it's just that ...'

'Yes, I know, you see the older generation as staid, as lifeless, a bunch of old farts, snorting in disapproval over their port while you gay young things disport yourselves among the joys of life and liberal morals. Every generation thinks thus of its elders, though if it were true the human race would be in a sorry state indeed.'

'Well, my father would certainly have disapproved.'

'No doubt, but he is, after all, your father. Who knows in what vices he may have indulged himself as a youth?'

'None, I'm sure. He's in the church, a rector. He's very strict.'

110

'Hence your urge to rebel and run nude through the streets of Chelsea – or almost nude. I must say, I find the boots most fetching when combined with an otherwise naked body . . . But I am being rude and have neglected the conventions. I am Percy Ottershaw, and you are?'

'Lauren, Lauren Green.'

'Then, Lauren, may I suggest a glass of wine to calm your nerves while you tell me exactly why you were running near-naked down the King's Road at close to midnight.'

'I ought to be getting back, really. I was at a party over the way, in Gertrude Street. My friends got caught and they'll be wondering what has happened to me.'

'If your friends got caught then the party doubtless includes some unwelcome guests at present – the police. They love this sort of thing: it gives them a chance to feel important without undergoing any of the dangers inherent in catching actual criminals.'

'They'll be sure to find out about me!'

'Do any of your friends know your home address off the top of their heads?'

'No, but . . .'

'Then it is unlikely that the police will make the effort of tracing you. They must, surely, have better things to do. So relax, enjoy a drink. Do you have a sweet tooth?'

'A bit, I suppose. I like rum-and-black – that's what I was drinking at the party.'

Percy gave a little shiver but said nothing and left the room, which gave me my first chance to look around. He was obviously well-off, but really old-fashioned. All the furniture was heavy, dark wood and obviously old, a bit like the stuff in my father's study and the living room at the rectory. The decorations were the same, with curtains of dark green velvet, a thick carpet in tones of green and gold and wallpaper to match. In fact, my father would have been right at home, at least until he saw the prints Percy had chosen to decorate his walls.

111

I'd been studying art, so nudes were nothing new to me, but these were something else. Among five, two of the artists were instantly recognisable: a Beardsley picture of a fleshy youth caressing an enormous erection out of all proportion to his body, and a Cocteau drawing of a naked man masturbating. The third was beautifully executed and when I stood I saw it was a Dali, but very different to anything I'd seen before. The main figure was a girl bending as she licked at one man's balls and handled another's hard cock. He in turn was holding apart the cheeks of her bottom with his fingers to show off not just the rear of her pussy but her bumhole, which just seemed impossibly rude. Two other figures were having sex and it looked as if the man's cock was not in the girl's pussy at all, but up her bottom.

The sight of it and the realisation of what they were doing sent a shiver right through my tummy and I pulled my gaze away quickly in case Percy came in and caught me. That left me looking at the wall on which the fourth print was hung. Unlike the others, it was not by an artist the Slade was ever likely to hold up as an example. It was well drawn but blatantly rude, showing a young girl across an older woman's lap, ready for spanking while an older man looked on, masturbating. There was a look of deep consternation on the victim's face, as well there might have been. Her skirt had been pulled up and her pants taken down, leaving her bum quite bare. As with the Dali, the pose left her pussy lips peeping out from between her thighs and her bumhole showing, but the lewd details made it clear that it was intended as a turn-on, with every little pink wrinkle of the poor girl's flesh precisely executed. I could really feel for her, bent over with her bottom bare for punishment while a man gloated over her exposure and made himself ready for her pussy once she'd been beaten.

I turned away, trembling and now with rather different thoughts about Percy. But I had to look at the fifth print, which was directly above my chair. Like the fourth it was by some artist unknown to me and was blatantly dirty. It showed a young girl seated on a stool and sucking the cock of a much older man. He was white-bearded and bald, his trousers dropped to the level of his knees and his shirt front tucked up beneath his waistcoat, his red-tipped penis just entering her mouth. She was a total contrast, young and fresh and pretty, with her long dress high and one leg cocked up so that her pussy showed beneath her thigh. It was rude enough anyway, but the thing that really brought it home was the expression on her face, which was one of calm, serenity almost, with her eyes closed and her mouth open around the penis of a man three times her age.

'Sadly anonymous,' Percy's voice sounded from behind me, 'which is a pity, because I feel it has a certain charm, not just in the innocence of the scene depicted but in its very lack of aggression. You're not shocked, I hope?'

'No, no,' I lied. 'I'm studying art . . . I just didn't recognise the artist.'

'I fear I am unable to enlighten you, although it would appear to have been done in the twenties from the style of dress. If she had any underwear on I could pinpoint it to within five years or so, but I suppose the fact that she is bare under her dress is part of the charm. Here is your wine: tell me what you think.'

He had changed the subject just at the right moment, saving me the embarrassment of finding a reply to his remarks about the picture. I sipped the wine, which was a rich gold colour and very sweet, taking my time in order to hide my thoughts. Everything I had been brought up to believe told me the picture was obscene, a deliberately titillating depiction of a dirty act. I'd done my best to change the way I thought at college, yet I knew that those tutors who would have approved of the

113

Cocteau or even the Dali would have considered this anonymous picture no more than crude pornography. Yet Percy was right: it wasn't aggressive, or nasty, or even coercive. The girl's expression suggested she was sucking the old man's penis as a favour, a kindness, no different to making him a mug of cocoa in the evening. Just that thought sent another shiver through me: cocksucking as a favour, or to show gratitude, and who had more reason to be grateful than me ...

I found myself blushing and suddenly very conscious of my naked body beneath the bathrobe. Percy paid no attention, apparently absorbed in the study of his wine. Clearly he was an expert and I determined not to say anything stupid, simply because I was so eager to please and not to offend.

'It's very rich,' I volunteered. 'Heady, like those big yellow grapes you get.'

'Yes,' he answered, 'the proportion of muscatel is perhaps a little high. Still, for a 'fifty-one it is really quite fine.'

'Nineteen fifty-one! It's older than me.'

'Really? A friend of mine used to say that decadence might be defined as enjoying one's wines older than one's women. A little exaggerated, I've always felt, but perhaps there's something in it, after all.'

'That's nonsense, Father often ... but then he's not decadent, I suppose.'

'Exactly. Most worthwhile wines take at least sixteen years to develop, or at least I think so.'

'And you *are* decadent, I suppose.'

I'd said it archly, perhaps wanting to challenge him, to see if he was all talk. Both dizzy with drink and flushed from the streak and my narrow escape, I felt bold. And his round, beaming face and soft, chubby body made it impossible to feel threatened by him. Then there was a resentment at knowing that everyone, not only my parents but my friends too, would have expected me to be shocked, even revolted, by Percy, by his taste in pictures, by his whole lifestyle. With a flicker of rebellion I decided that if he tried anything with me, or demanded some favour, then I would not stop him.

'Perhaps,' he answered. And his hand settled on to my skin, not on my bottom or leg, but in among the hair at the nape of my neck.

He began to stroke my neck and a delicious prickling sensation went through me, while my tummy began to flutter. We were still standing, looking at the picture with that beautiful young girl sucking on the old man's cock. The image was fixed in my mind: a penis in a girl's mouth, something so dirty, so rude, so improper, so wrong – and so desirable.

'Would you ... would you like a girl like that?' I asked.

He didn't answer, but his fingers kept working on the skin of my neck, stroking and teasing, and tugging the bathrobe down a little with each movement. I let him, allowing him to caress me as he liked, across my shoulders and then down my spine as he eased the robe open. My shoulder blades were bare, and the upper parts of my breasts. The belt was loose, and I knew that if I didn't tighten it ...

It went, falling open at the front so that my tummy was bare and my pubic triangle too. Percy's hand was moving down my spine, taking the robe with it so that it parted to show one breast. I felt the sleeve slip from my arm, then let the other one fall as I transferred my glass to my other hand. The robe fell to the floor and I was nude but for my boots, standing in a puddle of red silk with his hand snaking down my back and towards my bottom cheeks.

I was lost, and as Percy abandoned the subtle approach and took a handful of my bum flesh I did nothing to stop him. He began to fondle me, all the while sipping his glass and saying nothing. I had all but

115

offered to suck his cock, something men usually really had to push me into, yet he seemed happy to feel my bottom, stroking and squeezing first one cheek and then the other. It was when he gave my bottom a pat that I thought of the other picture, the one of the girl being spanked. The pat was gentle, not even enough to sting, but there was something paternal about it, something admonitory, as if I ought to be smacked, if only for letting him feel my bum. He did it again, a fraction harder and I felt my cheeks wobble. I was wondering if he'd like to see me like the punished girl in the picture, kicking and squirming over someone's lap, face full of consternation and bare bum warm and pink with my pussy showing from behind. I giggled.

'I *would* like a girl like that,' Percy said softly. 'And if there's not a pretty innocent with no drawers under her dress, then a naked blonde in knee boots will do very nicely.'

He put down his glass and his hands went to his fly. It was the old-fashioned kind, with buttons, and I looked down to watch. Men had got their cocks out for me before, and more than once they'd gone in my mouth. The men who had made me suck them had always been students, though, men of my own age, men full of confidence in their looks and virility. Not a fat man, though, not one like Percy.

I felt so dirty as he pushed me gently down to my knees. His cock was fully out, with his balls as well, all bulging from his fly. My knees touched the floor and my bottom bumped against the chair behind me. Percy's genitals were all in front of my face, inches away, a skinny pink worm protruding from under his belly with the wrinkled sac of his balls beneath it. I could barely believe I was going to do it, but my mouth was opening and he was guiding my head forwards. It touched my lip and I felt the rubbery texture of it. Then it was going in, Percy's cock followed by his balls, so that my whole mouth was full of male sex organ. I began to move it all

116

around in my mouth, sucking with my cheeks pulled in and rolling the balls around on my tongue.

As he began to swell I was thinking of the girl in the picture. She looked so serene, so complacent, quite happy that there was a cock in her mouth. I was finding it hard to be so cool. For one thing I could picture myself and I knew I looked anything but innocent. In fact, with my black boots coming up to my knees and not a stitch on beside I probably looked a proper little tart, more like the girl in the Dali, stark naked with her buttocks held wide for the inspection of her bumhole. My cheeks were open too, and I could feel the air cool on my pussy and up between the cheeks. I was showing everything, and rather wishing that Percy could see it all so that I'd feel even dirtier than I already did.

I looked up and found that he was looking down at me, feasting his little round eyes on my bare back and bottom, also on my face and the junction between my lips and his penis, or at least what he could see of it beneath the overhang of his belly. He looked really pleased with himself and so, so happy – smug, even, like a naughty little boy who had got away with something.

His balls slipped out of my mouth as his cock hardened and grew, until I was sucking on a little pink erection and holding his wet scrotum in my hand. I had begun to enjoy it: not just because it was such a rude thing to do but because Percy tasted male and his maturity and the way he had handled me made me feel that he had every right to expect his cock to be sucked. He was taking his time, too. Most of the men I knew would already have come by now, probably holding me by the hair and doing it down my throat, although I always told them not to. He was calmer, unhurried, just enjoying the feel of my mouth on his penis and the sight of me kneeling for him in the nude. I had even begun to wonder if I should touch myself and what he would think of me if I did. Then he pulled back.

I let his cock slip from my mouth, wondering what he expected of me. His hand had fastened on my hair, quite tight, and he started to pull me up. I responded to the pressure, allowing myself to be brought to my feet and then turned so that my face was to the wall – and to the picture of the girl getting her bottom smacked. Percy came behind me and I felt the stiff rod of his penis settle between my buttocks.

'You have the most beautiful bottom, Lauren,' he breathed from behind me. 'A true woman's bottom, full and feminine, like a little fat peach. Now play with yourself and I'll tell you about the picture.'

As he spoke his hands had come up, clasping my breasts and starting to knead them. He was rubbing his cock between my bum cheeks as well. I knew how rude it was, how shocked my friends would have been, how outraged at me being handled so intimately by a dirty old man. Yet I couldn't bring myself to make him stop, and I found my hands going to my pussy to do as I had been ordered. My lips felt swollen, with the silky hair parted and the middle wet. Before college I hadn't even known what happened when I touched myself. It was Pippa who had told me. I'd done it that very night and it had left me feeling confused and guilty after a moment of pure ecstasy. Now I was going to do it again, with a man's cock wedged between the cheeks of my bottom. All at once I felt simultaneously adored and abused, free and guilty, aroused and disgusted.

'Good girl,' Percy breathed as I began to rub at myself.

His cock was wedged right in between my bum cheeks, so that his balls were rubbing on the hole while his fat belly was squashed into the small of my back. The pressure was making me bend, forcing me to stick out my bottom to take his cock and balls ever more deeply into my crease. I was masturbating, though, and unable to stop myself.

'She is called Elaine,' Percy said softly into my ear, 'and the picture was drawn from life, drawn while she was being punished.'

My gaze locked on to poor Elaine's face with her expression of consternation and misery. I could really feel for her, as I was caught in a similar position, having my bum used for a man's sexual kick. She looked so sorry for herself, with her poor bum red and stinging from the beating while she stared at the cock being made hard over her pain and indignity. But no: she *wasn't* looking at the cock, she was looking beyond it and to one side, not at the woman spanking her, nor the man masturbating over her, but at the artist, at whoever was recording her degradation for posterity. My pussy tightened at the thought, then again at the memory that my bum had been shown off too, running nude through the streets. Now *I* was being punished, punished in just the way Father always said punishment came, fitting to the crime, with a dirty penalty for a dirty offence.

'They spanked her for being ill-mannered,' Percy went on. 'The artist was her boyfriend. The couple were dealers he wanted to impress. Elaine had been told to wear a miniskirt at dinner, with see-through knickers underneath so that they showed when she bent down. That would have been just a nice, teasing little thrill for the man, but she was selfish and she wouldn't do it, so she ended up showing a lot more than just her knickers.'

'That's so unfair,' I managed, panting it out as I rubbed hard at my clitty.

It was true. What they had done *was* awful – telling a girl to show her pants for some old man's thrill and then spanking her when she refused. She had every right to refuse and they had none whatever to punish her, let alone to take down her pants for her and smack her bare bottom. It was dreadful, but I was wishing it had been me and I was starting to come.

'Elaine came down in a long skirt, like a maxiskirt,' Percy went on. 'Her boyfriend asked her what she thought she was doing and she answered him back. There was a row, and it was the dealer woman who said Elaine ought to be spanked for her impudence. She really lost her temper at that, and swore at them and called them perverts. A moment later she was across the woman's lap, thinking how it's not wise to cheek someone bigger and stronger than yourself.'

He was really rubbing hard and I could tell he was about to come from the catch in his voice. My bum was stuck right out into his lap and my crease was all sweaty and damp. Percy's cock kept nudging my bumhole and his balls were slapping on my pussy. I was terrified he was going to go up me, but I was coming and couldn't stop it.

'She kicked and struggled,' he was saying, 'but it was no good. They pulled up her prissy skirt and they revealed her big white knickers. They told her she would be spanked twice as hard for not wearing see-throughs. They kicked her legs apart to show off her pussy and they told her they could see her anus. They held her like that while she was drawn and the men got their cocks ready. They spanked her bottom and fingered her hole. They made her suck the old dealer's cock and lick the woman who had beaten her. They stripped her nude and spanked her some more. Then her boyfriend buggered her.'

As Percy said it his cock slipped down and I felt it against my own bottom-hole. I could so easily have pulled away, and a voice in my head was screaming at me to do just that. I didn't, but instead I stuck out my bum and cried out as his cock invaded my bumhole. My ring was greasy with sweat and my own juice and his prick went in, filling my bottom as I grunted out my orgasm. I felt my bumhole tighten on his erection and I was in ecstasy even as I was thinking of how utterly filthy I was being. Also I was thinking of poor Elaine and just how she must have felt with her buttocks smacked red, sperm in her mouth and her boyfriend's cock up her bum.

My bumhole was on fire and I was coming and coming, grunting and crying my way through an orgasm far more intense than anything I had ever known. I could feel every movement of Percy's cock in my bottom and my head was swimming with dirty thoughts: streaking, being peeled out of the bathrobe, girls with their bum cheeks held apart, men with huge, hard cocks, young girls sucking old men, girls being spanked to punish them, then buggered.

'One thing they never knew,' Percy grunted as he jammed his cock deeper still up my bottom. 'She did it on purpose, she and her boyfriend, everything, because they knew the woman liked to smack girls' bottoms. And how do I know? I know because Elaine's my wife.'

And with that he came up my bottom.

7

Pippa in Panties

It was hilarious. My friend Lauren was shacked up with a dirty old man, and with his wife too!

It had happened the night we all got high and streaked. We did it down the King's Road, and we all got caught, except Lauren. The pigs really made a fuss, and our parents got told and the authorities at college. The way they went on you'd have thought we'd murdered someone!

Like I said, Lauren got away. What had happened was that she'd climbed in this guy's car and he hadn't given her away. I suppose it was only fair that she was grateful, but the little minx let him have her and the first thing we knew about it she had settled in as their lodger, and lover, with the wife as well!

Lauren was really shy about it, but we knew what they were up to. It wasn't just sex either, but kinky stuff. She was walking a bit funny one day, and Angel said it might mean she'd had it up the bum, or been whacked. We caught Lauren in the loo and pulled her skirt up and, sure enough, she had bruises on her bum. She got really embarrassed, but when she saw I was laughing and Angel said it was cool she calmed down.

Angel and I took down her panties to see the marks and made her tell us everything. The guy was called Percy and he got his kicks out of smacking her bottom. Lauren had had it up the bottom, too – the first night!

That wasn't all, either. They had taken her out, Percy and his wife, who was called Elaine. He drove right out in the country and they had a really posh lunch, champagne and everything. She'd been in bell-bottoms, and so had the wife, because Percy had asked. Lauren thought it was just because he liked to ogle her bum, but after the lunch they went out walking, miles and miles. After all the drink Lauren needed to pee, but when she said she was going to nip into the bushes they said not to, and that she ought to wet her panties. Lauren got all shy, but Elaine said she'd do it first!

Elaine bent over, sticking her bum out to let them see, and then she just let go. Lauren said she actually saw the pee coming out through the denim, like a little fountain, and this big wet patch formed on Elaine's seat. It was all down her legs, too, and really showed. Elaine said that now she'd done it Lauren had to as well. And she did, she actually peed her panties in front of them, with it all trickling out of her cunt and down her legs, and soaking into her clothes all up her tummy and round her bum.

Percy made them take their jeans and panties down and gave them both spankings, then put his cock in Elaine's mouth while Lauren watched. She got all horny and they whacked her with a belt and a piece of stick while she touched herself up, which was when she got the bruises. I didn't know if I should believe it or not, but the bruises were there and we made her show us again.

I felt so horny after that I had to do myself, so I skipped afternoon lectures and went back to the house. I'd taken Lauren's room when she had moved in with Percy and Elaine, because it was better than my old one and right next door to Angel, who was really cool. No one else was about, so I stripped off bare, put the right music on and got on the bed. First I had a joint, because I was really shaking and needed to cool it a bit. After a

123

while I started to touch my titties up to get going, making the nips hard and squeezing them and wishing they were a bit bigger, but getting really horny. I was thinking about Lauren, too, and thinking how she must have felt, wetting her panties in front of dirty old Percy and his wife.

It was funny, because I would never have thought that peeing my panties could be sexy. But the way Lauren had told it had made me feel really horny. She had been blushing and fidgety, and really embarrassed, but she hadn't even tried to make out that Percy had forced her, just that she took a bit of persuading. I'd have had to be made to do it, but I wondered if I wouldn't have been just as horny afterwards. The other thing that I'd noticed was what Lauren had had on under her skirt: big white granny panties, really tight and covering her bum right up. When they'd had to come down to show us the bruises she'd been a bit embarrassed about them, but said Percy liked her to wear them.

I liked to do myself with the big wooden crucifix Auntie June had bought me for confirmation. It was as thick as any cock and all smooth and shiny, and it wouldn't get a girl in trouble. I liked to hold the cross bit and put the long bit in me, then touch myself up while it was in my cunt hole. It hung above the bed where I could get it easily and I took it down now, sucked it a bit, then slid it up. I was soaking and it went right up really easily, all the way to the hilt. With one hand on it to fuck myself and my thumb on my button, I started to play, still stroking my titties with the other hand.

As I touched myself I made up a little story, which was always the best way, even with a man in me. I didn't mind pussy play and wondered if I ought to think about Lauren, or maybe Angel, or my friend Bobbie, who had streaked with us and had licked my titties to show a boy

124

when we'd got drunk once. None were right. I knew what I wanted: to think about being made to pee my knickers, not just talked into it like Lauren but really *made* to do it. It was hard, because it wasn't what I normally got off on, but after another couple of drags and a bit of pumping with the crucifix I managed to get it right.

I imagined it at a party first, with me in hot pants to really show my bum off and not a lot else. The girls would get jealous and tell the boys there was going to be a show. I wouldn't know they meant me, not until they grabbed me. They'd tie my hands and make me kneel down. They'd make me drink water and beer and cider, until my head was spinning. They'd leave me like that while my bladder filled. It would get worse, and worse, until finally I would wet myself, with the pee squirting out the back of my hot pants and running down my legs, all over the floor while they just laughed and laughed at me . . .

It wasn't right, not quite, good but not enough to get me there. I loved to strip off, and I knew if that ever happened I'd be the first one out of my panties. I wanted it ruder, more like what Lauren had done. I had it. I'd be at something really polite, perhaps with Aunt June, who always expected me to behave really well. I'd be sitting on a little chair, a covered chair, with a white seat. They'd all be talking, saying really boring things while I sat there, dead still, with my bladder getting worse and worse. I'd ask to get up but Aunt June would tell me to behave and mind my manners. Then it would just happen. I'd pee my panties, right there in front of them all, with the pee running out the front of my panties and over the chair. They'd all be staring as it dripped on the floor . . .

I was really hazy, right on the edge, when the door opened. It was Angel, but she didn't say a word, just stood there, looking down at the crucifix in my cunt. I started to say something and moved to cover myself, but she just put a finger to her lips and sat down on the bed. I was shaking. She'd really caught me out, feeling myself in my room, in the nude. I tried to get up, but she put a hand on my shoulder and rolled me back, then put a finger to her lips again. I looked at her – and I knew what she wanted.

I've done it before, a little with Bobbie and a lot with a girl at home, snogging, titty play, even putting our pussies together. Angel was cool, but Angel was scary too. I was high, high on my joint and high on sex, so I didn't even try and stop her as she bent over me and kissed me. I let my mouth open and we touched tongues. One of her arms was going around my neck and the other down across my tummy, which was fluttering really hard. She took the crucifix and began to fuck me with it and I was gone, really gone.

Angel's mouth came off mine and down my neck, kissing it and then moving on to my titties, nipping each and sucking them, all the while with the crucifix sliding in and out of my cunt. Her kisses went lower, on to my tummy, my pussy mound – and then she was kissing my cunt. No one had done that to me before, not boys, not girls, but it was lovely, so lovely I didn't ever want her to stop. Her tongue was at the top of my slit, licking round my button and making me wriggle and pant for it because I wanted her to take me there. She wouldn't, but kept licking and licking, taking me so high I could have screamed. The crucifix was gliding in and out of my cunt, my head was spinning, my titties were in my hands. Her tongue touched my button and I was going to come . . .

Angel stopped and sat up, leaving me shaking on the bed, still feeling my titties and with the crucifix sticking out of my cunt. My breath came out in a rush because I'd been right on the edge, but she put a hand over my mouth and a finger to her lips. She had gloves on, leather gloves, and I could taste them. Her fingers pressed down, into my mouth.

'Take your cross, Pippa darling. Wank yourself,' she said.

Angel was scaring me, but I did as I was told, starting to prod the crucifix in and out of my cunt. It was nice, and as I began to flick my clit with my thumb I knew I wouldn't take long to get there. She sat up, took my joint and drew deep on it, then blew the smoke in my face as I tried to get my head straight. Angel was bullying me, making me do myself so she could get off on it, but I couldn't stop it. The crucifix was moving in my cunt and I knew I was really going to do it, right in front of her.

Her eyes were really bright, her stare burning into me, and for the first time I realised they were green, the colour you get with cats. She licked her lips and it was like she was going to eat me, then she was bending down, opening her mouth, with the red lipstick glistening in the light. I let my mouth open and she kissed me again, really hard, with the taste of the smoke in her mouth.

I was gone, high and horny and shivery, with my cunt tight on the crucifix and my thumb playing my button. Angel kept kissing me, and stroking my tummy, and rubbing my titties. I'd been scared, but now I was loving it, melting into her arms, all hers, to play with, to cuddle, to hurt, to pee all over . . .

That was too much. I hit the top, thinking of how it would be if she just got on top and peed all over me. Not having to be asked, not getting all coy and giggly about it, just having her climb on me and pee on my body, on my titties and on my tummy, over my cunt and in my mouth, best of all, in my mouth . . .

It was the best, kissing as I came, feeling my cunt squeeze on the crucifix and my back pull tight to push my bum into the bed. Angel kept kissing, too, right until

I'd finished, doing everything for me. That was the best thing. She'd taken me there, not even getting her titties out but doing it all for me. Boys were greedy, it was them, them, them all the time – show your titties, suck my cock, spread your legs.

I was well high when I'd finished, stretching out and purring, really happy, while Angel looked down at me with her big green eyes and smiled, then started to stroke my hair, ever so gently. Neither of us said a thing for a long time. I think we both knew it was special, that what we'd done wasn't just pussy play. I'd always wondered if she was the other way. She liked to hang out with the boys but she never put out for them, not even for Carl who everyone went for. I'd thought it was because they didn't dare, what with her being so tall and, well, scary. Now I knew, and it was me she had hit on. It had been great, though, too good to go back on, even if I'd dared. I was hers and she didn't need to say anything to make it so. I guessed she'd want it herself after a bit and wondered how it would feel, licking pussy.

We shared the rest of my joint, then she told me straight out, as if she knew what I'd been thinking.

'You were wanking over Lauren, weren't you.'

I nodded.

'Tell me,' she demanded.

'I . . . I was thinking how she'd wet herself,' I started. 'How she must have felt with her pee going in her panties and people watching . . .'

'How about her spanking?' Angel interrupted.

'That must have hurt,' I answered, 'really hurt. What a pervert, spanking her bottom and making her pee herself . . .'

'Don't be a baby!' she cut in. 'A little spanking doesn't hurt! It's nice to have a warm bum, it gets you going.'

'Yeah, but this Percy bloke, he's old enough to be her dad!'

'Only if he started pretty early. Older men are cool, anyway, they know what to do.'

'And his wife joining in!'

'Don't be so square, Pippa.'

I didn't answer. It was me who was the cool one, flashing my titties at concerts, stripping off to streak and getting arrested, going with Carl in the back of his dad's car. Lauren was shy. She always needed to be pushed to be any fun. Now she was shacked up with Percy and Elaine, being spanked, taking it up the bum, peeing her panties – really wild stuff, really dirty stuff. It was stuff for old perverts, not for me, but Angel thought it was cool, and I'd come over it: I'd come over the idea of her peeing on me. I shivered, thinking of how dirty I'd been, how nice it had been. Angel had taken her hand off my hair and I knew I had to show her.

'Do you want me to do it for you?' I asked.

'Do what?'

She knew what I meant, but she wanted me to say it.

'Lick pussy?' I offered.

'You want to lick my pussy?'

Angel looked down at me, like she was amused that I wanted to lick her. I nodded.

'OK,' she said. 'If that's what you want, you get to lick pussy, my way.'

'Strip off, then,' I urged.

'No,' she said, 'I keep my clothes on, or at least some of them.'

'How am I supposed to do it, then?'

'You'll see. Roll over first.'

'Are you going to spank me?'

'I might. I like to see a girl's bum get red.'

I rolled over to show her my bum, feeling a bit scared and really shivery. She was going to smack my bottom, spank me like a naughty little girl, and she was going to get off on it. It was what I wanted, what I'd felt when I was coming, to really be hers, so she could punish me when she liked.

129

Angel climbed up on to the bed and settled her bum on my back, making me feel really helpless under her weight. I felt trapped, really controlled, and it was the nicest thing. She began to feel my bum, touching the cheeks and squeezing them, then pulling them wide to show off my hole. I stuck it up, letting her see, letting her know that if she wanted to spank me she could.

The smack still caught me unawares. It was really hard, right on my cheeks, and it really stung. I squealed out, but she just laughed and gave me another, then went for it. I'd forgotten what it felt like, and Mum was never as rough as Angel. She really spanked me, smacking and smacking, until I was kicking and struggling and biting the pillow my face was buried in. When I said to stop she just laughed and told me not to be a baby, then went right on smacking. My bum was burning and Angel was laughing and the more I kicked about and beat my fists and squealed the more she laughed, all the time with her bum planted firmly on my back so I couldn't do a thing. She stopped as suddenly as she had started, leaving me gasping for breath with my bum burning and throbbing.

It had hurt, really hurt, and I hated her for it, but I couldn't say it because I loved her, too. She was right as well: for all the pain I wanted the crucifix back in my cunt, and if my bum was burning I still wanted to lift it, to let my hole show like I was waiting for something to go inside. She stayed on my back, feeling my bum, pulling open the hot cheeks to look at my bumhole and wiggling her bottom on my back. I knew what came next: a licked pussy for her.

'Roll back, Pippa darling,' Angel said as she rose to her knees.

She said it sweetly but it was a command. I turned under her and I just had to spread my thighs, opening my cunt to the air. Angel laughed and moved forwards. I felt something touch me and the crucifix slid back up my cunt.

130

'I'm going to watch the cross in your pussy when I come,' she told me. 'Close your legs to hold it in.'

I did as I was told, closing my thighs to hold the thick wooden shaft tight in my cunt, with the top sticking out so she could see it. My bum was throbbing and I was really aware of my smacked cheeks, and that she'd done it, the girl who was about to put her pussy in my face. Angel had these leather trousers on, really tight over her bum which was right in front of me, lifted so I could do her in a sixty-nine if she crawled back. She was in boots, too, high-heeled and close to my head, the way she was kneeling. Her hands went to her belt and she moved back, pushing my arms high and posing her bum right over my face.

I'd done sixty-nine before, with boys, sucking their cocks with my bum pressed in their faces. Now it was a girl, and as she began to tug down her trousers I could only stare, watching her strip her bum, right in my face. She took her panties off with her trousers and I was staring at her naked bum, with her cunt open and wet and her bumhole showing. I'd always thought it funny where my own bumhole went when I did sixty-nine with a boy. Now I was going to get it.

Angel reached back and pulled open her cheeks, then sat down, right in my face. I'd thought she was going to bend, but she didn't. She sat upright, with her cunt on my mouth and my nose pushed right in her bumhole. It was all wet with her juice so the end went in and I could feel her ring round it. I tried to move, but she wriggled back on me and my nose went in her bumhole again. I don't know why, but it seemed right – after all, she had spanked me.

'Lick it, Pippa, right inside,' Angel said.

I put my tongue in her cunt and she wiggled in my face, squirming her holes around on my tongue and nose. It was wet and slippery between her cheeks and I couldn't see a thing, or breathe properly, with her bottom right in my face. I could hear, though, and she began to groan as I licked her. My tongue was right in her cunt, with her pussy spread on my face and her juice running down my chin and on over my neck. I felt her move and knew she had pulled her tits out, then her fingers went to her pussy and her bum cheeks began to squeeze on my head. She was using my face to rub on, getting off on having my nose up her bum, only that wasn't enough, and as she changed from squirming around to rubbing up and down I got her bottom-hole pushed against my mouth.

'Oh, yes, do it, do my bumhole,' Angel gasped.

Once more, she pushed it against my mouth, right over it so I could feel its ring on my lips. It was opening and closing, just like my cunt when I came, and I could feel the wet in the middle on my lips. I was kissing a bumhole. Then I just let go and my tongue was in it, right up her so I could feel the tight ring squeeze on it. She moaned really loudly as I started to lick her bum out, and just came in my face, wriggling and crying out my name as my tongue went deeper and deeper up her bumhole.

Even when Angel had finished she stayed there, sitting on my face so I couldn't even breathe. She only got off when I began to kick and struggle – and she didn't even say thank you! She did at least compliment me, sort of.

'Nice,' she said. 'You're a good little licker. Ever kissed a bumhole before?'

'No,' I admitted.

'Well, you'd better get used to it.'

That was it. No question or discussion, just that. I did want to be hers, but maybe a bit more on my terms. I was tongue-tied and couldn't think of anything to say, so I just let it be. Angel pulled up her panties and trousers and took another drag on the relit joint, then sat back down on the bed, looking at me with a little smile. Then she kissed me, right on the mouth. Maybe

I was looking for reassurance or maybe it was because if she kissed me after I'd licked her then it wasn't like she really thought I was beneath her or anything.

We smoked a bit more and talked, mainly about men. Angel wasn't really into men, not for sex. They exploited women, so she said, but I reckoned it was more that she liked to be in control. We got back on to the more extreme varieties of sex, and I asked her if she thought getting off on wetting my panties was weird.

'Not weird, just unusual,' she answered. 'You've got to accept what you are.'

'And what's that?'

'You like to be the centre of attention, don't you?'

'Sure, who doesn't?'

'Lots of people. You're what's called a submissive: you like things done to you, or to be made to do things that bring sexual attention to you. Like wetting your pants, or getting a spanking. You love to show off, too, don't you?'

'Yeah,' I admitted.

'Then how about this?' she went on. 'From now on, when you're in the house you only wear pants.'

'What's the big deal? I go completely nude sometimes.'

'The thrill will come from knowing that you're doing it because I say so – and I don't mean any old pants. You're to be in special pants, tight white pants like Lauren wears.'

'I don't have any!' I laughed. 'I like skimpies, see-through ones, the sort the boys like to see us in.'

'Tight, white, cotton,' Angel answered.

I went to buy my new panties the next day. It shouldn't have been a big deal. I mean, I was only buying some panties, wasn't I?

I was, but it wasn't like any other panties-buying trip I'd been on. I was sure everyone in the store knew I was

133

having a lesbian relationship and that my new panties were part of a kinky game. By the time I'd paid for them I was blushing really red and I walked home feeling acutely embarrassed, even though I was only holding a carrier bag from the store I'd been into, and it was one of the biggest and smartest shops around!

Angel had really got to me. I didn't know if I was in love with her or what, but what she had done to me had really turned me on and I couldn't get it out of my head. I wasn't sure I even liked her that much, but with her I could make fantasy reality, and I wanted that thrill so badly.

Back at the house I went to my room and changed into the panties. I'd done as I'd been told and got them two sizes too small, so that they really hugged my bum and the flesh spilled out at the sides. If nothing else I looked really girly, almost innocent and very vulnerable, which I suppose was mainly what Angel was getting off on. I'd wondered before if she was into Lauren and now I was sure, because that was Lauren all through: innocent and girly.

The other girl in the house was Sophie. She was an English student and hoping to be a journalist, only nineteen and a Catholic like me. She was used to me, so she didn't say anything when I came down to the communal room in just the panties, my socks and shoes. I was glad, because I wanted it to build up slowly, until Angel got back and saw I'd done as I'd been told. Then I'd be taken upstairs, and Sophie would probably guess, and that would make it even hornier.

It was ages until Angel turned up, but when she did it was really something. She was in her leather trousers and boots that came right up to her knees and was also wearing a white shirt, like a man might wear. I was making a coffee and she looked at me, smiling as she saw I was topless and in the white panties. I'd left my shoes and socks on because I'd thought it made the look even better, but when she saw them I knew I was in trouble. Her face changed, the naughty smile turning to a wicked grin.

Angel nodded to Sophie and put down what she was carrying, then walked right over to me. Before I knew what was happening she had me by the ear. She just did it, right there in front of Sophie. I was pulled down as she dropped on to the sofa, hard over her lap, with my bum going up in the air. Sophie just sat there with her hand to her mouth, looking on as Angel took me round the middle and pushed a leg up to bring my bum up even more. I wasn't at all sure I wanted to get it in front of Sophie and I kicked and struggled, but Angel was too strong for me. My panties were pulled down and I got spanked.

It was really hard, like the first spanking, and again I kicked and struggled and made a right show of myself, all the while with Sophie demanding to know why I was getting it and Angel just smacking away. I'm sure Sophie was scared she'd be next, because she suddenly ran for the door, only to stop just as she reached it. She gave a gasp of shock and I craned my head to look past Angel's legs. In the doorway was Lauren, along with a fat man who could only be Percy and another, younger man standing behind them. My bum was stuck out right at them, red and open, with everything showing. I tried to get up, but Angel only tightened her grip on my waist.

'What's happening?' Lauren demanded, her mouth and eyes wide in her surprise.

'A little domestic discipline, I imagine,' Percy remarked. 'Don't mind us.'

'Watch if you like,' Angel remarked. 'I don't care.'

'I should be delighted.' Percy smirked. 'But what is the young miscreant's name, and what has she done to merit such a stern rebuke?'

'Pippa,' Angel answered. 'Get off on seeing young girls get spanked, do you?'

'Naturally,' Percy answered. 'But I am being rude. I'm Percy Ottershaw. This is my friend Charles, Charles Carlisle. You, I presume, are Angel?'

'You've got it, fatso,' Angel answered.

Percy ignored her rude comment and looked at Sophie, who introduced herself really shyly. All this had been going on with my bare red bum stuck up in the air, and I was blushing like crazy. But I was turned on, too, because I knew Percy was into it – and Charles was a really good-looking guy. He was embarrassed, though, and I saw him and Sophie exchange looks. Angel didn't care. She went on with the punishment, slapping away at my bum as if it didn't matter at all that five people were staring at me, right up my cunt.

They watched me get it, all of them: Lauren giggling, Percy smirking, Charles and Sophie shy but not so shy that they looked away. Angel really put on a show, too, spanking me really hard so that I lost control completely and kicked and wriggled and made a right exhibition of myself. I got hot, though, and when she had finished she took me by the ear and dragged me upstairs. They all knew what was happening, and that made it so horny. Angel told me to kneel on the bed, which I did while she took off her leather trousers, socks and boots. I was shivering, and as she pulled down her panties I was thinking of how it had felt to kiss and lick her bumhole, certain I was to be made to do it again.

Sure enough, she climbed on the bed and put her bum in my face, then pulled her cheeks open so I could see the tight little hole between. I puckered up and kissed it, feeling humiliated and punished – and very, very excited.

'Good girl,' Angel told me. 'Now put the crucifix in, then pull up your panties over it.'

I reached up and took down my crucifix, trembling as I set my thighs apart. I was soaking and it slid right into my cunt, until the hilt was against my pussy and between my cheeks. Pulling my big white panties up, I jammed the cross into place, the material holding it deep in me. Angel had turned and was looking down, watching me.

'Now wank off,' she ordered.

She didn't need to tell me. Her pussy was right in front of my face, so close I could feel her warmth. I put my hand down the front of the panties, feeling the crucifix in my cunt. The crosspiece was right on my clitty, and by wiggling it I could rub myself and also make my smacked cheeks wobble. I kissed Angel's pussy and thought of how she had punished me, in public, with Sophie watching as my panties were pulled down. Not just Sophie, either, but Lauren and fatso Percy and Charles, all fully dressed and quite proper while I was in nothing more than a pair of lowered panties. I burrowed my tongue down between Angel's pussy lips, feeling incredibly horny and also grateful for the spanking, the pain and the public humiliation. They'd seen everything: my cunt, my bumhole but, most importantly, they'd seen that I got discipline . . .

I started to come and licked harder, hoping to make my beautiful Angel come with me. She moaned and took my hair, pulling me in, then abruptly back so that her pussy was right in front of my face, hot and musky.

'So you like to pee yourself?' she asked.

My climax was so close that I couldn't speak. I was right on the edge, but I managed to nod.

She just did it, right in my face. I even saw the little pee-hole open and then it came out, a great gush of pee, full into my open mouth, up my nose, in my eyes – everywhere. She laughed at the sight and I started to choke on what was in my mouth, but I was coming and I couldn't stop as the pee ran down over my titties and tummy, down the front of my panties where I was rubbing and on to my cunt. I felt it, hot and wet over my pussy as I coughed out my mouthful over the bed, and then I was screaming out my pleasure, really loud as I was peed over – soiled on my own bed, stripped, spanked and peed on while I came.

Angel put me into a routine, so that all the time I was in the house I was in the tight white panties, nothing else. They became really important for me, as a constant reminder that I got my bum spanked. Pulling them down got to be a real turn-on, even when I was just undressing to go in the bath or for bed. Sometimes I'd even spank myself if Angel wasn't around, just to get that glow. Not often, though, because I usually got plenty of attention.

Each evening my panties would come down and my bum would be out, pink and rosy. Sometimes it would be in front of Sophie, who didn't seem to care much once she knew she wasn't going to get the same. Quite often there were other people there, because Angel loved to show me off, and it became quite a thing for them to come round and watch me get it across her lap. Not that so very many people knew, but quite enough to make it really embarrassing. Still, anyone who came into the house got an eyeful of my titties and, as the red part of my bum often showed below the edge of the panties, they had a chance to guess what had been done to me.

In fact, it was really getting out of hand. I did like to show off, and Angel was right, the best times were always in front of other people, and when I came later it would be something else. The problem was the way I got treated. People thought that just because I enjoyed a spanking it meant I liked being pushed around. Percy and Lauren and Elaine were all right, because they understood – Sophie too, once she got used to it. Carl knew and used to really take liberties, along with some of his friends.

Angel's answer was that I shouldn't be worried because I was her girlfriend and she would look after me, but that was a fat lot of help when she wasn't around. I couldn't even tell the others to go to hell, because then it would have been right round college and everyone would have been calling me a dyke and a pervert and things.

The other thing was that I knew why Angel wanted me in the tight white panties. It was because Lauren had to wear them for Percy and Angel fancied Lauren. That meant I had to be the same, so she too could have a girl wearing embarrassing panties to her order.

I wanted some advice, and I also wanted Angel to know how I felt so she would cool it a bit. She wouldn't let *me* spank *her*, though, because she said a relationship like ours could only work if one person was firmly in charge. As a naturally dominant person she would always be the one to dish it out, while I would always get it. I didn't agree. It struck me that when it comes to sex what's good for one ought to be good for the other. All I wanted was to give her bum a couple of pats, just to make me feel good, but she wouldn't go for it.

Advice I could get, because Lauren was getting spanked too. I talked to her and she said Percy didn't think the same way as Angel. He said it was just fun, and that what happened in the bedroom, or over the kitchen table, shouldn't matter when sex wasn't going on. She said he had done a lot of spanking in his time, and had it all worked out, and that I should come and have a chat.

I agreed and went round to Percy's place off the King's Road. When I arrived he was unloading cases of wine from his big Rover, and I stood and chatted while he finished. The cases were big wooden ones, and by the time he had moved twelve into the house he was puffing and blowing. I tried to help, seeing how he was so fat, but when I tried to lift a case I had to put it down again because it was so heavy.

Inside the house I explained my problem. I was a bit worried in case Percy tried something, but he never even suggested it and took my troubles really seriously. In the end he suggested that he should talk to Angel, and with luck she would listen. I couldn't see it myself but was willing to try, while I'd thought of another idea too.

Sure enough, Angel was not going to take any lip from Percy when he dropped in at my invitation the next day. She told him he was a male chauvinist pig just for trying to give her some advice. I mentioned Lauren's name, which got Angel even crosser. She wouldn't even leave it when Sophie and Charles came in. They had started going out together and had watched me spanked many a time. Sophie had even seen me with the crucifix in my cunt, so they knew, but I was surprised at Angel because she usually liked to keep her emotions hidden in front of others. The argument had got really heated, and Angel was trying to get Percy to admit to spanking girls against their will.

'I suppose you think it's right for women to be given physical discipline?' she was asking Percy. 'Keep the little woman in order and all that.'

'Not at all,' Percy answered. 'It is true that some girls like to see their spankings as punishment for wrongdoing, or laziness, or whatever, but I strongly disagree with giving a spanking against the victim's will.'

'Yeah, sure,' Angel sneered. 'I can just see it: some poor little secretary given the choice of a spanking or the sack. Oh no, not against her will at all.'

'I assure you that I have never done such a thing,' Percy stated firmly, only for Angel to interrupt him.

'You've never got a girl drunk and put her across your knee either, I suppose?' she accused. 'Or paid for it?'

'I've paid for it,' Percy admitted. 'Once or twice, before I was married, and, yes, I suppose one or two of my girlfriends might have been a little tipsy the first time they . . .'

'Like I said,' Angel cut in, 'you push them into it. It doesn't mean they want it.'

I thought that was pretty rich after the way she had done me, but I didn't say it. I had something else in mind.

'Be fair, Angel,' I cut in. 'If he was like that he'd have done it to you before now. Like when you called him fatso.'

'Ha!' Angel laughed. 'That's because he wouldn't dare. And he couldn't, anyway, the fat pig. But you can bet he'd like to.'

'Certainly I would enjoy it,' Percy answered her. 'You have a magnificent bottom, and being taught a few manners would certainly do you no harm.'

'Oh yeah? Fucking try it, then!' Angel snapped.

'I wouldn't dream of it,' Percy answered. 'As I say, I only spank willing girls, even though you clearly need it.'

'You couldn't do it, Percy,' I put in. 'She's very strong.'

'The point is moot . . .' he said softly.

'You're just trying to back out!' I laughed. 'Go on, Angel, let him try. Show him up!'

'Come on, fatso, try it!' Angel said. 'Try and spank me, just like you have all the poor little girls you've spanked before! Come on!'

She had gone for the bait! I'd been sure she wouldn't be able to resist it. It was too much for her, with her jealousy over Lauren and her general low opinion of men. She was confident, too, and she just *knew* he couldn't do it. I knew different: I'd seen Percy carrying wine cases that I couldn't lift even an inch off the ground. He tried to back off but the further he attempted to retreat the more she went for it. In the end she scribbled a note, giving him permission to punish her if he could. At that Percy finally gave in to the taunting.

Maybe Angel wanted it, deep down. Maybe she was just too stubborn to back off. She fought like anything, scratching and kicking and thumping, but it was obvious from the start that Percy was stronger than her. He didn't even use his weight, but just forced her down over his lap where he was sitting. All the time I backed her up, yelling for her to sort him out, until she was helpless. Then I stopped. Percy had got her arms up behind her back and a leg hooked around one of hers. She couldn't move and her thighs were spread out across his leg, so that her pussy was pressed against him, which must really have wound her up. He held her there for a bit, getting his breath back and ignoring her swearing and attempts to struggle.

'Now,' he told her, 'I'm going to take down your trousers and knickers and spank you on your bare bottom. Is that understood?'

Angel just called him a string of names, mainly to do with his weight. Percy gave a little chuckle and reached under her tummy for her trousers button. She went berserk, yelling and trying to bite and kick, but it was no good. He got the button open and pulled her zip down, then put his hand in the back of her trousers and began to tug them down.

It was something else. Her face was bright red and she had this great look, with her lower lip pouted out, really sulky and determined, in between bouts of swearing as her bum came out of her trousers bit by bit. Percy took no notice, holding her firmly and taking his time, until her leather trousers were down around her thighs and her lovely big bum was only covered by a tiny pair of black satin panties.

'Don't you fucking dare!' she gasped, but his thumb was already hooked into her waistband.

I was holding my breath, wondering if he really did have the guts to pull the panties down. He did. I was sideways on to Angel and could see both her face and her bum. Sophie and Charles were across the kitchen, holding hands and watching in absolute fascination as

Angel's bottom was stripped. Percy did it slowly, easing the black satin down and admiring the swell of her bum cheeks as they came on show. She had stopped struggling, but her face was set in a look of petulant bad temper that had me giggling behind my hand, for all that I was trying to pretend to be on her side. Down her panties came, over her bum, showing the crease, inch by inch. She gave a little choking sob as the plumpest bit of her bum came on show, the chubby tuck of her cheeks, which I had kissed so often before having to kiss her bumhole.

Then it was bare: a big pink moon, all lovely and nude over his lap. Angel, with her bum showing while everyone else was fully dressed! Angel, about to get a spanking, in public! She had given in, and was lying limp over Percy's lap, waiting for her punishment to start. Percy adjusted his leg, pulling her trousers and panties well down and then putting his foot through the waistband, to trap her with her cunt pressed to his thighs. That really showed her off, with her lips pouting out behind and the pinky bit showing, just like mine did when she punished me. Her cheeks were right up high too, and looked very big and very vulnerable.

Percy was in no hurry, savouring the moment. Then he began to feel her bum up. She just gave another sob and let him do it. He groped her cheeks and smirked, even putting a finger and thumb in her crease and prising it open to get a look at her bumhole. I was behind and saw the little dark hole, the hole I'd been made to kiss and lick – only now it was revealed to a dirty old man!

He let her crease close and gave her bottom a thoughtful pat. Then he cupped one fleshy cheek, weighing it judiciously.

'On the of subject of fat,' Percy remarked, 'any girl with such a well-upholstered posterior might do well to keep her opinions on another's weight to herself.'

That set Angel off again. And me too: I laughed out loud as she started to kick her free leg and swear at him. I couldn't help it, because she just looked so silly, with her nude bum wobbling about and one leg going up and down in the air. She cursed and swore, but Percy just gave his dirty little chuckle and then started to spank her.

Angel kept at it, right through the spanking, kicking out and yelling blue murder, but never once actually telling him to stop. That was the give-away – that, and the way her cunt had begun to get all juicy!

I was laughing and running around, wanting to be at both ends at once. Her face was a picture, varying between a miserable pained look when the slaps hit her and consternation in between. The other end was even better, with her thighs wide and her wet cunt showing, with a smear of juice on Percy's leg where she kept bucking up and down so that it slapped on his thigh. I could see her bumhole, too, each time her cheeks opened, and I told her so.

Her bum was purple when it happened. Charles and Sophie had come round behind to see it properly and were obviously getting pretty excited. I certainly was, with my pussy juicy in my tight white panties. Angel was still kicking, but not so hard, and she had started to snivel. Percy was going strong, spanking away merrily. He kept putting his leg up, so her cunt was pressed tight against his trousers, with her own trousers and panties locking her in place.

She called him a fat bastard one last time, and then she stopped kicking and began to move her bum in time to Percy's smacks, rubbing herself on his leg. Sophie gave a nervous little giggle and I laughed out loud. Percy cocked his leg up higher still and tightened his grip on her arms. He began to smack the lower part of her bum, right over her pussy. Angel gave another sob and her squirming became firmer, pushing her open

144

pussy hard against the rough tweed of his trousers. The beating had become rhythmic, one smack per rub, and was getting faster. She was going to come on his leg!

Angel's breathing was getting faster too, and so was mine. I wanted to touch myself and I didn't care who saw, because they'd all seen me naked before, spanked and humiliated, just like Angel. I heard her groan and I was struggling with the belt of my bell-bottoms. They were down as she cried out and my hand was on the front of my panties. Percy saw and smiled as I tugged them hard into my pussy. Angel screamed and I was rubbing the cotton against my clit, tight white cotton moving on me as she bucked and squirmed, her cheeks parting to show off her bumhole . . .

And then my face was buried in her bum and I was licking, tasting her cunt and tasting her bumhole with my panties pulled tight up my cleft. She really screamed and I was coming too, licking and kissing at her juicy rear and her beaten cheeks, indifferent to Sophie's exclamation of shock and Percy's dry laugh.

We came together, Angel and I, snogging and hugging on the floor as she rolled off Percy's lap, sharing the taste of her bum and cunt, kissing and whispering soothing words. The others left quickly, leaving us to our moment, and as Percy shut the door I caught his words.

'As I said,' he remarked, 'she needed a spanking.'

8

Sophie in Chablis

Percy Ottershaw was a pervert: there was no other word for it. He and Charles had got me drunk, teased me into a sexy mood, covered me with food and stuck sausages up my fanny and my bottom. They had then eaten the food, every scrap, with Charles feeding me the mess from his mouth. The sausage had been a local *andouillette*, fat and white and made from an assortment of offal. Percy had even eaten the one that had been in my bottom and, to add the final filthy touch, he had sodomised me.

Worse still, I had enjoyed it. I couldn't remember how many times I'd come but it was a lot. I'd certainly come with Percy's cock up my bottom, because he'd reminded me the next day while he and Charles had been discussing which of the wines we'd drunk had gone best with me!

I'd actually felt sorry for Percy on the drive down from Calais, because he had just been through a divorce. If he had treated his wife the way he had treated me then I wasn't surprised, although they had been together for years. Now all I could do was sit in silence as we drove through the hills to the north of Chablis, pretending to have a hangover but all the while burning with guilt and shame for what I'd done.

I needed to confess, badly, but I couldn't bear to admit it to the men. Charles was always sympathetic to my beliefs, although he didn't share them. Percy would just have laughed. Nor was there likely to be a chance to get away, because Percy had lined up a long series of tastings for us. He was being helpful, because with Charles trying to get a toehold in the wine trade and me struggling to get recognised for my writing on the subject, it was really very good of him to take so much trouble. Not that it excused his sodomising me.

We tasted all morning, going from domaine to domaine in the town of Chablis. I spat out every sip but still felt tipsy by lunchtime, while Percy had guzzled down every glass he'd been offered and still seemed to be sober. Everybody seemed to know him and we were welcomed with open arms, the normally reserved French *vignerons* bringing out bread and cheese and opening old bottles and generally treating us as honoured guests. As Percy had for years been the buyer for a big importer I suppose many of them had cause to be grateful, while without being vain I can say that my own looks contributed. Twice I had my bottom pinched and one old boy of about eighty simply took a handful and had a good feel while his son opened the bottles for us.

Lunch was at the house of a grower Percy particularly favoured. We were served oysters with his Chablis, an *andouillette* with his Fourchaume and goose with his Valmur. I could only just get the *andouillette* down, all the while thinking of how it had felt when one was pushed up my bottom. Percy ate his with gusto. The meal ended with an older vintage of Valmur and strong, soft cheese, then a marc, by which time my head was spinning and Charles was sitting back with his hands folded across his lap, barely awake. Percy and our host were finishing the cheese and discussing the merits of different vintages, especially the quality of the 'seventy-five, which was just being bottled. I should have been taking notes, but it was all I could do to keep my eyes open.

After lunch we set off for Maligny, where we had an appointment later in the afternoon, but as we drove into La Chapelle Percy spotted a sign by the road advertising *foie gras*. Nothing would do but that they had to go and get some, but they couldn't agree which way to go. The sign was a big yellow goose, but there was no arrow on it. Charles reasoned that the beak would point in the right direction and I agreed. Only Percy could have thought the goose's rear end would be the pointer.

The spire of a church was visible among the trees and I saw my chance to make my confession. Besides, I knew what was going to happen if I went with them for the *foie gras*. I would end up in the woods with it smeared all over me while their tongues burrowed into every little fold and hole of my body, doubtless with some suitably rich old *Grand Cru* to wash it down.

'Look, you boys find your pâté,' I told them. 'I want to see if anybody in the village does a *l'Homme Mort*.'

'Fine idea!' Percy answered enthusiastically. 'Do you know, I've never seen one, but here would be the place, if any. Try and get an old one and we'll have it for tea with the *foie gras*.'

I climbed out of the car, leaving them to their goose chase. My tummy felt bloated and I needed the loo, but the fresh cool air was a blessed relief and I just stood for a while, looking out across the valley and sucking in lungfuls of air. I knew I was drunk, very drunk, so much so, in fact, that what we had done the night before didn't seem so dreadful any more. I was even giggling a bit as I started into the village and thinking of all those orgasms, one after another, enough to make Germaine Greer put out a revised edition of her best-seller.

Not that that meant I could skip my confession. To the contrary, I needed it all the more badly, to clean away my sins and start afresh so that they could have me again, one in each entry to my body, filling me, making me scream . . .

No, I was *not* going to do that. I was going to confess – and I hoped the priest would give me a heavy penance. Yes, that was what I was going to do, only first I had to try and find a sample from a respectable 'sixties vintage, or bang would go the reputation I was trying to build up.

On the fifth attempt I succeeded, by which time I had tasted a further fourteen assorted Chablis. I had in fact tasted two different *l'Homme Mort* across three vintages, which for the first time meant that I had tasted something Percy had not, nor Charles. That in itself was a triumph and I had a quick glass of cognac at the café to celebrate.

By luck the priest was in the café at the same time, taking a leisurely Ricard and reading the paper. He happily agreed to hear my confession and we walked up to the church together, chatting mainly in French. I was glad of this, because for all my determination to confess I didn't mind taking the chance that he wouldn't understand some of the dirtier details. Certainly I didn't know the right French phrases for having two men at once in vagina and anus, sodomy with a sausage or face-sitting, which I vaguely remembered as the last thing I'd done to Percy.

The inside of the church had that atmosphere of sanctity and age that always makes me feel so cosseted and so small. Obedience is appropriate in such an atmosphere, and as the great door creaked to behind us I felt my guilt coming back with a vengeance. What I had done was dreadful, an appalling thing, for which I desperately needed to be absolved.

The priest took my hand and led me to the confessional. Inside it was dark and warm, with only a faint light from the grid to throw a pattern on my skirt as I seated myself. I heard him settle into his place as he mumbled a prayer. We went through the formal responses and I admitted to a couple of little things. Then

I took my courage in both hands and admitted carnal thoughts – and acts.

'And what form did these thoughts and acts take, my child?' the priest asked.

'Pleasure in my intended, Father,' I admitted, 'and the act itself, and with one other.'

'What act?'

'Carnal acts, Father: touching, and with my mouth.'

'Just that?'

'*In* my mouth, actually, Father. Intercourse also, only with my intended.'

'And the other?'

'With my mouth, Father, and . . . and sodomy.'

'Sodomy?'

'Sodomy, Father.'

'With a man, or a beast?'

'A man!'

'Yes, of course . . . Hmm, and how old are you, my child?'

'Twenty, Father.'

'I would have thought you younger.'

'No, Father, twenty.'

'It seems very young to be so . . . so depraved.'

'I'm not depraved, Father!'

'You confess to sodomy with a man not your husband, not even your intended, and you deny depravity? Come, my child, accept the nature of your sins.'

'Yes, Father. Sorry. Forgive me, Father.'

'Tell me of it, so that you may unburden your soul.'

'Everything, Father?'

'Everything, my child.'

I began to tell him, trying to tell him what had happened before my last confession and what after. It seemed pointless to mention Pippa, or how Charles had first taken my virginity and then sodomised me. I kept to events in France, how Percy and Charles had teased me and made me drunk, the hotel near Epineuil, persuading me to strip to my undies, playing with the food. The priest stopped me at the point where Charles had put the *andouillette* up my fanny. His breathing was hoarse and uneven. I was burning with shame, but my nipples were stiff and my fanny felt tingly. There was an odd shuffling noise coming from his half of the confessional, rustling, like cloth moving over cloth, and a meaty sound. He was masturbating, masturbating over what Percy and Charles had done to me – him, a priest!

Not that I was any better, because I had an urgent need to touch my fanny and I knew I was wet. It was impossible to describe such a thing and not get turned on, and in my drunken haze I decided that if he was going to do it then so was I. I kept talking, but leaned back on the bench, opening my thighs. A hand went down my tights and into my panties. I found my fanny and started to rub.

'They covered me in pâté,' I admitted. 'In my mouth and everywhere, even in my most private places. They ate it, all of it, and fed me from their mouths, even eating the sausages that had been inside me. When they were done my intended, Charles, lay on the floor and I climbed on top of him. As I did so Percy came behind and he sodomised me. After that . . .'

I had nearly come but the priest suddenly told me to stop. He ordered me to get out of the confessional and I thought he was going to throw me out of the church, but as I quickly adjusted my clothing he ordered me into the sacristy. I knew what was going to happen, because it had happened before. He was turned on and I was going to be made to make him come, then we would probably pray together and I would be let off with some mild penance. When the trick had first been played on me I had let it happen, but I'd sworn I would be stronger the next time and tell the priest to go to hell. I had been wrong. I was drunk and aroused and I was going to let him do it, in my hand or in my mouth, maybe even up my fanny.

The priest strode to the sacristy, his robe pushed out at the front by his erect cock. It looked big, and I found myself licking my lips. Inside I was told to kneel at his feet, which I did while he gave me a brief lecture on my sins. Then he announced that he was going to have me and that I should open my mouth.

I obeyed and he reached up under his robe, pushed down his underwear at the front and pulled the robe up, exposing himself. His cock was already hard, a rigid column with the head swollen and purple, really big, bigger than Charles, much bigger than Percy. If the priest's cock was big, his balls were huge, dangling in a loose scrotum, hanging a good few inches beneath his cock. I gaped wide and he took me by the hair, then fed me his cock, right to the back of my throat. I wanted to suck, but he was holding me hard and began to fuck my mouth. So I pursed my lips and made the best of it, wondering if he was going to come down my throat or go the whole way and fuck me. It was a lovely cock: it seemed a shame not to have it put properly in me and, as he tugged my hair back, I felt sure I would get my wish. His big prick came out of my mouth and I sat back on my bottom, awaiting instructions.

'On the floor,' he ordered. 'Right down, bottom up.'

'Are you . . . are you going to fuck me?' I stammered.

'No,' he answered. 'Do you think I would break my vows? Just get down and you will see how I treat dirty whores.'

I scrabbled round, wondering what he meant as I presented my bottom to him. Was I to be beaten? Just exposed to bring home my shame to me while he masturbated over what I was showing? Maybe he would push a candle up my vagina and light it as my penance, as had been done to me once before. Or a crucifix, the same way that my friend Pippa liked to masturbate. He began to interfere with my clothing, pulling up my skirt. My tights came down next, my knickers with them,

152

leaving my bare bottom thrust out with the hole showing and my fanny too.

As I looked back between my thighs I could see the priest's legs and balls, with his hand gripping the base of his cock. He shuffled forward and laid it between my bum cheeks. I felt the rounded head press against my anus and now I knew what he meant. He wasn't going to fuck me, or beat me, or shame me. He was going to sodomise me, to do it in my back passage, just like Percy had. He was right, though: I *was* a dirty whore, fit only to be sodomised, and I made no move to stop him – it was going to happen anyway. But at least Percy had lubricated me first, and it hurt now as my bottom-hole flinched against the unnatural pressure. It wasn't my first time, and I remembered what Charles had said as he took my anal virginity: pretend you're on the loo. I relaxed my ring, pushing out, and felt it open against his cock, my anus's wet centre spreading like a little flower, opening to him, letting him into my body by the back door.

A sudden stab of pain made me think the priest had split me, but he kept on pushing, forcing his prick in and cursing to himself as my ring stretched. By the time his cockhead was in I was clenching my fists and gritting my teeth. Then it was his shaft, and even with my hole stretched wide it took a lot of effort to get it in. It went in, though, bit by bit, while he complained about me being so tight and said English girls ought to be sodomised more frequently. Only at the end did it get easier. He pulled out a little and there was a wet, squelching sound. Then he was going back up and his last few inches slid into my back passage. His thighs met my buttocks and I knew it was all up, that I was being well and truly sodomised.

I could barely take it in. He was up my bum – a priest, right in, filling my passage. He was bigger than Percy, a lot bigger, and my poor bottom-hole was really

153

straining, but as he used me his huge balls slapped on my empty fanny, bringing me more and more on heat. Sometimes bits of ball hair would tickle my button, and if it hadn't been for the pain I think I would have come. Every push of his cock was jamming into my bladder and I was wishing I'd gone to the loo in the bar. And it wasn't just my bladder that felt pressured. I was amazed by the way I felt so bloated, really stuffed, with a strained feeling in my back passage, and a squashy, wet sensation each time he pushed into me.

The priest was mumbling in French as he sodomised me, calling me filthy names, especially the word *sale*, again and again. With the pain in my bladder and bottom that almost had me crying. It was so unfair. He was the one who'd put his cock up my bottom, and it wasn't my fault if I hadn't been to the loo before. I hadn't thought I was going to be sodomised, or I would have done!

Then my bladder gave way. I couldn't help it: it was just too much, with all the wine I'd drunk and my bottom-hole stretched around his cock. I cried out in a final effort to keep it in, but it was too late. As the pee burst from my fanny I gave a choking scream and sank my face to the floor. I felt it spray out, backwards from my peehole, all over his balls and the floor, into my knickers and tights, down my thighs and over my fanny mound. It even ran forwards, to soil my skirt and drip from my belly. He never stopped, but just called me a dirty whore and rammed his cock even deeper up my back passage.

The pain was going, though, draining away as my bladder emptied and the warm pee washed down over my body. I'd never pissed with a man up me before. It was bliss, a really lovely, yielding sensation, warm and dirty, that took me higher and made me sigh with relief.

The priest stopped just as the last of my pee trickled away. He pulled slowly out, leaving my bottom-hole gaping and sore. I thought he'd come, only when I turned my head I found him reaching for a half-empty bottle on the table. Complaining that his balls were too hot and that my bottom and fanny needed washing, he emptied it down my crease. Some went up my bottom, which hadn't closed, more in my fanny, and more over his genitals and into my tights and knickers, adding to the pee puddle on the floor.

As he entered me again, still up my back passage, my fanny farted and sprayed his balls with wine. Unlike before, this time he got in without difficulty, sliding up my greasy back passage until the full length was in me. I grunted as my bottom filled, then again as he leaned forwards on to my back, wrenched up my blouse and bra and caught my breasts in his hands as they tumbled free. The sodomising started again as he began to squeeze my breasts, now mounted on me like a dog with only about half his cock up my bumhole. It wasn't enough, because his balls were no longer slapping my fanny and the scrotum hairs no longer tickling my button. I had been near coming and had been sure I could make it. Now I was just on a plateau of pleasure, kneeling in my own pee puddle with the priest's erection in my back passage and his hands on my breasts, but still a hair's breadth from the ecstasy I needed to come.

I was going to reach back to masturbate, but the priest's kneading suddenly became firmer and the movement of his cock in my bottom-hole harder. The pain started again and the squelching noise of my being buggered became louder along with his gasps and grunts. He jerked inside me and I knew he had come up my bottom. Again it happened, and a third time, as I thought of the state I was in and wished I had come while he was still buggering me.

The priest pulled out, mumbling prayers and curses to himself as his erection eased from my anus. I wanted to come myself and asked for his tongue, only to be called a whore. I hung my head, my hair trailing in a trickle of pee that had escaped the main pool, and asked again, begging him to make me come.

'Do it yourself, little whore,' he answered and stood up, holding his clothes clear of his genitals.

I stayed down, watching as he washed his cock at a tiny sink, hoping he would take mercy on me. Instead he finished and strode to the doorway, stepped part-way through and briefly turned back to me.

'You are bound for hell,' the priest spat. 'As surely as if you were the very daughter of Lucifer.'

The door slammed and I was alone, kneeling, sodomised and filthy with my bottom in the air and my lowered tights and panties full of pee and wine. The liquid was under me, too, a big golden pool, the same colour as the richest, oldest Chablis. He had had me, really used me, in my mouth and up my bottom. Now I was going to come, and it didn't matter if I was kneeling in my own filth on the sacristy floor.

I sat down squashily, right in the pool of pee. My fanny was soiled and my skirt was in the puddle, while my knickers and tights were ruined. I didn't care – all I could think of was the need in my fanny and the warm, wet feeling on my bottom and thighs. I took my knickers and pulled them in, rubbing the gusset over my fanny and on to my button. My lips felt swollen and fat under the wet cotton, the centre of my quim a wet, slimy, slippery mush. I let go and caught my breasts up, weighing them in my hands and feeling the nipples, soiling them with my dirty fingers.

It was bliss, pure heaven, with my bottom in the mess and my breasts in my hands, while the wine sang in my head and my bottom-hole dribbled the priest's come – and more – on to the floor. Or maybe it was pure hell, as he had said but all I wanted to do was come, and come in the puddle of my own mess. Keeping one hand free to caress my breasts I started to masturbate again with the other, rubbing my fanny through my knicker crotch and occasionally dipping down beneath myself to put a finger in my vagina or up my bottom to pull out more mess and slime it over my fanny. It felt wonderful, soggy and squashy and wet, up between my cheeks and over my cunt. Soon I was wriggling my bottom in it, squirming my cheeks about to make them open and rub my sore bottom-hole on the floor.

My button was on fire, the burning heart of my soiled fanny sending wave after wave of ecstasy through me as I rubbed and rubbed and my bottom squirmed and squelched in the mess. As my cunt began to pulse I lost control of my bottom-hole and it all came out, on the floor between my cheeks. I came, calling out for Charles, wishing he was there to take charge of me, or that it was his come oozing from my bottom-hole. Then, right at the peak, Percy invaded my head, ramming his cock into my gaping anus as I was mounted on Charles, and the priest too, taking my mouth so that every hole was full of cock and then every hole was running with men's come.

I was screaming aloud and bouncing my bottom up and down in the mess, showering the walls with drops of it and splashing my legs, my clothes and even my belly. At the last instant I grabbed my knicker crotch again and pulled the cotton hard against my button, hitting a final peak that made me scream. I stuffed the hand that had been feeling my breasts into my mouth, tasting myself on my fingers and half stifling my cries as I came down. My climax faded slowly, leaving me squatting in my puddle and panting hard as my head slowly cleared. At least, it cleared a little. But I was still drunk, and felt little of the overpowering guilt that I should have.

The sacristy was an appalling mess, but I wasn't cleaning it up. The priest had had me up the bottom and it was his outsize cock that had made me wet myself, so he could clean up the results. I badly needed to wash myself, though. A tiny sink allowed me to sluice my hands and breasts, but it looked too weak to sit in and wasn't really large enough for my bottom anyway. For a moment I stood there, tights and knickers around my thighs, top up, with everything showing, dreading the return of the priest. He didn't come, but in any case my best choice seemed to be to run up into the woods behind the church, then somehow to try and find Charles and Percy. I could strip off completely and put on a surplice. Either way there would be some embarrassing questions to answer if I got caught.

Fortunately there was a sort of fountain affair at the back of the church, completely hidden by high walls. I washed my bottom and then my clothes, bare from the waist down and terrified someone would catch me. In the end I abandoned my tights and knickers and went naked under my wet skirt, which was embarrassing but better than wandering around the village with my fanny and bottom showing.

With the priest around I didn't want to linger so I left as soon as I decently could, keeping to the little lanes at the top of the village in the hope of avoiding people. Two locals saw me and both gave me funny looks, but no one else appeared and I soon found myself at the junction where I had got out of the car. Charles and Percy were there, leaning on the vehicle's bonnet and eating pastries.

'Are you all right?' Charles greeted me. 'Good heavens, your skirt's soaking!'

'I slipped in the mud,' I lied. 'I had to wash it in the stream.'

Percy glanced at my legs. I was sure he guessed I had no knickers on but he said nothing.

'How did you get on?' Charles asked.

'I've got some samples,' I told him, 'including a l'*Homme Mort* 'sixty-nine.'

'Splendid,' Percy put in. 'But where are they?'

'I left them in the little café,' I admitted. 'Behind the bar. Be a sweetie and get them, Charles. I feel really embarrassed like this.'

'Certainly,' he said. 'A pity, though. I was hoping to take some time to look around.'

'It's a charming village,' Percy remarked. 'You would both be interested in the church, especially you, Sophie. It's built in front of a spring where some saint or other washed her feet. Very sacred, apparently. It's supposed to restore virginity or purify fallen women, or some such nonsense.'

9

Proper in Public

July in London, and everybody flushed with optimism and money. Everybody except me, that was, or so it seemed. Fresh out of school with less than wonderful exam results, I was finding it hard to share the general air of enthusiasm, but at least I had the chance of a job. Not that I was entirely happy about that, because it was as a waitress in a restaurant owned by a friend of my mother's. His name was Percy Ottershaw and he was a fat, red-faced man of about fifty. The few times I'd met him he had been perfectly polite and entirely friendly, but never leery or over-familiar or anything. That surprised me, because I knew what he was really like.

I knew because I'd read Mum's diary from soon after she came over, before she'd married Dad. Percy used to spank her, and they got off on it together. He used to do other things, too, but mainly he used to spank her. It had really shocked me, because I'd always thought of her as very sensible. I'd also felt bad for reading the diary but I was glad I had because I was sure he'd want to give me the same treatment and I wanted to be ready for it. Not that I wanted to be spanked – just the opposite. In fact, I'd never even realised that women could enjoy anything so obviously degrading. I knew it happened, but only as the sort of thing male chauvinist pigs did to girls to humiliate them. Fortunately, feminism has put a stop to that sort of thing, but I didn't imagine Percy would have much time for feminism. He was like that: old-fashioned, formal and not at all the sort to be impressed by modern ideas.

Despite telling myself that Mum would never have suggested I take the job if she thought I'd end up across old Percy's knee, I wasn't at all sure about it. I could even imagine how he would go about it. Nothing would happen for a few weeks and then he would set something up so that I broke something, or was rude to a customer, whatever, as long as it was bad enough for him to consider sacking me. I would then be called into his office and given the choice: the sack or a smacked bottom. He knew how badly I needed the job, and doubtless thought that with poor qualifications and so many people out of work I would opt for a few smacks on my behind rather than the sack and a bad reference. Possibly he would even accuse me of taking money from the till and threaten me with the police if I didn't do as I was told. Then it would be over his fat legs with my panties pulled down for a spanking.

The thought made me shudder and put a lump in my throat. It was just such a horribly undignified thing to happen to anybody, especially me. I mean, imagine lying over some dirty old man's lap with your skirt up and your panties down, bare-bottomed for punishment, then being spanked while all the while his cock gets harder and harder against your tummy. It was more than I could bear to think about.

I put it off for two weeks, but all my other attempts to get a job came to nothing and so I accepted Percy's offer. The restaurant was *Au Boeuf Farci* in Charlotte Street, a smart place that specialised in French cooking. In order to avoid giving him any excuse to present me with the awful choice I was really careful, on my best behaviour at all times and as helpful as I could possibly be. I even dressed down, never wearing tight jeans or short skirts, even though I wore a uniform at work. This was a simple black-and-white affair, very practical and demure, with a skirt reaching just below the knees and a little ribbon tie at the neck. The uniform meant that we had to change at work, so I even bought some plain white panties, just in case Percy ever peeped and got the wrong idea from me wearing sexy underwear.

For the first month everything was perfect. Percy behaved like the perfect gentleman, always polite, never rude or suggestive. He was a good boss, too, while I got on well with my fellow staff and the regular customers. Many of these were Percy's friends from the wine trade, which he had been in before he started the restaurant, and that was where I came unstuck.

Percy's main supplier was a man called Charles Carlisle. He was a dapper little man, very cool and correct and would never, ever dirty his fingers with carrying cases or anything of the sort. All that was done by his driver. This was Nick, who was as different as could be, a real gorilla of a man with great hairy arms and legs like tree trunks. He also had unusually bright, dark eyes and was highly sexed, to say the least. He would always tease me and the other girls, sometimes mercilessly, but there was something about him that it was impossible not to feel attracted to.

Jilly was the first to fall for him, letting him have her on the grass in Regent's Park after work one evening. She had a regular boyfriend, too, but just got carried away. I couldn't get the thought out of my mind, especially when she admitted he'd made her kneel to take it from the rear. They'd been seen by at least two people as well, which I found a real turn-on. It was ages since I'd had sex, and I wanted the same. As Jilly had no intention of leaving her boyfriend there seemed to be a good chance that I would get it. Nick was keen on me, too, and made no secret of it, but the problem was not giving Percy his excuse.

Charles came in for a drink on most evenings, sometimes on his own, sometimes with his wife Sophie, who was a wine journalist. If there was a delivery to be made Nick would be there, too. Not alone, though, even after closing, because both Jilly and Susan would always be there. After a while I began to get really frustrated, but when it did come it took me by surprise.

I was in the cellar, trying to get the right bottles from our bewildering selection of wine. There were still a few people in the restaurant, including Charles, Sophie and Nick, while it was Susan's night off. That left Jilly and I to do all the work, along with the cook, Mary, as Percy only did what took his fancy, which was very little. I was a bit flustered and had got right in among the stacks of cases, trying to find the last bottle I needed. The case I wanted was right at the bottom and hard to open, so I was bent over, and I suppose I must have looked a bit of a sight with my bum stuck right up and my legs braced apart as I pulled at the cardboard.

'Nice arse, Anna,' Nick said from right behind me.

It was typical Nick, crude and direct. I fancied him enough not to be angry, but his next remark still took me aback.

'How would you like your cunt licked in that position?' he asked.

I managed to laugh, thinking he was joking. Then I answered, determined that I could give as good as I got.

'Oh yes, please,' I said.

Nick came straight up behind me and pulled up my skirt. I gave a little squeak at the sudden exposure of my panties – and then they were down, just like that, and his face was going in between my thighs. It was such a shock that I cried out in protest, even though it was really just what I wanted. He took no notice, just pushing my back down with one strong arm, then kissing my pussy from the rear. I gave in at that, it was just too nice, although a weak voice of common sense was telling me to stop him. As he started to lick me out his tongue burrowed into my pussy, really deep to get

163

the taste of me. All I could manage was to groan in pleasure and, feeling thoroughly wanton, I stuck my bottom in his face for more.

I was in heaven as Nick licked me and was soon too far gone to think about where I was, or what might happen to me if we were caught. He was a really dirty bastard as well, and a tease, because he was wriggling the tip of his nose on my bumhole and licking in little circles around my clit. I do like having my bumhole touched, but not all men like to do it, or to lick pussy for that matter. Nick had no such inhibitions, and after a while he put his hands between my cheeks. A finger went up my pussy. He touched my bumhole and then went a little way in there, too. I squeezed myself tight on him with my orgasm building in my head.

It was simply glorious, all that attention being paid to me, fingers in both holes and a skilled tongue on my sex. I was right on the edge for what seemed like an age before Nick suddenly began to flick my clit with his tongue and I tipped over and came and came right in his face. My pussy was squeezing on his finger and my thighs and bum cheeks tightening over and over. He had begun to finger-fuck me and was going deeper and deeper up my bum as its hole clamped on him. I wanted my tits out because the top thought in my mind was of how nice it was to be showing off and I wanted to be bare, stark naked in my ecstasy. That thought held as I came, the desire to be worshipped naked, licked and fingered, stroked and teased, kissed and sucked on, tickled and spanked . . .

The thought of having my bottom smacked brought me down. It was really unexpected, but it had come at the very peak of my ecstasy, the outrageous idea that getting my bottom spanked could be part of the turn-on. Nick thought I'd finished coming and stopped licking, leaving me in a welter of shame and confusion.

He didn't know, and, not surprisingly, wanted to fuck me. Before I'd got my breath back his cock was at my pussy, then in me. I was taken by the hips and he began to hump away merrily on my bottom. I didn't try to stop him but held my pose, just bracing myself a little to stop my body being pushed down over the cases. Despite my pussy being full of cock my mind was full of what I'd been thinking of when I'd come. I tried to tell myself it was because I'd been thinking so much about how to avoid getting spanked by Percy but that didn't really explain why it had popped up in my fantasy. The idea of a slapped bottom had turned me on, that was all there was to it, and the realisation of what I was like was almost unbearable.

One other thing did manage to get through the jumble of my thoughts. Nick was about to come up me without a condom sheathing his cock. I gasped out for him to stop and said I'd suck him, and fortunately he took notice. He didn't wait to put it in my mouth, though, but grabbed his cock and began to jerk it over my bottom. I felt his knuckles rubbing up and down in my crease, realised what he was doing and cried out, but it was too late. Nick gave an ape-like grunt and I felt something warm and wet splash into my bum crease. He put his cock in it and finished himself off, rubbing in his own sperm as more and more spilled out into my slimy cleft. It felt really disgusting, with his thick shaft all slippery between my cheeks and hot come running down into my bumhole. I was grimacing and I called him a bastard, but he just kept on, smearing the spunk around in my crease and then on my cheeks. He finished off by wiping his prick on my skirt, and I was about to really give him a piece of my mind when I heard Percy's voice calling me.

'Shit!' Nick swore.

I was up in a second, struggling with my panties as he stuffed his cock back inside his jeans. My skirt fell back into place of its own accord, so I was spared the embarrassment of showing my bum, but that was about all. Percy appeared at the end of the row of cases with Charles and Sophie behind him. It was obvious what we'd been doing, because the scent of sex was strong in the air; Nick's fly was still down and I hadn't quite finished pulling up my panties. Percy's round, red face had gone redder than ever. Charles looked stern, Sophie also, and a bit flushed.

'Er . . . sorry,' Nick managed as he did up his zip.

'Sorry, Mr Ottershaw,' I echoed.

'For goodness' sake,' Percy snapped. 'Go and get cleaned up, the pair of you. Anna, I'll talk to you about this afterwards.'

My panties were still half down, but I couldn't very well adjust them, so had to walk like that all the way to the staff toilet, with Nick's spunk squishing about between my bum cheeks. I kept my head bowed to hide my furious blushes and there was a huge lump in my throat: I was on the edge of tears. Cleaning up was really humiliating. I had to stand in the tiny cubicle with my panties right down and my bum stuck out towards the mirror while I wiped myself. My panties were all right, luckily, but it took ages to get the come off my skirt. Nick had managed to get some on my stockings, too, which were expensive hold-ups, and I was really cursing him by the time I had finished. It wasn't just for spunking on my bottom and clothes, either. It was also because I'd now given Percy the prime excuse he needed and I knew exactly what was going to happen after work.

I thought about it for the rest of the evening, trying to steel myself to tell Percy to go to hell but failing miserably. If the customers hadn't lingered so long I might just have succeeded, but my courage faded with the frustration of waiting. By the time Jilly and I had finished with the washing-up I knew I was going to let him play his filthy little game with me. As I dried my hands I decided to appeal to Sophie Carlisle, who seemed far too sensible and modern to let a fellow woman suffer a spanking. But when I came out of the kitchen I found that she had left, along with Charles and Nick.

Being done in front of Jilly and Mary would have been truly unendurable for me, though I'm sure Percy would have got a big kick out of it. But, fortunately, he couldn't punish me in front of witnesses. I would be spanked in private, that at least I was sure of, but it didn't stop the knot in my stomach growing tighter and tighter as the other girls packed up to go home. They knew something was up, of course, and gave me sympathetic looks as they left. Neither of them stood up for me, though, and as the door clicked shut behind them I found myself alone with Percy: fat Percy, Percy the spanker.

I had played the scenario over in my mind so often that I found myself acting it out. First there would be the lecture, and as I came to stand in front of Percy I found myself instinctively bowing my head and folding my hands in my lap. I was shivering inside, and there was a lump in my throat so big it felt as if I was choking. He took a sip of his wine, shook his head sadly and then folded his hands over his stomach. It was all just as I had imagined it would be. Suddenly I just couldn't bear to go through with the pretence before he demanded what we both knew he wanted.

'Don't,' I interrupted as he began to speak. 'You can spank me if you really have to.'

Percy must have been expecting a fight, because he stopped dead and his face took on the expression of a dead fish. Then he began to smile and his eyebrows lifted.

'I know you used to do it to Mum,' I told him. 'So there's no use pretending.'

'Ah, ha,' he answered. 'Well, then, I suppose you had better come across my knee.'

167

I had never heard anybody sound so pleased with themselves, so smug. As I bent forwards to lay myself across his lap it was with a sense of bitter injustice, but also of resignation. I was surrendering to having my bottom smacked by a fifty-year-old man, and it was a pretty abject surrender at that, without even a cross word. In my thoughts I'd always planned to tell Percy what a dirty old man he was when it happened. But I couldn't, not now, not with my tummy pressed to his fat legs and my toes and head down as I waited for punishment.

'Stick it up a little, please, my dear,' he said.

Feeling meek and pathetic, I did as I was told, edging myself forwards so that my bottom went up. Percy gave a dirty little chuckle at the sight, making me feel worse than ever. It wasn't just that I was to be punished, nor that it was to be in such an ignominious fashion, but that he was going to get turned on by doing it.

'So,' he went on, 'shall I put an arm around your waist, hold you still by your wrist, or would you just like to kick and wriggle?'

The old bastard was really enjoying himself, tormenting me, as if it wasn't enough to get his rocks off from just beating me. I knew what he'd like best, to have me thrash and kick and probably cry, so I determined not to give him the satisfaction.

'You'd better hold me by the wrist,' I told him and put my arm up behind my back.

My hand was immediately caught and twisted high into the middle of my back, making me squeak despite my best efforts.

'You're hurting me!' I protested, even though I knew that was the idea of it.

To my surprise Percy slackened his grip a little, still holding me firmly but a good deal less painfully.

'Now let me see,' he mused. 'How hard do you think you deserve your spanking?'

168

'I suppose you're going to do it as hard as you can,' I answered bitterly.

Percy chuckled and smacked his lips, then took hold of the hem of my skirt.

'Here we go, then,' he continued cheerfully. 'Skirt up, and let's see what taste you have in knickers.'

I swallowed the lump in my throat again as my skirt was lifted, quite casually, as if the exposure of a young woman's bottom for punishment were an everyday, unimportant event. He pulled the skirt right up and tucked it into my uniform belt, leaving a little of my back showing.

'White cotton, a little too tight for you, and stockings – how sweet,' Percy remarked. 'Ideal for being spanked in as well.'

That really brought home to me the fact that my panties were showing. My bum felt really big inside them, and I could feel his gaze feasting on them and enjoying the way my bottom filled them out. I was expecting to be fondled a bit, so it didn't surprise me when he began to stroke my bottom through my panties. It made my shame worse, though, but I hung my head and kept quiet, ignoring the feel of his hand on my bum as best I could. He had a good feel, too, stroking my panty seat and the flesh that spilled out at the sides, then squeezing my bum cheeks and all the while humming to himself quietly. He even had the nerve to put his hand between my legs and cup my pussy, which was doubly humiliating for me because I was wet. He gave his dirty little chuckle at the discovery, then abruptly stopped feeling me.

'Very pretty, but I think they had better come down, don't you?' Percy said merrily as his podgy hand took a firm hold of my waistband.

I gave a miserable nod, knowing that it was inevitable that my panties would come down. Mum's always had, and I knew why. Percy didn't think a spanking had been done properly if the victim's bottom wasn't bare. It was supposed to be good for the girl's sense of humility. The question had been asked just to make me more aware of it when my bottom was laid bare, and it worked, because it put me on the edge of tears as he peeled them slowly down over my cheeks and settled them around my thighs. My bum was bare, and it now felt huge, really fat, stuck up in the air for him to gloat over and then spank.

Percy began to touch me again. This time on the bare skin, stroking my cheeks in a really lecherous way, feeling their texture and weight, then pulling them apart. I knew he'd done it to get a look at my bumhole, which was just the sort of filthy thing I'd have expected from him. He'd have enjoyed my protests, so I held back, all the while thinking of the little brown hole I'd seen in the mirror when I washed myself and hoping he didn't decide to finger it. I realised that my pussy was showing, too, pouting and hairy with the pink bits all wet, again just like it had looked in the mirror. He lingered over the inspection but at last it was over and as he let go of my cheeks I braced myself for the spanking.

I'd never had my bum smacked before: I was sure it couldn't be too bad, more degrading than painful, really. The first slap dispelled all such silly ideas, landing hard across my cheeks to make me cry out and kick my legs. Another slap caught me before I could catch my breath to complain and after that all my intentions of remaining cool and dignified just evaporated. The smacks stung crazily, and for all my wriggles and kicks and cries nothing seemed to reduce the pain. Through it all I could hear Percy chuckling and the ringing *smack* noises from the contact of his hand on my poor bottom. I was vaguely aware how ridiculous I would look, with my thighs going up and down to show off my pussy from the back, my pulled-down panties taut between them one moment and then slack the next. As for the idea of anybody actually *enjoying* a spanking, it seemed inconceivable.

That was what I was thinking as Percy beat me, over and over: how much it hurt and how it was anything but sexy. Obviously it was for *him*, because he had my naked bum dancing about across his lap and his cock was hard against my belly. Not for me, though. For me it was just painful and humiliating. Then it changed.

First my bottom began to feel numb, then just hot, and my pussy too. I realised that my juice was running free, between my thighs and down under my pussy where it was pressed against his leg. Knowing that I was getting turned on just made my humiliation worse, but Percy was still spanking merrily away and I was just out of control. When I started to stick my bum up to the smacks he laughed, and then suddenly he had cocked a leg up between mine and my pussy was right on his thigh, pressed hard against the rough cloth. His other leg curled around mine and I was held tight, bum high, with each spank forcing my pussy hard on to his leg.

It was a mean trick and I managed to gasp out my opinion of him, calling him a fat bastard and a pervert, but my clit was right on his trouser leg and I was already rubbing myself. His slaps became less frequent and aimed lower, catching the chubby bit of my bum where it joined my thighs. That made the contact between my clit and his legs even firmer, and now I knew for sure that Percy was bringing me off on purpose. I swore at him again, but I didn't want him to stop, because the most wonderful, warm feeling was building up in my belly and I knew I was going to come.

I began to sigh, then to moan, listening to myself and hardly able to believe what I was doing. My bottom was glowing with heat, fat and ripe and open, with my sex a hot hole at the centre and Percy's spanking hand as needed as any man's cock had ever been. Then I was coming, coming in a hot, golden haze of pleasure and begging for him to beat me, harder, faster . . .

As I came I screamed, completely lost in the ecstasy of spanking. I didn't care for my dignity any more, but was babbling out 'Spank me, spank me, spank me', again and again as the orgasm swept over me. All the while Percy kept smacking, attending to my bare bum, giving me what I needed: a hard, bare-bottomed spanking across his lap.

He stopped the moment my climax subsided, and I found myself lying there, limp and beaten, over his knee, still with my thighs cocked apart and my pussy and bumhole on plain view to the man who had taken me in hand. I knew what came next, too. After her spanking sessions Mum had either brought Percy off by hand or in her mouth, even in her pussy sometimes. I was resigned to it.

I slid off his knee to land hard on my sore, bare bottom and stayed there, leaning in to him. He parted his knees obligingly and pulled down his zip, releasing a stiff little prick. I took it and began to wank him. Percy smiled benignly down at me, picked up his glass and swallowed a mouthful.

My feelings of resentment returned as I pulled at his cock. He had really used me, after all, pushing me into taking a spanking and then tricking me to make me come against his leg. Now I was wanking his cock, every bit the beaten, obedient girl he wanted me to be, with my bum still bare and his prick in my hand. He seemed to be taking ages, too, which was frustrating. Feeling irritable and more used than ever, I tugged open the buttons of my blouse and undid my neck tie, then pulled my bra up over my breasts.

'There, have something to wank over,' I snapped.

Percy didn't answer and I went back to work, tugging his skinny little erection as fast as I could manage. My tits were bouncing up and down with the rhythm and I must have looked a sight, topless with my panties around my knees as I sat splay-legged on the floor. It didn't seem to bother him, because he took another sip of his wine.

Then Percy came. It was totally unexpected, with none of the grunting and groaning most men make but just a deep, satisfied sigh as a great jet of come erupted from his prick, right over my face and tits. I hate spunk and I gasped in disgust as it caught me, hitting my eye and falling in a long sticky streamer over my cheek and lips. There was a bit hanging down from my chin, more had gone on my tits and soiled my bra, and as I hurriedly let go of his cock he just took it and emptied himself all over my front.

I hadn't expected there to be much, because of his age and his having a small cock. I was wrong: if anything, he produced more than Nick had. It was in my hair and in my mouth, on my neck and on both breasts, on my face and in one eye, while my blouse and bra were filthy with it. I could do nothing but sit, filthy with come, and wait for Percy to help me.

'Terribly sorry,' Percy remarked casually. 'Here, do have a handkerchief.'

I took it and began to clean myself up, all the while feeling ever more used and resentful.

'I hope you're pleased with yourself,' I said as I got up.

My face must have been as red as my poor bum, which was stinging terribly. Despite what I'd done I felt immensely resentful towards him for spanking me, and I made no effort to hide this in my expression as I put my hands to my bottom.

'Immensely,' he answered me. 'But no more than you are with yourself, I feel sure.'

I could hardly deny it after the way I had behaved and only managed a sulky look in response, at which he laughed. It seemed pointless to cover myself after what he had seen, and my bottom needed a good rub. So I stood there with my panties around my thighs and my skirt in my belt and my tits showing, feeling sorry for myself.

'I'm glad to find that you share your mother's enthusiasm for a smacked bottom,' he remarked. 'It's such a rare virtue among modern girls.'

'But I don't!' I protested, rubbing at one smarting cheek. 'Or, at least, I didn't know I did.'

'Then why did you ask for it?' he enquired.

'Before you *demanded* it!'

'You suggested it yourself.'

'Only because I knew *you* would!'

'But you even explained how you wanted it!'

'No, I didn't!'

'You most certainly did! Hard and with your arm twisted – you said so yourself! You even agreed to have your knickers taken down!'

'I ... I ... thought you were asking, so I felt worse ...'

'I was asking to help perfect your fantasy, Anna. Come, come, you can't expect me to believe that you didn't want it?'

'No, I just thought you wanted to get off on beating me.'

'You mistake me, my dear. It is true that you have a delightful bottom and I will not deny that the thought of smacking it had occurred to me. Yet I would never have done it had you not asked! To Gabriella's daughter! To an employee! Nor did I know that you were aware of my little agreement with your dear mother. You do me an injustice, Anna, you really do!'

I knew it was true, just from the tone of his voice, and as I realised exactly what I had done I found my mouth dropping open in dismay. I hadn't wanted it, I really hadn't, but I did now – and that was the worst of it.

10

Consequences

I wouldn't have believed it if I hadn't seen it myself, but Percy was having an affair with Anna! Nick had told me he suspected something and we had stayed back at the restaurant, pretending to leave and then sneaking round to watch through the screen between restaurant and kitchen. It wasn't just an ordinary affair, either, because what they were doing was so rude! First she had given him a little show, exposing her panties for him in a number of dirty poses while he sipped brandy and squeezed his crotch. He had then spanked her bottom, across his lap with her panties pulled down and her bum on show, all bare with her pussy peeping out from between her thighs and her bum pushed up to show off the hole. The smacks had been hard, until poor Anna was kicking and wriggling with a cherry-red bottom and her boobs out at the front, all of her exposed flesh wobbling and bouncing around to the rhythm of the slaps.

'How would you like that to be you, Jilly?' Nick whispered into my ear. 'Spanked over fat Percy's lap. I'd love it. I'd make you suck me afterwards.'

I tried to give him a dirty look but it failed.

'Do you reckon he pays her?' Nick asked quietly.

I shook my head. Anna was too proud to take money for sex, I was sure of it. I could only suppose that Percy had caught her out in some way and blackmailed her.

She was such a pretty girl, with her dark Mediterranean looks, and so proper. It was impossible to imagine her voluntarily having sex of any sort with Percy, let alone what they were doing now. He was fifty and fat; she was just out of school and fresh and beautiful – which made watching her get a spanking from him all the more dirty.

Nick and I were in the dark, lying flat on the floor, face down as we peered through the gaps in the screen. It gave us a great view, while we were totally hidden, and Nick had begun to feel me up as we watched, which was more than welcome. Once Anna had been thoroughly spanked she climbed off Percy's lap and started to take off her panties, only to have him stop her and tell her to pull them back up. She did, right into her crease, so that the spanked cheeks stuck out at the sides, all red and goose-pimpled. She stayed like that, posing her smacked bum while Percy unzipped himself and took out his cock. It was skinny and pale, a lot smaller than Nick's. He took his balls out, too, rather fat ones in a pink, wrinkly sac that went well with his cock. She looked back to watch as he got himself stiff at the sight of her smacked bum, occasionally wiggling or smoothing her hands over her cheeks.

I thought he was just going to wank off over her bottom, but Percy had other ideas. Anna was told to get lengthwise over a table and did so, sticking her bum up at one end and holding on tight to the other. She was side-on to us, her breasts squashed out on the table-cloth, her skirt raised and her panties taut across her rear, with the rosy bum-cheeks sticking out right at his face. Percy stood up and gave a little chuckle, then went behind the counter. For one awful moment I thought he was going to come into the kitchen, but he ducked down to the fridge. When he came up he was holding a jug of mayonnaise and a fat little chorizo sausage. He showed it to Anna and gave a dirty little chuckle, then dipped it into the mayonnaise. Anna's mouth opened wide and she said something I didn't catch but which must have been a protest, because he hadn't got that sausage out to eat it!

Percy just chuckled again and walked round behind Anna, with her eyes following him in an expression of outrage. When he was right behind her she closed her eyes tight and took a harder grip on the table. He took down her panties, his little piggy eyes feasting on her bum as he stripped her. They weren't pulled off, but turned down around her thighs so the inside showed. Percy dipped his finger in the mayonnaise and put it between her bum cheeks. It was too high up for her pussy, and I almost gave us away as I realised that he was greasing her bumhole. She took it with her eyes screwed up tight and her mouth set in a firm line of misery, only for her expression to soften and her lower lip to go loose as he wriggled his finger about up her bum. I liked a finger up the bum myself as much as the next girl – but not from Percy!

Anna enjoyed it, though, the little tart, and to think I always thought of her as a bit prim and proper. Not now, though, not with Percy's finger up her bumhole and her bottom all glowing from her spanking. She started to play with her boobs, too, and her nipples were soon sticking out from between her fingers, all hard and swollen and really big. His finger came out with a wet, sucking sound and she farted, which made him chuckle again as he pulled the sausage out of the jug, dripping with mayonnaise.

The chorizo went up Anna's pussy, squashed in from behind so that we could see the mayonnaise dribbling down her leg as it came out. Percy got right behind her, his stiff little cock pointing up between her bare red bum cheeks and I knew he was going to bum-fuck her. We watched it go in, Anna grunting and gasping as her anus took the strain, then giving a squeak of alarm as her ring popped and it went up. He got well in, holding her hips until his gut was wedged on top of her bottom as he buggered her.

It was wonderful to see, with Anna's soft, fleshy buttocks moving to the rhythm of Percy's fat stomach and knowing that his cock was up her anus. Her expression was great, too: open-mouthed disbelief at what she was doing while the tears ran from her eyes and her hands clutched at the tablecloth in the ecstasy of buggery.

I knew what it was like, because Nick had had me up my bottom in my bedsit, not even bothering to ask but fucking me until I was too high to care, putting a finger in and then his cock, lubricated with my tangerine-and-pineapple body rub! Now he was watching with me, as rapt as I was, enthralled at seeing sweet little Anna get her bottom fucked by Percy Ottershaw.

Nick's hand had been on my bottom almost since the start, but I had hardly been aware of it. Now it was getting harder to ignore, with my uniform skirt rucked up over my panties and his fingers pushing the material down into my bum crease. I was too excited to stop him as his finger pushed deeper and he found my bumhole. It went in, opening me. I should have been cross at having a piece of my panties pushed up my bum, but with what Percy was doing to Anna it didn't seem wrong at all. I knew Nick liked girls' bumholes, and I knew what he liked to do to them. With his finger in mine and Percy's cock up Anna's I knew it wouldn't be long before my own little arsehole was full of cock.

What I didn't expect was to be buggered on the kitchen floor, but that was what Nick did to me. Percy was taking his time, as what dirty old git wouldn't with his prick sheathed in a young girl's back passage? My skirt was already up and my hole open where Nick's finger had pushed in my panties. He mounted me and the next thing I knew his hard cock was prodding at my bum between my thighs. My pussy was soaking and I knew it would go in easily if he just pulled my panties aside, while with his weight pressing down on me I could do nothing to resist physically.

'No, don't fuck me, not here!' I whispered, scared of getting caught spying but even more desperate that if we were I would not be being fucked at the time.

'I won't, I promise,' Nick said as he twitched my panties out of my bumhole and to one side.

'No!' I gasped as his cock slid into the sweaty, slick crease between my cheeks.

It was too late. My anus had been opened and his cock was already wedged a little way in. I moaned in resignation and let him up me, his erection easing up my back passage bit by bit until its full length was wedged up my bum.

I watched Percy and Anna while Nick buggered me, wishing I could get at my pussy for a sneaky frig at the view. Just knowing that Anna and I had cocks up our arseholes at the same time would have been enough to give me an orgasm, never mind the feel of Nick's erection in my anus and the weight of his body on mine. He was still holding my panties aside, and his other arm was under me, feeling my boobs. I was ready to have him spunk up my bum, and then he started to talk.

'I'd like to see you where Anna is now,' he whispered, 'bent over the table with fat old Percy's willy up your arse, just like mine is. I'd like to watch him spank you, too, spank you and fuck your arse, just like Anna's. In fact, I'd like to watch you spanked side by side, Susan too, the three of you bent over together with your skirts high and your knickers down, your arses all red and your cunts on show. Then he'd fuck your arseholes, one by one, finger them and fuck them, and make you suck his cock in between. That's right, Jilly, you'd suck his cock for him, suck his cock after it had been up your arse . . .'

I grunted as Nick's cock jammed deep up my bum. He had come, and as my box filled with spunk I was rubbing my pussy on the floor, desperately trying to get to my own orgasm. It came, not well but it came, and as Nick relaxed on to me with a sigh I was biting the floor and trying not to scream.

After watching Percy spank and bum-fuck Anna it was impossible to see him in the same light. To me he had always been something of a father figure: kindly, paternal and a good employer, if rather pompous and pedantic. Now I couldn't look at him without seeing his red, puffing face as he had come to orgasm up Anna's bum.

Nick made it worse. Every time he saw me he would tease me, and he didn't bother to keep it a secret from Anna, either. He not only told her we'd watched but that he had bum-fucked me while we did it! That left both of us red-faced and speechless, but he just laughed and suggested a threesome in the toilet. I slapped him for that, but if he'd pushed it I know I'd have gone along with his proposition.

Him being so open did mean we got to find out about Percy and Anna. Her mum had been Percy's girlfriend for a while back in the 1950s, long before Anna was born. Gabriella, Anna's mum, had kept a diary and in it she had recorded getting spankings from Percy, which she had thoroughly enjoyed. They'd done harder things, too, some of them very dirty, but it was the spankings that Percy had really got off on. Anna had assumed that Percy would try and find an excuse to get her across his knee, pretending it was a genuine punishment, and in the end she'd more or less managed to talk herself right into it. I suspected she had wanted it all along underneath – after all, like mother, like daughter. I didn't push it, but berated Nick for licking and fucking Anna in the cellar, which was ostensibly what Percy had spanked her for.

Nick just shrugged and I held my tongue. After all, I was supposed to be engaged to Gordon, so I wasn't exactly one to talk. Instead we teased Nick, telling him that *he* was the one who deserved a spanking, to which he simply replied that we were welcome if we could do it. I knew we couldn't and would just end up in trouble ourselves. Besides, it might have lifted a few eyebrows since we were in the middle of the restaurant at the time.

Anna was a bit defensive about letting Percy spank her on a regular basis, but it seemed that once she'd had it done she felt she needed more. It made her really hot, and the deal had been a sucked cock in return for her spanking: she would frig herself while he watched and simultaneously got sucked off. I was astonished, because it seemed so dirty for her, but I'd seen it. The anal sex had started when she got carried away and said he could have her. He'd declined but had fucked her up the bum instead. Why he should refuse to fuck her pussy I had no idea.

The conversation took place in snatches while Anna and I served and Nick stacked wine. By closing time I was incredibly horny and hoping Nick would be able to stick around. He did, and so did Anna, and I knew something was going to happen. We took a couple of bottles and made for my bedsit, which was closest. All the way I was getting higher and higher, while Nick had his arms around both of us and must have thought all his Christmases had arrived at once.

I knew I was going to get spanked for the first time in my life. After seeing Anna get it the idea really turned me on, and we hadn't been inside for ten minutes before Anna and I were kneeling over the bed with our bottoms stuck out. We were giggling and looking back at Nick, who was doing his best imitation of Percy, with his cheeks blown out and a pillow under his jumper. It was too funny to be taken seriously, which I suppose was why I could handle kneeling next to another girl and waiting for my bum to be shown off.

He lifted our uniform skirts and made a big deal of inspecting our panties, licking his lips and saying how

181

sexy our bottoms looked. Mine were white and lacy, while Anna had on a tight, plain pair just like the ones she'd worn to her spanking before. Nick lifted our skirts up on our backs and that's when it began to get serious. My bum was showing, stuck out in just my panties, always a sexy position, but not one I had ever adopted to take a spanking, nor with another girl looking.

'Down they come, then. Arses out,' Nick announced as he put his hands into the back of our waistbands.

There was a jerk and suddenly my panties were down – Anna's, too – with our bare bums sticking out and Nick gloating over the sight of two girls ready to play at once. I was shivering, a lump in my throat, and then he had kneeled down, patted our bottoms and begun to spank us.

It wasn't hard, but it stung, at least at first. Soon my bottom was warm and glowing, a lovely sexy feeling that made me wish someone had taken the trouble to spank me long, long before. Anna was obviously having fun, too, moaning and sticking her bum up for more, then unbuttoning her blouse to pull out her boobs and feel them, just as she had while Percy had done her. The sight of her two big breasts so close to me really had me going, and as Nick continued to slap our bums and tell us off I began to get mine out too. Soon they were bare, soft and sensitive in my hands as I massaged them, squeezing in time to the slaps on my bum and watching Anna.

When Nick finally stopped my bottom was a hot, glowing ball and my juice was running down the insides of my thighs. We must have made a fine sight with our pussies open and I wasn't surprised Nick had decided it was time we were fucked. I was willing, and Anna too, from the way she kept pushing her bum up and tightening her cheeks. He got his cock out and quickly made it hard, staring at us as he stroked himself. When it was ready he took off his trousers and rolled on a condom, then stood over us with his hands on his hips and his erection sticking up in readiness for our holes. It must have been hard to choose, with two willing girls with their red bottoms stuck up and their pussies gaping for his cock.

'I'm going to fuck you both,' he declared. 'In your cunts, then up your arses. Anna first, because I've only had her the once.'

He did it, too: all four holes while he held his erection. Anna got fucked first, while I watched and played with my pussy. He was in her from behind, with her reddened cheeks bouncing and wobbling, just like they had with Percy. As I watched I kept thinking of Nick's cock going up my bum and before long I had my thumb in my arsehole while I fingered my pussy and rubbed at my clit. Anna was watching me, too, her face set in an expression of bliss.

When Nick tired of Anna's pussy he greased her bumhole with my hand cream and put it up there. Anna grunted a lot as her box filled and was clutching and biting at the bed cover as he bum-fucked her. I was nearly coming, just from the expression on her face and the noises she was making. When Nick finally pulled out I was begging for it and sticking my rear up on to my finger and thumb.

He changed his condom, which was really frustrating, then got behind me and took me by the hips. I pulled my hand out and his cock touched my pussy, filling me so that I cried out and shut my eyes. Something soft touched me. I knew it was Anna and I didn't care. I'd never played with a girl before but my bottom was hot from spanking and my pussy full of cock. She wriggled up to me, pressing her breasts into my face as she masturbated with her hand down between her legs. Nick was fucking me harder and harder and I was sure he was going to come. But just then he pulled back.

I knew what that meant and was lifting my bottom as Anna slipped a nipple into my mouth. Nick's cockhead touched my bumhole as I started to suck her and then it was going up, forcing me open, filling my box until his balls nudged my empty pussy. I put a hand back to frig, revelling in the sheer bliss of being spanked, bum-fucked and made to suck my friend's boobs. My bumhole clamped on Nick's cock and I was coming, nuzzling my mouthful of boob and kicking my feet as the most lovely orgasm swept through me, leaving me limp and panting just as Nick came up my bum.

It had been great playing with Nick, and although I felt a little guilty I was happier than before, if only for having such a lovely memory to dwell on. Anna and I didn't make a big deal of having played together and we got on as before, only closer. What I did do was talk about it with her, especially about spanking. Somehow getting a kick out of that was worse than allowing men up our bums, perhaps because spanking is supposed to be a punishment and suggests a low status for the one who gets spanked. We told Susan as well, as she had guessed something had happened, and that was how she explained it.

Sexual spanking, Susan told us, was all about exerting authority over a girl, or a man for that matter, by punishing them in a sexual way. I could see what she meant, because having Nick pull our panties down had made me feel weak and compliant as well as eager. Submitting to a spanking was surrender, she said, with the implication that women shouldn't really do it.

I could understand what Susan meant, but I hated that feeling, of being supposed to be 'a woman' and not me, an individual female. It was the pressure that made me stay slim when I'd have liked to eat as Percy did – what he liked, when he liked. It was the pressure that made me buy fashionable clothes when I'd have liked to be slobbing around in an old pair of jeans. It was the pressure that kept my panties up when I ought to have been letting them down. Spanking was the same, and now I understood the turn-on. It wasn't just because it was naughty to do it, but because it was a release to do it, a relief from stifling social restrictions. Then there was the physical pleasure, the way it brought blood to the bottom and the genitals, which was undeniable.

Susan and I argued this out, and while she was generally as liberated as anyone she was really quite shocked by what I was saying. At first, anyway, because after a while she suddenly changed and went quiet, then swallowed her drink in one go. She left and I wondered if I'd upset her, but that evening at work she was as cheerful as ever and it was she who started to tease Percy.

It was the middle of the week and we weren't busy, with just one party of businessmen and a handful of regulars. As the name of the restaurant, *Au Boeuf Farci*, implied, the style was for plenty of really grand food, very much against the fashion for *nouvelle cuisine*. We didn't actually do stuffed ox, or at least not then, but Percy had served a truly extravagant dish to the businessmen. This was a turkey stuffed with a chicken, which in turn was stuffed with a pheasant which, finally, was stuffed with a quail. He had prepared it himself, and had it hung with sausages and served with wild mushrooms and roast vegetables. I had to help Anna carry it out, and it did look ridiculous, with the huge, fat breast sticking up and the legs forced out at an angle by all the stuff that had been put in it.

When Susan joked that it looked a bit like Percy I could hardly believe my ears. She was normally so polite to him – none of us ever cheeked him – and for a moment I really thought he was going to sack her on the spot. As it was he contented himself with an arch look and went back to sharpening the carving knife. I wondered if she was trying to put him down because he'd seduced Anna, but the remark hadn't really been nasty, just cheeky, the sort of remark a girl might make in the hope of getting her bottom spanked.

I was sure that Susan was putting an extra wiggle into her walk as well, especially when Percy was watching, and as the evening went on it became plain that she was deliberately taunting him. He didn't react, which made her worse, dipping her back as she served so that her bottom stuck out and generally flaunting herself and flirting. The customers loved it, and Percy was beaming happily and the businessmen's bill piled up to a truly impressive total. When Anna started to join in I couldn't help but start to play a little myself, if only so as not to be thought boring.

'What are you doing?' I demanded when I finally managed to corner Susan alone in the cellar.

'I'm going to get a spanking,' she said. 'I'm going to tease Percy and flirt with the customers, then after work he'll put me across his lap, just like he did to Anna. My knickers'll come down and he'll smack my bottom.'

'You're joking! I thought you said . . . what was it . . . inappropriate behaviour.'

'I've changed my mind. Now I want my bum smacked, and he's just the man to do it.'

'Percy? Why not Nick, if you really want to try spanking? He's a lot more attractive!'

'Not to give a punishment, he isn't. Percy's perfect. Besides, he's the boss and we ought to be given discipline by him now and then.'

'Susan!'

The door opened and Percy himself appeared, so we both shut up quickly. We had joked about holding Susan down and letting Nick spank her, but she'd been less than keen. Now she wanted it done by Percy, and she wanted us to know as well! I was happy to watch her get it, and when I told Anna she agreed that there could be no better end to the evening than seeing Susan get put across Percy's lap.

186

For the rest of the evening we really played it up, doing our very best to get Susan in trouble but never going so far as to actually annoy Percy. He took it well and didn't seem to realise anything was unusual, or at least he gave no sign of noticing it. The businessmen left, then the regulars and finally Mary the cook, leaving the three of us girls to finish clearing up.

We had been working hard and there was the pause that always came when the last dish was washed and the last piece of cutlery returned to its place. Percy was sitting at his favourite table, sipping a glass of Sauternes, which he always liked last thing in the evening. He seemed happy, and doubtless was hoping that Anna would stay behind for a smacked bum – and, perhaps, a cock up it. Not that he was overeager, because rather than chivvy us out he suggested a drink and opened another expensive bottle of Sauternes for us.

I had expected Susan to put on a little show, maybe apologising for her behaviour and suggesting a spanking as suitable punishment. When nothing happened I began to wonder if she had got cold feet. I had really built myself up to the thought of watching her get a spanking and so I followed when she went to the loo, along with Anna.

'Well, are you going to ask him?' I goaded Susan as soon as we were out of Percy's hearing.

'You'll have to, you know,' Anna put in. 'He won't ask unless he thinks you're up for it.'

'Well, I ...' Susan began, looking flustered and fiddling with her fingers.

She stopped and began to make a big deal of adjusting her dress while we waited for her answer. I could see she was having second thoughts, but I was half drunk and horny and not about to pass up the chance of seeing her get it. It was Anna who broke the silence.

'You'd better,' she announced. 'Or I'll do it for you, *and* say you like to be buggered afterwards.'

'No!' Susan squeaked.

'Go and ask for your spanking, then.'

It was said pretty firmly, and we all knew Anna would carry out her threat, although it might not mean that Susan ended up getting it.

'We'll do it ourselves, in front of him, panties down,' I threatened.

Susan glanced from one of us to the other and nodded.

Back in the restaurant Percy was quietly sipping his wine, and he looked up with a questioning glance when the three of us trooped in and formed a line in front of him. In fact, I think he expected us to ask for a rise, as there was something distinctly worried about his expression. Susan was in the middle and I nudged her. Her face went gradually red and she bit her lip, then spoke.

'Might ... I mean, would it,' she stammered. 'Oh God, I think you ought to spank me, Mr Ottershaw, right now.'

I was feeling pretty nervous myself, and horny, with the prospect of Susan's panties coming down, but her face was crimson and she was shuffling from foot to foot in an agony of embarrassment. Percy had paused with the glass halfway to his mouth. His gaze flicked back and forth between us and I could see he was trying to decide if we were joking. I knew the whole thing was going to fall to pieces if someone didn't make a move, and I was about to speak when he suddenly broke into a smile and put his glass down.

'A well-deserved spanking,' he declared, 'after your behaviour tonight, very well deserved. Anna, I take it you suggested this?'

'No,' Anna answered quickly, seeing exactly where he was going.

Percy's eyebrows rose a fraction. I tried to hold back a smile, realising that I might get to see not just one but *two* bums get reddened.

'Well, sort of,' Anna admitted sheepishly, then suddenly changed her tone. 'No, it wasn't! Nick and Jilly spied on us and told me, then Nick did us both, together.'

'Indeed?' Percy queried. 'Jilly?'

Suddenly it was my turn to blush. I hadn't bargained for this at all, but it was quite obvious I was to be offered a chance to join in and if I didn't take it I could see the girls doing me anyway.

'Oh God, OK, spank me too,' I breathed, unable to face being slowly manoeuvred into it.

Percy gave his dirty little chuckle and Anna giggled.

'So the three of you are willing to be spanked?' he asked.

We nodded, Susan and I blushing, Anna smiling mischievously.

'Spanked one at a time, in private, or spanked together?' he asked.

'Together,' Anna answered before either of us could speak.

I nodded, feeling trapped and even a bit frightened but too horny to back out. Susan gave each of us a nervous glance, then nodded too. I am sure she had wanted it alone, in the back room, where she could get through the shame of it without us watching. But, like me, she didn't feel she could back out now.

'Bare bottoms, I hope?' Percy went on.

Anna nodded immediately. But it was all very well for her: she had been over his lap before. For Susan and I it was different: we were being asked to surrender our modesty, to show out to him, bare bums and doubtless pussies too. Skirts-up was one thing: that was reasonable, that if we were to be spanked it should at least be across the seats of our panties, but bare, that was

189

different. It would take it beyond sexy punishment to actual sex, with my hole vulnerable to his cock. I'd wanted to see Susan's panties come down, though. In fact, I'd been sure they would, but my own – that was different.

'OK, you can pull my knickers down,' Susan blurted out.

It had come out in a rush, showing how much emotion was packed into what she had said. Before, when I had tried to persuade Susan that it was all right to let a man spank her, I had only been half serious, arguing more for the sake of mischief than from any real conviction. It had backfired on me with a vengeance, because the idea of having her spanking virginity taken had obviously really got to her.

'Jilly?' Percy asked gently.

I nodded. It was hopeless, because I was sure if I tried to hold back the girls would have me down in a trice and it probably wouldn't just be my knickers that came down. I'd have it all shown off and I'd be the one getting spanked, on my own while the others enjoyed the view. The sole consolation if I went along with Percy's proposition was that I wouldn't be alone; if my bare bum was going to get an airing, then I wanted Susan's and Anna's beside me.

'Good,' Percy said. 'I am glad. A spanking just isn't a spanking without the girl's bottom bare.'

He was right. The moment Nick had pulled my panties down had been really strong, but something told me that with Percy it would be stronger still.

'Well, then,' he remarked. 'If this is to be done it should be done properly. Breasts out first, I think. It always adds a little something if a spanked girl has her breasts showing, don't you think?'

Yes, humiliation, I thought as I nodded dumbly and began to undo the buttons of my blouse. As each one popped open I felt a little more vulnerable, a little less in control. I was thinking of how I'd talked Susan into accepting the idea of a spanked bottom and was wishing I hadn't, or at least that I'd kept it to Nick.

Percy watched us undo our blouses, his little eyes feasting on each detail as our cleavages came on show, then our bras. Mine was lacy, like my panties, and as I pulled my blouse wide I thought of how I'd soon be showing those, too. To either side of me the others had also obeyed. Anna's breasts were already out, big and round, with their olive skin and dark nipples. Susan's, too, resting on her bra where she had pulled the cups down, each plump and white with the deep pink nipple hardening in her excitement. I swallowed hard and added my own contribution to the peep-show, popping the button at the front of my bra and letting them free, bare and pink, with my perky nipples betraying my feelings.

'How sweet,' Percy remarked. 'Yes, breasts out for a spanking – after all, the removal of her modesty is important when a girl is to be punished. Now, how to make the best display of you? Yes, if you could each kneel on a bar stool and place your hands flat on the top, along the main bar, so that you will be able to see yourselves in the mirror.'

He began to move a table, ensuring that when we were in position all we would have to do was look back over our shoulders for an unobstructed view of our bare bums. My hands were shaking as I took a bar stool and pushed it into position, then climbed on and put my hands on the bar. Susan and Anna got up beside me, each kneeling on her stool with her bottom stuck out and her boobs swinging in her open blouse. The tops of the stools were so small that we had to keep our knees together, but I still knew I'd be showing the lot once my panties were down.

Percy came up behind us and began to interfere with our clothing, chuckling occasionally at our blushes or treating himself to a quick feel. It was our blouses first, pulled wide and tucked up into our collars so that our boobs swung free under our chests. Our skirts came next, taken by the hem and turned up on to our backs, then tucked into the waistband. He did Anna first, showing off her stockings and suspender straps and the tight white panties she seemed to like, absolutely bulging with chubby teenage bottom. Susan was done next, exposing black satin panties with a broad lace edge, very expensive and pretty too, tight over her well-fleshed bottom with the crease showing as a shallow valley in the shiny material. I had tights on and an old pair of pale blue panties, as I hadn't expected to be showing them off. Now I felt distinctly ashamed of myself as Percy tweaked up my skirt, tugged my tights down with a cluck of disapproval and the others saw what I was wearing.

'Hmm,' Percy remarked from behind us as he admired our panty-clad bums. 'A few remarks on underwear for girls, if you don't mind. In my view the perfect knickers for a girl to wear to a spanking are large, white cotton, plain or with a slight frill, and one or two sizes too small, the better to show off the target before it is stripped. Anna's are perfect, and the suspenders make a nice touch, so rare these days. Susan's are pretentious and vain, black satin with lace – really, who *do* you think you are? Jilly's are better, now those dreadful tights are out of the way. I like the ragamuffin look on a girl. So, Susan will get an extra dozen slaps on each cheek for being pretentious. Jilly will get the same for wearing tights and another three on each cheek for her knickers.'

I had been feeling more and more humiliated as the panty inspection went on and made a little gasp of protest when he said I was to get more smacks than the others. It wasn't fair and I had to swallow hard to stop myself beginning to snivel. But if having our panties inspected was bad, having them pulled down was almost unbearable. I watched it all. Percy came up behind Anna and peeled hers down, really slowly, exposing her full bum. I watched her face as he did it, and she showed that same odd mixture of misery and bliss I had seen before. Only now I understood, because the same was about to happen to me.

With Anna's panties inverted down around her thighs Percy came up behind Susan. Her eyes were shut and she was clenching her hands, obviously really feeling it as he took hold of her expensive panties and peeled them down over her bum. She made a little choking sound as it all came on show, and I caught the scent of her pussy.

It was my turn, but where the others had kept their eyes to the front while they were exposed I just had to look. He saw and stepped a little to one side, as polite as ever, in order to allow me an unobstructed view of my own humiliation. I felt his fingers in my waistband, pressing into my flesh, then they were coming down, the cotton tickling as they were eased lower and lower, exposing my crease, my bumhole and the lips of my pussy, all of it showing, blatantly rude in the mirror. Percy stepped away, beaming smugly at our nude rear views.

'Very pretty,' he declared. 'I've had two side by side before, when I was married, but never three. Yes, delectable: I shall enjoy spanking you immensely. May I assume this is to be a regular occurrence? Not as discipline, you understand, but just for the fun of spanking such pretty bottoms.'

None of us spoke, each too wrapped up in her private feelings to answer, and perhaps unwilling to be the one to admit that our bottoms would be available to him in future.

'Now pull your backs in,' Percy ordered. 'Yes, good girl, Anna. Right, that's it. It makes your bottom-holes show, you see, which I feel is even more important for a spanked girl than having her breasts bare. Your pussies look prettier, too, but it's your bottom-holes that really must not remain hidden. There is something about showing a girl's anus that is essential to her proper punishment.'

We had dipped our backs in and our bottoms had spread, just as he said. I could see it in the mirror: three female bottoms, bare, with our pussies showing, our bumholes too, the way he wanted. Being slimmer than the others my cheeks were really open and I could see every little wrinkle and fold of my sex, along with the star-shaped lines leading down into the pucker of my anus. Not that Susan was exactly demure, with her pale cheeks wide and bumhole on show in a little oval of dark skin. She had shaved her pussy, too, which made the display of her sex lips that much more blatant. Anna was nearly as bad, with her darker skin and hair a pretty contrast to Susan and me. Her pussy lips were poking out and she looked very ready, while her bumhole was just a dark area in a nest of hair. Percy tapped the small of her back and she dipped further, her full cheeks opening to make her anus pout.

'Good,' he declared, 'three neat little bottom-holes, and clean, too – which I prefer, although some gentlemen have different tastes. Now let me guess . . . Susan, I do believe you are a virgin.'

'No,' Susan answered softly.

'No, no,' Percy went on. 'I mean in your anus.'

'Yes,' Susan answered, her voice no more than a squeak as the blushes once more rose to her face.

If her face was red, mine must have been crimson, because if he could tell she was a virgin in her bumhole then it had to be obvious that I wasn't! Three times Nick had put his cock up my bottom, and already it showed. I hung my head. I knew that the intimate inspection of our bumholes was just designed to humiliate us, but that didn't stop it working. All three of us were shaking, and Susan had tears starting in her eyes, but none of us made to get up. I was dying to be spanked, but he hadn't finished.

'Shaved, too,' he remarked, 'even between your cheeks. I am glad you make an effort with yourself. Now, Anna is like her mother, naturally hairy and best that way. Jilly here is more classic, furry on the pussy and slick around the anus.'

I winced at his remark, but less than Anna had at the casual description of her mother's sex. Then Percy began to take his jacket off and I knew the painful bit was coming at last. Not that he hurried, taking it off slowly and hanging it carefully on the back of a chair, then rolling one sleeve up and removing his watch. Anna knew she was going to be first and was looking at him, as was Susan, round-eyed with her jaw trembling. Percy took a sip of Sauternes, walked to the far side of Anna's stool so that we could see properly, took her firmly around the waist, patted her bottom and then laid in.

Percy spanked hard, much harder than Nick had, and Anna was kicking her feet and squealing almost immediately. He was skilled, though, I could see it, not just smacking away merrily but periodically changing the way he held his hand to slap her flesh and making sure each cheek got a good even covering. I knew I was going to get thirty more than she did and tried to count, but soon lost track. When it did end her whole bottom was red, her nipples were rock hard and her pussy was simply dripping. She was moaning, too, really eager and uninhibited.

Susan got it next, taken around the waist just like Anna and given the same treatment, spanked and spanked across her naked bottom until she was writhing and kicking in Percy's grip, out of control and indifferent to the display she was making of herself. She cried,

195

too, first snivelling and then really bawling as her bum cheeks bounced and quivered and her boobs wobbled in time with the slaps. I thought she would try and get up, but she didn't, taking the punishment she had wished on herself until it left her sobbing and gasping with her head hung low and her hair draped over the bar, wet with her tears. Her pussy was wet too, though, I could see it in the mirror, as wet as Anna's, while Susan's bumhole was pulsing slowly as if she was trying to keep something in it.

It was my turn. I braced myself as Percy came to my side and his arm encircled my waist, soft with fat but strong all the same. The pressure pushed my back down and I caught a whiff of my own pussy as my cheeks spread further. Then his hand came down on my bum and it was happening – I was getting my bare-bottom spanking from a dirty old man. It hurt, far more than when Nick had done it, and during the first flurry of firm slaps I was wondering what the hell I was doing. I let myself go, though, squealing and mouthing protests in my pain, tears welling in my eyes, no more dignified than either of my friends. After the punishment from Nick I knew the warmth would come, and sure enough, soon my bum began to feel numb, then like a big, warm ball with the anus a tight point at the centre, and my pussy felt glowing and wet. In fact, I was worse than the others, because by the end I had began to really moan in arousal and had one hand on my boobs, and when Percy stopped I felt only regret.

After a moment to recover myself I looked back again, finding the same rude view of three naked, girly bottoms with pussies and bumholes on show, only now our skin was flushed red and covered in goose pimples, well spanked, punished, given physical discipline, as girls should be . . .

I don't know where the thought had come from, but that was what went through my head as I kneeled there with my smarting bottom stuck up in the air. It was right for Anna and Susan and me to be spanked, right that we had had our panties pulled down for it, right that we were made to snivel and kick and show ourselves off in our lewd poses.

None of us tried to move, all three waiting for what we knew was inevitable: the obligation for one or all of us to relieve Percy's cock and so say thank you for our beating. The only question was, who was going to get it, and where? He was already undoing his fly, and I knew that it was my last chance to protest if I didn't want it to go further. I said nothing, but watched as he took his prick out and stroked it to full erection, all the while admiring our well-spanked bums and ready pussies.

'Who's game, then?' he asked, glancing between us. 'Anna?'

'Have Susan or Jilly,' she answered. 'I'll pose for you.'

'A delightful prospect,' he answered. 'So, who is it to be? I rather fancy a bottom-hole, I think, given what a pretty display you three are making of them. Besides, fucking pussy is more intimate, in a way, and I wouldn't want to bruise your boyfriends' feelings.'

'You ... you can have me,' Susan said, choking the words out. 'I'm not with anyone just now.'

'Thank you, my dear,' Percy answered. 'But you are virgin, and when a girl loses her anal virginity it should be an important occasion, the full focus of the erotic pleasure. No, tonight,' he declared, 'I shall take my pleasure in Jilly's sweet little anus, if she is willing?'

I nodded, feeling foolish and dirty even as the pang of excitement at being chosen went through me.

'Splendid,' Percy answered. 'Then, if Anna and Susan would be so kind as to hold their poses, perhaps you would come down?'

It was going to happen, just as Nick had said. Percy was going to bum-fuck me. He was going to stick his cock in my box and his fat belly would slap on my rosy bare cheeks as he did it. He had spanked us and now he was going to bugger me, and I wasn't going to stop it.

I climbed down from my stool. Percy was sitting back, his cock protruding from his fly, positioned so that I could sit on it and plunge it in my bottom, effectively controlling the bum-fucking, effectively bum-fucking myself.

'I'll get the mayonnaise, shall I?' I offered, seeing that he had no intention of moving himself.

'As you please,' he answered. 'Although there is butter, or the fat from the duck. Yes, use duck fat: I adore the smell of roast duck.'

I ran to get it, my hot bottom jiggling about under my skirt as I went, my lowered panties and tights catching at my thighs. In the kitchen I found the jug of duck fat and dipped my finger into it, pulling out a thick blob. It glistened in the light as it began to ooze down my finger, a truly disgusting thing to be greasing my bumhole with – and totally appropriate to what was about to happen to me. I wanted it in, and bent, flicking my skirt up with my free hand. My finger went down between my cheeks, finding the little hole that had been so blatantly displayed and popping through the tight entrance. It went in easily, the duck fat greasing my passage and letting me ease my finger deep into my box. I felt around for a bit, enjoying the hot feel of the flesh in my box, then pulled out and gave my hands a quick wash.

In the restaurant I tried to act playful and nonchalant, giving the others a twirl and then lifting my skirt and spreading my cheeks to show my greased bumhole. Percy had been wanking over their bums and looked fit to burst, so I found myself hurrying so that he could get it up my bum before he came. I went to him, looked back at the stiff spike of his cock and then sat down, wiggling my bottom on to his erection. His hand was on it and he guided himself to my bumhole, and then I was taking him, with the smell of pussy and duck fat thick in the air. My ring stretched to let his cockhead in, then the shaft, which slid up my bottom until my spanked cheeks came to rest on his lap.

I was in ecstasy as Percy took my bum in his hands and began to bounce me on his shaft. In front of me Anna and Susan were still in their spanking poses, red bums stuck out, pussies and bumholes on show. Mine had been, too, and now it was full of hard little cock, filling my box and making me gasp as Percy fucked my ring. I wanted to come, to come while I watched the girls and while I could feel him in my bum. Anna had reached back and started to masturbate, with one hand working her pussy and the other between her cheeks so that she could finger her anus. Her front was down on the bar, with her big boobs squashed out to either side, and she was watching us, frigging to the sight of me on Percy's cock. Susan watched, gaping at Anna's filthy display and then slowly, shyly sliding a hand back between her own thighs and finding her pussy.

The bum-fucking got harder then, with both girls masturbating in front of us, and my breath was coming in ragged pants as Percy buggered me, holding my hips and ramming his cock in and out of my smarting hole. Anna came first and I saw her holes tighten on her fingers and her bottom cheeks clench as it hit her. Percy was next, ejaculating his load up my bum even as my ring began to contract on his shaft. Susan came when I did, whimpering to herself as she rubbed her clitty with long strokes of a finger. Her rear was so beautiful, with the wet, pink, shaved pussy and the little dark bumhole between her beaten cheeks, and I just had to kiss it.

I wanted to do everything – come with Percy's cock in my bumhole, lick Susan's pussy, feel and kiss and lick both girls all over – but I was coming, and even as Percy's erection slid free of my ring I knew it was too late. I came, sinking to my knees on the floor in a welter of pussy juice and spunk, with the contents of my box dribbling out over the floor and into my hand. I kissed Susan's bum, just as she was finishing her climax, right on her ring. She gave the sweetest little cry and my knees gave way and I collapsed to the floor, gasping and panting as I rubbed and rubbed at myself. I'd been bum-fucked, there was spunk in my box again, Percy's spunk, and as my climax hit a peak that was what I was thinking of: the thick white fluid oozing out of my open bumhole between two cherry-red bum cheeks -- spanked bum cheeks.

11

Candles and Carew

We stopped at the church and I got out of the car, feeling small and vulnerable and fragile. Suddenly I was a teenager again, being told off for wearing my skirts too short, being refused permission to have my ears pierced and, above all, being nagged by the vicar for refusing to go to church to be confirmed. That had been my best effort at rebellion and it had failed. After tears and cross words I had ended up trailing after my family with my head down, sulking in a demure white cotton dress with loads of really embarrassing frills; fourteen and fed up, with my family, with life and with the religion that was forced down my throat day after day.

Carew had been his name, the Reverend Benjamin Underwood Naughton Carew, a man capable of gathering the young of the parish around him to sing hymns to his guitar and actually imagining we liked it. We had called him Bunker, partly from his initials and partly from a rumour that he liked to go out to the old coastal defences and masturbate over girls on the beach. It had been false, or at least I was pretty sure it had been, but it was a nice idea.

'I'll, er ... take a walk down to the sea, shall I, Susan?' Percy's voice came from behind me.

'Sure,' I answered. 'I won't be long. I've just got a ghost or two to lay.'

He nodded his understanding and ambled off down the path that led to the cliff. Like me, Percy had always resented the strictness of his upbringing, although he had cleverly turned it to his advantage, learning to take pleasure in the very things that had been the source of his repression. That was why he liked caning me across my bare bottom, and in turn why I had come to like the feel of being caned. Well, caned *and* spanked *and* buggered *and* made to wet my knickers outdoors – but at the end of the day, Percy was a dirty bastard and that was why I loved him. He was going to the beach to watch the girls, he had told me, happily discussing the chances of someone being topless or even nude in the heat of the July afternoon. That was the difference with Percy. Seventeen years I'd lived in Walwich and I'd never known if Bunker was really a Peeping Tom. I'd known Percy for less than two years and I knew exactly what he was like.

All I wanted to do was go into the church and remember what it had been like, and hopefully my memories of the past would stop troubling me. That was the idea, anyway, because it didn't work. In fact, in the cool silence of the church I felt worse. I had to do something, something bad. I'm no vandal, although it would have been easy. I liked the idea of doing something naughty, like masturbating on the altar, but I didn't dare in case I got caught. Then, as I reached the end of the aisle, I turned to look out of a window towards where we had parked the car.

I could see the path in distorted image through the stained glass, as well as the gate, some gravestones and part of a buttress. It was easy. All I had to do was sit on the top of the pew, tuck my skirt up at the front, pop my hand down the front of my knickers and I'd be there, coming with my pussy spread to the rows of pews. The chance was too good to miss. I could be rude, really rude, in Bunker's church, in the very place I had kneeled and mumbled meaningless responses to his patronising drawl, all the while wishing I had the guts to get up and run. Where once I had kneeled humbly in my silly dress with all the ridiculous lace and bows when what I had wanted to be wearing was a microskirt and a torn top advertising the Clash, I would show my open, wet, gaping pussy.

It would be revenge, belated but glorious, as I could well imagine Bunker's fury at learning a girl had masturbated in his precious church. I would even leave a token to make sure he discovered – perhaps my stained knickers, hidden where he would find them at some awkward moment. It came to me in a flash, and I was already peeling them off under my skirt as the delight and outrage of the act sank in. I would put them in the big Bible on the lectern, flat so that the heavy pages would weigh them down but where they would be sure to be found. With luck Bunker wouldn't realise immediately and would lift them up in the middle of a service: a pair of soiled white knickers.

My heart was in my mouth as I wriggled them to the floor and pulled them off. A glance through the window showed that the coast was clear and I ran up to the lectern, opening the Bible at the beginning and sandwiching them carefully down. Next time Bunker read out a passage from Genesis he would get a surprise!

I was feeling wonderfully naughty as I climbed down. For a start I was knickerless under my skirt, which has always turned me on. Percy prefers me in knickers, preferably white cotton ones a couple of sizes too small, but I like to be bare and know that a puff of wind might show my bare pussy or bum at any moment.

The idea of a quick frig with my skirt up at the front was no longer enough. I wanted more, something really dirty, something the mere thought of which would have had Bunker red with fury. I glanced towards the altar and I had my answer. A tall candelabrum stood at either side, and in each was a thick cream-coloured candle, ideal for a naughty girl's pussy. A moment later I had them in my hands and was seating myself on the pew top, my view of the gate clear as I wiggled my bottom to spread my cheeks. I had both candles. One was going in my pussy and I would then use it to frig myself. The other was going up my bumhole.

I was really shaking as I tucked up my skirt into my belt, exposing bum and pussy and leaving myself naked from my waist to the tops of my socks. Just being bare in the church was glorious, and when I put my hand to my pussy I discovered I was soaking. The candle went in easily, sliding up my open vagina despite being a good two inches thick. Nearly half of it was up me before it bumped against my cervix, by which time I was panting with pleasure and desperate to get my bumhole filled.

My finger went to my mouth, my tongue lapping saliva on to it to leave it wet and slippery. I stuck my bum out over the back of the pew and reached behind myself, delving between my cheeks to find the tight little hole at the centre. It gave reluctantly, slowly accepting the top joint of my finger so that I had to lick it twice more before I was juicy enough. Then it was in, the tight, hot tube of my back passage squeezing on the intruding digit as I fed it in and out, opening myself for something larger by far. I was going to put the candle's thick end in, not the tapered one that would have slid gracefully up my bum, but the thick, round stub, which would bully its way in and make my ring stretch and strain to take it. It hurt, but not enough to make me stop, and soon my rectum was stuffed as full as my pussy, both holes straining on thick candle stems.

I posed for a bit, getting into rude positions. Between each pose I would check the window. First it was just standing, my back to the pews, legs apart, with my bare bottom showing and the candles sticking out behind. Then it was up on the lectern, imagining myself reading the sermon while the ornate book-rest concealed my rude lower view from the congregation. Next I kneeled, just as I had to take my confirmation, at the end of the aisle, only now, instead of my bottom pushing out a ball of lacy white, it was naked, with candles sprouting obscenely from both orifices. For a while I stayed like that, fucking myself with the candle in my pussy and rubbing at my clit, until the risk of discovery overcame my pleasure.

Quickly resuming my original seat, I began to masturbate. The candles were either side of the pew top, jammed against my holes as I spread my thighs to the imaginary congregation. With my pussy lips spread and my hand working the cunt candle in and out, I showed off, imagining row after row of horror-struck, outraged churchgoers watching my filthy, self-indulgent little display. That was the key phrase, the one that brought me to the edge: self-indulgent – Bunker's favourite put-down for anybody who dared to think for themselves or do something of which he did not approve. Little skirts were self-indulgent because they showed your legs and that was vanity. Boyfriends were self-indulgent, because they took your mind off your duty to the church. Even sweets were self-indulgent because the money would have been better spent on some holy cause. How much more self-indulgent would masturbation have been, then, female masturbation, dirty masturbation, with a candle in my cunt and another up my bottom-hole. I pulled the candle from my pussy and put it to my clit, rubbing hard as my head spun and my dirty thoughts brought my climax nearer and nearer . . .

Only by luck was I not caught. I was just starting to come and my attention had wandered, but in the instant before I shut my eyes for the final ride to orgasm I caught a flicker of movement through the window. For a moment I thought it was Percy but there just wasn't enough bulk and I dragged myself back from the edge of my climax. I threw my cunt candle under the pew but had no time to get the anal one out. Instead I jumped down and simply let my skirt drop, then pretended to be reading the legend on one of the tombs in the floor.

It was Bunker himself, entering and looking up in surprise at the sight of me. The smell of pussy was heavy in the air and I was sure the candle up my bum was pushing out the back of my skirt, but I could do nothing, only smile politely as he approached. He gave his oiliest grin in response, the sort reserved for strangers and his wealthiest parishioners. It changed as he recognised me, through a flicker of uncertainty to a patronising smirk.

'Well, if it isn't little Susan St Clair,' he said.

'Not so little,' I answered, rather lamely as I tried to think of an excuse for being there. 'Anyway, it's Susan Ottershaw now.'

'Drawn back to your alma mater, I see.' He supplied the explanation for me. 'Do you know, it is remarkable how many of those paying a return visit come to my church first, especially those who needed more guidance to see the light. I find it comforting.'

'Er . . . right.'

'Do sit down, my dear,' he went on. 'Take a pew, as it were, ha, ha.'

He had not laughed but had spoken the last two words, an irritating mannerism I remembered from before. I sat, suddenly unable to disobey, just as if I was still a teenager. Immediately the candle jammed deeper up my bottom and I gave a little involuntary grunt. I had to sit slowly, feeling a really deep humiliation as the candle slid up my rectum bit by bit.

'Are you all right, my dear?' Bunker asked as the final inch of the candle was crammed into my bottom and my anus closed reluctantly over its end.

'Yes, thank you,' I managed.

We talked for a while. He delivered a stream of questions and remarks with just the sort of smug certainty that had always annoyed me. I had never been able to argue with him and nor could I now. I just answered with what he wanted to hear. I even apologised for not getting married there. Finally it was over and I was left feeling small and weak, just as I always had before I met Percy. Once again I was the little girl sinner, grateful that such a good man would condescend to make time for me.

I had to do something, anything to try and get my confidence back. The naughty play I had been taking so much pleasure in now seemed a dreadful thing to have done, a wicked, awful sin. I could imagine Bunker's stern disapproval when he found my knickers, then, worse, his prayer of forgiveness, chiding and smug as he looked down on me from his inaccessible moral perch. I could have screamed, but at least I had Percy, Percy who would laugh at Bunker, Percy who would make me feel good again, and special, and naughty without being wrong.

We left the church together and I pretended to need something in the car. Bunker made a few parting remarks, made me promise to attend church in London regularly and left, walking briskly in the direction of the beach. I paused, wondering. Could the rumours have been right? Could the wonderful, righteous Reverend Carew really be a Peeping Tom?

There was a lump in his pocket, possibly binoculars, possibly a camera. Maybe he was just going for a healthy walk, maybe not. I had to find out, because I knew that if I could catch him at it then I really would break the spell, once and for all. I followed at a distance, walking rather awkwardly because of the candle in my rectum.

Percy was standing at the cliff top, the very image of the English gentleman taking the sea air. But I knew that his attention would not be on the distant horizon but on a pair of girls in skimpy bikinis who were playing chase with their boyfriends through the water.

'I have no knickers and a candle up my bottom,' I greeted him, determined to be playful.

He turned and smiled, immediately making me feel better, at least a little.

'Which do you think is the prettier?' he asked, nodding down towards the beach.

'The one in blue,' I answered.

'A sound choice,' he responded. 'Her bottom is perhaps too fat for fashionable tastes, but she is ideal spanking material. In fact, she has rather started me off, not to mention your reference to whatever perversions you have been indulging in with your candle. Do you fancy a spot yourself?'

'Later,' I promised. 'For now, do you see the man in the black suit walking along the cliff path?'

'Indeed,' he answered. 'Your insufferable priest?'

'Yes, and I think he's going to peep at girls. We're going to follow him.'

'We are? I rather thought I'd take you into the bushes for a light spanking and then try and find somewhere that does oysters, or perhaps lobster.'

'It's not even twelve yet. Come on.'

'Very well, but if we miss lunch you will be in frillies for a week, and a very short skirt.'

'Promises, promises, Percy.'

We followed Bunker along the cliff path, stopping as soon as we were safely clear of the village for me to get the candle out of my bottom. It was difficult, and my struggles had Percy laughing so hard he could hardly stand, but eventually it was out. Squatting with my bottom spread in front of him brought back my naughty feelings and I frigged off for him on demand, rubbing my clit in abandoned display until I came. I felt a lot better for my orgasm and more determined than ever to see what Bunker was up to, so after a hasty clean-up we went on.

Bunker had got well ahead, walking faster than either of us. I knew he would never be so stupid as to do anything obvious, and expected him to go to the row of fortifications where the cliff dipped at Wick. Their gun slits covered both the beach and the path, while the doors opened into trenches, making them ideal places for a bit of surreptitious peeping and even a quick wank. That was one of the things I'd learned from Percy: how to be dirty and get away with it. I explained all this to Percy, who agreed that it was what he would have done in Bunker's shoes.

He also agreed that we ought to approach from behind, through Wenmere Marsh, although only at the expense of a caning for me directly we got home. I still wasn't sure, but it was exciting to try in any case, and as we pushed through the woods and then along the edge of the reeds I was in an ever better mood. At last we reached the line of trees behind the three bunkers. I could see the access trenches, each with a beaten path to show that someone, if not necessarily Bunker, used them. He seemed likely to be in the right-hand one, as it covered the path back to Walwich, so we crept forward, me with my heart in my mouth, Percy grumbling about brambles and threatening dire retribution on my bottom.

I went really slowly, picking my way step by step, and all the time thinking what an idiot I would feel if I was wrong. I wasn't. As I reached the bunker and peered around the rusting door I saw what I wanted, the Reverend Benjamin Carew, binoculars aimed at the beach, fly wide open and cock in hand. He had a nice one, actually, big and pink and very smooth, and I watched him tug at it for a while before making my grand entrance.

It was great. I coughed and he jumped around, his cock still in his hand and his face going absolutely crimson as he saw me. His cock was so hard he couldn't get it back in his trousers, and Percy came in as he was struggling to cover himself, which made it worse. I said nothing, simply crossing my arms and watching until Carew's cock was tucked away and he was stammering incoherent excuses about birdwatching and needing to pee.

'You were wanking,' I told him.

'Masturbating,' Percy agreed as he peered out of the gun slit that covered the beach. 'Hmm, yes.'

I stepped forward to see. On the beach below were three girls, their ages suggesting a mother and two daughters. Mother was topless, with her green bikini top laid aside and her good-sized breasts bare as she rubbed lotion into them. She was at least forty, but far from unattractive. The older girl was on her front, sunbathing, with the top of her one-piece rolled down to her waist. With only her back on show she was still cute, but when she rolled over it was likely to be a fine show. The younger girl was best, also on her front, but topless and with a minuscule black bikini bottom pulled up tight between her bum cheeks. She was blonde, with an air of fragility about her, ideal dirty old man's wanking material. Her legs were even slightly apart to show the tiny triangle of material that covered her pussy, a sight that would have had any red-blooded man hard in his trousers.

'Tut, tut, Reverend,' Percy remarked, although I knew it wasn't what he was thinking.

'Look,' Bunker stammered, 'you won't report this or anything, will you? I mean . . . surely not . . .'

'No,' I answered. 'I'm not going to report you. I want you to wank off.'

'*What?*'

'Wank off, all the way, until you come, all over your hand while you watch that little cute blonde and think what you'd like to do with her. How old do you think she is? Seventeen? Sixteen?'

'Look . . . I . . .'

Bunker was lost for words. For the first time since I'd known him he was lost for words. I felt high, drunk with elation.

'Oh, but I'm being rude,' I went on. 'Percy, this is the Reverend Carew, the Reverend Benjamin Underwood Naughton Carew, the Vicar of Walwich. He likes to be called Ben, but I prefer his nickname, Bunker, so we'll call him that, shall we? Bunker, this is Percy Ottershaw, my husband. Say hello.'

'What ho, Bunker,' Percy said cheerfully.

'Er ... hello ...' Bunker managed.

'Well,' I continued, 'I'm sure Percy doesn't want to watch you jerk your little cock, so he can keep watch outside.'

Percy nodded and left, doubtless heading for the next bunker where he could take his time wanking over the three girls. Bunker immediately began to bluster but I wagged my finger at him and he shut up.

'No, no,' I told him, 'not this time. Come on, cock out. Let's see you.'

He hesitated but his hand went to his fly. I watched as he pulled out his cock, no longer stiff but still turgid with his earlier excitement. A glance out of the gun slit showed the scene much as before, only Mum had walked down to the water's edge and was looking back along the beach towards Walwich. I wondered if she had overheard us, but as she stepped back towards the cliff I realised that she had another reason for her uneasiness. To either side of us the cliff stuck out a few metres, forming the miniature cove in which the girls were sunbathing. Directly below the bunker a tangle of bushes had grown, where the concrete foundations stopped the cliff eroding. Mum went to this, and with a last, nervous glance she stuck her bottom out towards us and pulled down her pants.

I watched with a delicious voyeuristic thrill as her bum came on show. She was quite fleshy, but firm and very womanly, with well-cleft cheeks and a lot of dark hair between them. As she stuck it out I caught a glimpse of her anus, dark and puckered in between her

211

spread cheeks. She was holding her bikini pants down with one hand, ready to jerk them up if anybody came, although the next group of sunbathers was a good four hundred yards away and quite out of sight. Her uncertainty and embarrassment made watching her all the more lovely, and as she started to pee I watched the trickle of wet run out from beneath her.

'That should give you something to get hard over,' I whispered to Bunker.

He was still looking nonplussed, although he had watched Mum pee, so I gave a stern nod to his cock. It was still limp, but he started to wank and I smiled encouragingly.

Outside, Mum had gone back to her towel, but rather than pull her pants back up she was now nude, face down with her fine bottom towards us. Bunker was watching, his cock bobbing up and down in his hand. It was still limp, my presence doubtless having destroyed his confidence, and I realised that I was going to have to do something.

He made an odd noise as I pushed his fingers aside and took him in hand, halfway between a groan and a sigh. I began to wank him, revelling in my power as the thick, rubbery shaft began to swell. I watched it grow, thickening and lengthening in my hand until he was fully erect, the bulbous head poking out from between my fingers, fat and bloated.

'Watch them,' I whispered to him. 'Watch her bum, all bare for you to stare at, naked on the beach and she doesn't know you're watching her, wanking over her. And her daughters, too – wouldn't it be nice if they decided to strip as well? They'd peel their swimsuits down over their bums, showing you their pussies and their tight little arseholes. You'd like that, wouldn't you, the three of them lined up, bare-breasted, bare-bottomed, pussies on show, all of it on show, to you – you dirty, filthy, wanking bastard!'

Bunker had come as I mentioned their pussies, his sperm erupting over my hand as he gave a defeated groan. I flicked his spunk away, mostly over his trousers, and with that gesture the last glimmer of his hold over me just vanished.

12

Lydia, Lydia

I wanted to shock someone. I mean really shock them.
I had to: I was so fucking bored. I wanted to be in
London, with my friends, not stuck in the middle of
fucking nowhere with my parents. That was bad
enough, but they'd met up with that fat old git Percy
Ottershaw, who was staying at the same hotel.

Every day in Burgundy was the same. We'd get up,
visit some winemaker, taste his wine and be very polite
and thankful, and then go on to the next one, who'd be
exactly the fucking same. I didn't mind the wine,
because at least I could get pissed, but the talking really
got me down. They went on and on and on, mostly in
French, so I couldn't even understand what they were
saying. The blokes used to stare at me as well, and make
little remarks about how pretty I was and how lucky
Mum and Dad where to have such an attractive
daughter. I knew what they meant. They wanted their
grubby fingers down my pants. I'd have let them, too, if
they hadn't been such a bunch of old farts.

On the third day I couldn't take it any more. We'd
been at this place for hours and the guy had been really
leching over me, staring at my tits and legs and making
his dirty little comments. When Mum and Dad weren't
listening he made some remark to fat Percy. I'd learned
enough French to know it was something about my
bum, and I just lost it.

'This is what you want, isn't it? You fucking old perve!' I yelled.

I turned round, flicked my skirt up and jerked down my panties, showing them my bum, with the cheeks held open so they could see the hole – and my cunt, too. They just stared, so I gave them all a V-sign and walked out, laughing. Mum came after me, really cross, and started going on about how I ought to show some respect and all that crap. When I told her to fuck off and leave me alone she actually threatened to spank me. I mean, spank me, at my age! I just laughed at her. I mean, over Mum's knee with my knickers down? It wouldn't even hurt!

'All right, Lydia,' she answered. 'If that's the way you want it then how about this. Do that again and I won't spank you, nor will Dad. We'll send you to Percy for a spanking. How would you like that?'

I told her she wouldn't dare, but she knew she'd got to me. I knew what Percy was like, you see. He got off on spanking girls. I'd heard things from when he used to run a restaurant, how he used to make the waitresses line up on the bar stools with their panties down. He'd spank them and fuck one afterwards. It wasn't bullshit, either, because I'd heard it from Nick, who managed one of Dad's shops. He'd been out with Jilly, who'd been one of the waitresses. Nick said they'd actually got off on it. I didn't believe him, or I didn't want to anyway, but one of them had married Percy. It hadn't lasted, but she'd still done it.

That was what got to me, not the threat of a spanking, not the thought of getting it over fat Percy's knee, not even the thought of him jacking off over it afterwards. I can take a spanking, and I know dirty old men like to jack off over young girls. What got to me was that getting spanked might do it for me. Sure, I'd been spanked before, but only by Mum, and that was different. Nick said spanking made girls horny, and I

215

really couldn't handle it if I got spanked by Percy and found I had a wet cunt afterwards. I knew he could do it, too, because even though he's a fat bastard and pushing sixty, he's really strong.

I was good all the rest of the day, even though I kept telling myself I was being a chicken. What I should have done was to've given them all another flash of my bum and let Percy do it, right in front of some old winemaker, panties down and all. Then, when he'd done me, I'd just have laughed at them. That would have been it. After that they wouldn't have been able to threaten me with anything. Only I just didn't dare.

As usual they had a really big dinner at the hotel, pissing it up half the night. I managed to nick a bottle when I went up to my room and sat drinking it with the TV on with no sound and the light off. There was one of those French sex films on, with a load of people getting really worked up over nothing much and then bonking each other. I watched it anyway, because they show cocks and I hadn't had it since we'd left England. It was actually getting quite good, with this big black guy and two nuns, and I decided I wanted to play with myself a bit.

I was already down to my panties, with the sheets pushed off and my thighs open. In between drinks I'd rub the bottle on my pussy, pushing it down and thinking of the guy's cock. The nuns were sucking on it, taking it in turns to have it in their mouths while the other one licked and sucked the guy's balls. I was getting well horny, with my panties pushed hard against my pussy, and I decided I was going to take it all the way. I curled up my legs to pull my panties down and left them around one ankle. With the bottle between my tits and my hand on my pussy I started to frig, all the time staring at the long black cock going in and out of the nun's mouth.

Sometimes when I frig I get really dirty, thinking of other girls, or taking it up the bum, even being pissed on. Now I was determined to keep it clean, just focusing on a nice, big cock and, whatever happened, not to think about spanking.

I was getting close by the time the black guy decided to fuck the nuns. He had them on the floor of this church they were in, with their robe thingies turned up over their bare arses. They prayed while they got fucked, with their hands together while he took them in turn, doggy-fashion. The camera got really close in, and I could see their bumholes and the way their cunts went in and out with the motion of his cock. I was wishing it was me, and I drained the bottle and put it up myself, fucking myself with it and frigging my clit as I watched. He was right up one of them and suddenly he whipped it out and his cock shot a great wad of come over her bum. I was wishing I could lick it off and my clit was burning. I was going to come . . .

Then it changed, and it really caught me out. One moment it was the black guy, spunking all over a nun's cunt and arse, then it wasn't. Instead there was this fat bloke in a purple robe, and he had a girl over his lap, a schoolgirl, with her skirt turned up and her little white panties taken down. He was spanking her, bare-bottomed, a fat old man, just like Percy, spanking a young girl like me. Her tits were out, too, swinging under her chest to the rhythm of the smacks, and her face was a picture, eyes tight shut, mouth coming open each time his hand hit her bum . . .

. . . and it was me being spanked. Me with my panties pulled down and my bum showing. Me with my blouse up and my tits swinging. Me squealing in pain as I was punished, only not by the bloke on the TV, but by Percy, fat Percy, holding me down for a fucking good spanking while his cock got hard and my cunt got juicy.

I came, crying out loud and filling with shame for what I was frigging myself over even as I hit the peak. At that moment, right at the peak, I was praying

Percy'd just come in, find me frigging, turn me over, spank me until I was in tears, make me pray while he fucked me and at the end just spunk up all over my bare bottom. Then my shame got the better of me and my orgasm broke, right in the middle, leaving me half finished.

I lay there for ages, naked, with the bottle up my cunt, just thinking of what I had done. The bishop finished spanking the schoolgirl and she sucked him off and got spunk in her face, and I wondered if that was what fat Percy would expect if he did me. It was an awful thought, because I knew I'd probably do it.

The next day I just couldn't look Percy in the face. I kept looking at his hands, though, which were fat and red, with really thick fingers, just right for spanking my naughty bottom. Mum must have thought her threat had done the trick, because I stayed on my best behaviour all day, as bored as ever except that I couldn't stop thinking about getting my naked bum slapped over Percy's lap.

I didn't frig that evening, or try and find anything sexy on the TV, because I knew what would happen if I started. It would be back across Percy's lap in my mind, and the whole spanking ritual, up with my skirt, down with my panties, out with my tits, then *smack, smack, smack* until I was snivelling and ready to have his cock put in my mouth.

In the end I managed to get to sleep, only to have vivid dreams all about spankings and nuns in white panties. Then there was a great fat pig with Percy's face that caught me and fucked me, with its corkscrew cock winding in and out of my cunt as it gave *his* dirty little chuckle, over and over. I woke up in a sweat. I had to do it; I just couldn't stop myself. Turning on to my face I lifted my bum and eased down my panties at the back, just far enough to show my cheeks. I threw the sheets off and imagined how I looked, bare-bottomed, as if waiting for a spanking with my panties pushed low in meek obedience. My hand went to my pussy, the other to my bum, both stroking and feeling, touching my sex lips, caressing the cool, smooth surface of my bottom skin and thinking how it would feel when I'd been spanked until I cried.

I knew Percy would want to show me off when he beat me, too. I'd shown him my bumhole, taunting him, but this would be different. He would pull open my cheeks and look at it, inspecting it, seeing if I was clean. Maybe he'd even touch it, or put his finger in, deep up my bottom between my red spanked cheeks while I lay over his lap, thoroughly punished and feeling sorry for myself. I'd be too humbled to tell him to take it out, and I'd just let him feel around, right in my box.

My bottom crease was under my hand and I was doing it, touching my bumhole and imagining it was Percy doing it as I started to rub my clit. Twice I slapped myself, making each cheek tingle, then again, bringing a warm, spanked feeling. My finger went back down, finding my bumhole, tight but moist where my juice had run down in my sleep. I felt the little ridges and tucks, imagining Percy exploring my anus, feeling every little fold of flesh. As I pushed at the centre my little hole opened and my finger was in, up my box, feeling the tight, deep ring and the wet flesh beyond it.

I was sobbing as I frigged, feeling so dirty and so good, with my clit wobbling under one finger and another deep, deep in my bottom, right up. That was what I wanted, to be spanked and then fingered, with his fat, strong fingers in both my holes, feeling about up my cunt and bum. He'd fuck my cunt and tell me I was dirty up my bottom to shame me. He'd make me suck his fingers and go down on my knees. He'd make me frig my pussy with my fingers in my bumhole. He'd make me get right down and he'd stick it up my hole, my bumhole, my arsehole, the filthy little box my own finger was working in, squashing around, feeling, probing . . .

I came, biting the pillow and kicking my feet, rubbing my pussy and jamming my finger up my bum, squealing and shaking and panting. My ring clamped really tight on my finger, just as if there was a cock in my bumhole, and on that thought I let it ride, on and on, spanked and buggered, spanked and buggered, just like I deserved it.

This time the climax didn't break, but I felt just as bad afterwards. Worse, in fact, because if getting a kick over the thought of Percy spanking me was bad, then wanting him up my bum was worse. At least with a spanking I could pretend not to like it. Once his cock was up my box I wouldn't be able to hold back at all.

I was good again the next day, very good. Even when one of the winemakers called me a little girl I kept my mouth shut. I *am* small, and I suppose he thought I was about eleven. I've got tits, though, and hips, and normally I don't take that sort of shit from anyone. This time I did, just giving him a girly little laugh and asking if he'd like to see my passport. He said nothing, but stuck out his lower lip in a way that suggested it didn't matter what was on my passport, to him I was eleven.

He kept joking with me, and if I hadn't been on my best behaviour I'd really have let him have it. He was about fifty, I suppose, a squat, wrinkled old git with a face the colour of tobacco, a paunch and a low-slung arse. He had these huge hands, too. They all did, I suppose from picking all the grapes and such, but this guy's were enormous, like spades. There was no way he could seriously have imagined I'd fancy him, but he kept flirting and even said he could do with a young wife if I was free. He was joking, but it was just such a fucking arrogant thing to say that I really had to bite my tongue to hold back.

It got worse as the tasting went on. He put his arm round me and pinched my bum, which earns any man a slap in the face unless I want it. The others were all looking at one of those big maps that show all the vineyards, so I pushed his hand away. He gave me a look, like it was me who had done something wrong, then said, in plain English, 'No, no, little lady, you don't want to stop a pinch, or you may find out it turns to a slap.'

I was going to answer him back, to call him a filthy old toad and tell him to keep his hands to himself. I wanted to flash my tits and ask if he wanted a good feel. That always puts old bastards in their place when they try to flirt. Only I didn't dare, because Percy was there, and if it happened it was going to be in front of the winemaker. At the thought of how much he would enjoy seeing me get my panties hauled down for a spanking I choked my words back and walked over to the map to ask Mum if we shouldn't be thinking about lunch.

She looked a bit cross, because it was good wine and there was more to taste. Percy wasn't so keen and said that lunch was a great idea. We tasted a couple more wines, bought some bottles and left, driving up into the woods above the village for a picnic. I was already a bit pissed, even though I'd spat most of what we had been given. If I got drunk I knew I was likely to get lippy and I knew where that would lead. I'd have got my spanking in the middle of the picnic rug, so I did my best not to misbehave. I knew it was going to happen, though. It just seemed inevitable. Something would happen, something that would give them an excuse to punish me. Then up would go my skirt and down would come my panties and I'd be getting it, the spanking I needed so badly . . .

I didn't know how the thought had got into my head. It wasn't true. The last thing I wanted was to get my bare bottom spanked. Yet I'd thought it, thought it when I was pissed and off guard, which is always when the truth comes out. It was bad enough having frigged over it, but now, in the day, when I wasn't horny, it was really too much. Suddenly I just had to be alone. I needed to think, to get my head straight, to clear it of the awful need for utter, unbearable humiliation across Percy Ottershaw's lap. I said I needed to clear my head and that I'd catch them up at the next domaine, then set off walking.

It wouldn't go, but only got worse. There was the squat winemaker, too, who had as good as threatened to spank me. François, he was called, and he had known Percy for years, so I wondered if he hadn't been put up to it. I could see Percy doing it, or it might just be that they were two of a kind, dirty old bastards who liked the idea of spanking young girls' bottoms – bare bottoms, because I had no doubt whatever that if it happened my panties would be coming down.

I walked along the belt of scrub above the vineyards, thinking of what it meant to be spanked by a man, how humiliating it would be, how helpless I'd feel with my bottom nude and Percy's arm holding me hard around the waist, raising that big, fat hand . . .

It was their hands that really got to me. Percy's were fat and heavy; François's were like spades: both perfect for giving little girls a much-needed piece of discipline. I was shaking as I thought of it: my skirt being pulled up, a big thumb in the waistband of my panties, the exposure of my bum, then the spanking, long and hard and painful, until I was crying and pleading and my pussy juice was running down my legs.

That was already true. I was so wet it was like I'd peed myself, with my panty gusset sodden against my pussy and all wet up between my bum cheeks. It was awful. I was going to be punished, I mean really punished, sent to fat Percy Ottershaw for a spanking, and at my age! It should have had me furious with indignation, but instead I had wet panties. I was almost in tears with the frustration of it, of not being able to control my feelings.

I should have been defiant, doing something that would really wind Mum up, like taking one of the waiters at the hotel back to my room for a good suck-and-fuck session. The next morning I'd tell them and I'd be sent to Percy's room, where I'd take my spanking without a sound and then laugh at him. Only I wouldn't. I'd snivel and squeal and if he wanted me to suck him afterwards I'd do it. I'd even let him bugger me. After all, that was what I'd been thinking of in the middle of the night when my defences were down: his cock working about up my bumhole.

My eyes were moist and half closed, my head swimming with dirty thoughts. Below me were the vineyards and the village, hazy through my tears. I was going to do it, but not with Percy, not when it might get round at home. No, François had as good as offered it. He would be willing, a good spanking for me and a suck of his cock. A warm bum and spunk in my throat as I came, and it wouldn't have been a punishment. That was it, my defiance, taking what had been used to threaten me, but for kicks, not as a punishment.

I struck down between the vines, thinking it out. I was supposed to catch them up in a village called Pommard, the next one along. The appointment wasn't even until half past two, so I had plenty of time, while at the moment François would be taking his lunch. Sure enough, the yard gates had been closed and when I rang on the bell he appeared with a piece of bread and pâté in his hand. He didn't look too pleased at first, but smiled when he saw me and ushered me in with a pat on my bottom. I'd been thinking how to get around to it, but from the way he touched me I knew it wouldn't be hard.

He poured me a glass of wine, which I downed at a gulp. My hand was shaking as I put the glass down, and he saw and threw me a quizzical look. I had to say it, but I didn't know the French for spanking. So, with my cheeks blushing scarlet with humiliation I pointed to him, then stuck out my bottom and gave it a slap. He looked at me and stuck out his lower lip in exactly the way he had when doubting my age. I smiled encouragingly. He shrugged, swallowed his own wine, got up, and took me by the arm.

I'd done it, and now it was going to happen, because his grip was like having my wrist in a vice. My heart was beating like a hammer as he led me out of the kitchen and down the cellar steps. It was a good private place to spank me, with no risk of being seen from the windows, for which I was grateful. It was cool, too, which made me really aware of my wet panties.

He may have guessed he'd got to me earlier; he may have even thought I'd been sent to him for punishment by my parents. Either way he didn't question me, but simply sat down on a chair and patted his lap. I came forwards, shaking hard, and then I saw Percy's glasses on top of a barrel. He only wore them to write his notes and was always leaving them around, but he was sure to notice eventually. I wasn't safe any more. He might come back. Worse, my parents might come in, too, maybe while I was getting my spanking. I hesitated and François patted his lap again, impatiently. I pointed at Percy's glasses, trying to explain in my schoolgirl French. He shook his head, not understanding and doubtless thinking I was trying to back out. Then he had taken my wrist and I was going down over his lap.

When Mum spanked me she would always let me get comfortable. Not François, he just pulled hard and I sprawled across his legs. His left arm went around my waist, taking me in a grip I knew I could never break.

His hand touched my thighs and my little skirt was coming up, high up over my bum, showing off my panties, the little white panties that were so wet at the crotch. He sniffed, perhaps smelling my pussy in the air, then his thumb was in my waistband, just as I'd imagined it, and my panties were sliding down over my bum, baring me, exposing me for spanking. He didn't just take them down, he pulled them off, jerking them free of my trainers and then balling them in his hand. I was looking back, acutely aware of my bare bottom and wondering what he was doing, only to find out as my wadded panties were pushed at my face.

I let him stuff them into my mouth, tasting cunt and sweat, gagged to stop my squeals. He held me tighter around my waist. I shut my eyes and gritted my teeth. His hand found my bum, covering almost all of it, squeezing both cheeks, then bouncing them in his palm. He gave a grunt as his hand left my bottom and came down again. I heard the meaty smack sound even as the stinging pain of the slap shot through me and my whole body was jolted forwards. I gave a muffled squeal of shock and pain and kicked out. He just laughed and brought his hand down again, even harder. I almost swallowed my panties, it was such a shock, jarring my back and knocking the breath from my body. Again he did it, and again, bringing his huge hand down on my poor bum, over and over until I was gagging on my panties and thrashing my legs, kicking and writhing and making a shameless display of my cunt and bum.

It went on and on, *smack, smack, smack*, with my poor bum bouncing about under his hand, wobbling and opening and showing the little hole down between my cheeks. All I could do was grunt and kick and snort through my nose because of the panties in my mouth, and all the time I could taste my own pussy and smell the scent of my own excitement. I'd expected humiliation, and I'd got it, but this was something else – gross, undignified punishment as I was handled like a little rag doll and spanked and spanked and spanked.

The panties fell out of my mouth after a while and I began to squeal, but he just kept on, grunting to himself occasionally as he punished me, never once stopping or even slowing down, until I finally lost control completely and farted, really loudly. At that I burst into tears, but even then he didn't stop.

He beat me well, really well, until my bottom was numb and my whole rear end was throbbing. When he stopped I could only lie there panting, wide-eyed and breathless, wondering what could ever have made me submit to such pain. I knew I'd be purple behind, really well spanked, worse than the girl in the film. Yet if I couldn't understand it in my head, I could in my pussy. I was wet, soaking, with juice trickling down my thighs. There was even a puddle of it on the floor underneath me where I could see back through the legs of the chair, thick and white, a total giveaway of my excitement.

François had a good, leisurely feel of my spanked bum, stroking the hot skin and squeezing the cheeks, even opening them with his fingers to get a good look at the cleft. I was too shocked to stop him, too dizzy to even kick out as a thick, callused finger invaded my cunt. He began to finger-fuck me, working it in and out. A lot of boys have had their fingers up me, but this was different. His finger was as thick as some cocks, and really rough, making the mouth of my cunt squirm and pulse as it went in and out. I was soon sighing and ready for the expected demand for cocksucking – or just for getting his cock stuffed in my cunt, for that matter.

His thumb was between my smarting cheeks, touching my bumhole, and I thought he was going to put it up when the doorbell went. François cursed, hesitated, then dumped me on the ground. It was unexpected and I sat down hard on my sore bum, then just stayed there, feeling dazed. The blood had gone to my head from having been held with it upside down for so long, while the effect of the spanking and fingering had me dizzy with pain and arousal. It never even occurred to me that it might be Percy at the door, come for his glasses, not until he walked down the cellar steps, chatting merrily with François and laughing.

'Ah, Lydia,' he greeted me. 'Nothing like a good spanking, eh?'

I didn't answer. I didn't even move, but just sat there. My skirt was still up and my pussy was showing, while my wet panties were lying on the floor beside me. He obviously knew anyway, because of the way they'd been laughing together.

'Do you think I might?' he went on. 'After all, you'll admit you've acted the brat to me, and Charles said Sophie was going to send you to me if you got any worse.'

There was no answer, which Percy took for assent. He spoke a stream of rapid French to François, who nodded his understanding. Percy pushed two chairs together as François helped me to my feet. They sat down, facing each other with their knees interlocked and I was pulled down, over their laps. My skirt was pulled unceremoniously up over my bum and it was bare again, already red and hot from spanking, and really high because Percy had one knee cocked up. That left my cheeks open and my cunt and bumhole showing, but I was too far gone to care.

'Good heavens, you have given her a whacking,' Percy remarked, then repeated the comment in French.

François gave a happy grunt and Percy began to rearrange the rest of my clothing. My top was tugged out of my skirt and turned up over my tits. I had no bra, so they were left hanging nude immediately. Then it was my skirt, tucked up into its own waistband so everything was showing, everything that mattered to them. That left me feeling all the more vulnerable, and I remembered the unfortunate schoolgirl in the film, with her tits swinging as she got her spanking from the priest.

Percy began to spank me, not hard like François had, but with the tips of his fingers, producing a mild, stinging pain that just had me wanting to stick my bum up and have a cock pushed home up my hole. Percy talked as he spanked, and then François joined in, using the same technique on my other bum cheek. It was all done in French, but I could understand enough to know they were using my bum for Percy to teach François how to spank a girl properly. At least, how to spank a girl to turn her on, because he certainly knew how to punish one, as I'd found out.

First it was the fingertips, then a cupped hand to make a lot of noise, with each smack of my bum like a clap. That was harder, and had me grunting and panting, but they took no notice whatever. It was hard smacks, next, right under my seat, each one pushing against my cunt. Even my cunt lips got smacked a bit, making me squeal and writhe. They just tightened their grips on my waist and went right on spanking, smacking and smacking as my juice got smeared on my pussy and bum cheeks.

The last thing Percy did was pull my cheeks apart and use a finger to smack my hole. Twelve times he did it, until my ring was smarting and felt all puffy and swollen. It hurt, too, an odd stinging feeling, but it left me shivering and thinking of cocks in girly bumholes.

They let me up, and told me to put my hands on my head. I did it, stood there, skirt rucked up and top over my tits, everything on show, not even allowed to cover my pussy. Percy indicated that I should turn and I did, shuffling around on my feet to show off my red bum. I stopped with my back to them, feeling their eyes on my naked, spanked bottom. A chair grated on the ground and I heard the rasp of a zip. It was going to happen. I was going to be made to give them blow jobs. Maybe I was going to be fucked, maybe even fucked in my bum.

My jaw was shivering and I couldn't help myself, so I turned to look. François had his blue work coverall pushed down and his cock and balls out of his underpants. They were big, two full handfuls for me, easily, with his fat cock dark and heavily hooded and his ball sac almost hidden in a thick tangle of hair. Percy had his out, too, a little pink thing half the size of François's, along with fat pink balls out of proportion to his cock. He was wanking it and admiring my bum, and his prick was already half hard.

'Come and sit in my lap, my dear,' Percy offered.

I knew what he meant: sit on his knee and wank his cock. He'd feel my hot, smacked bum while I did it and think of what they'd done to me. I obeyed as he opened his legs, perching my bottom on one thigh. It was comfy, because he was fat and my bum was only small, but it made me feel the beaten state of my bottom more easily. I was feeling like I had imagined I would when I'd frigged off: horny and willing after a beating. So I took his cock and began to jerk it up and down. If anyone had told me a week before that I'd end up wanking Percy Ottershaw, I'd have hit them, but here I was, spanked and with his cock in my hand. Not only that, but willing for more.

As I had expected he put a hand under my bum, fondling one well-smacked cheek. His cock was small and thin, but very hard, with the head popping in and out of my clenched fist as I wanked him.

'Not large, it is true,' Percy said, obviously following my thoughts. 'Perfect for the rear entrance, so I'm told.'

He didn't mean doggy-fashion, and he chuckled as he saw me start. His finger slid in between my bum cheeks, and before I really knew what I was doing I was pushing my bum out to let him get at my anus. He touched it and rubbed the tip of his finger in the wet of my cunt juice. I expected him to finger my anus and I was shutting my eyes in shame at the thought but relaxing my bumhole. For a moment my ring was open around his fingertip, and then he had withdrawn it and moved his hand to my hip.

I kept my eyes tight shut, filled with shame and despair as he moved me. I felt his cock shaft bump my bottom, then it was between my cheeks. He rubbed it in the crease, then his hands were under my bum, fat and clammy against my sore skin. His knob touched my bumhole and I let out a long sigh of mixed ecstasy and misery as he started to lower me on to his cock.

He was right to say he fitted girls' bumholes. His cock slid up without more than a twinge of pain, right up my box, all the way, until it was packed up my bum, with my hole stretched taut on his shaft and my cheeks pressed firm against his fat belly and big thighs. He was up my bum, and it was just too good to resist. I began to move on his lap, wiggling to get the feel of him in my box, then starting to bounce and make my hole move in and out. My box felt really full, bloated despite the small size of his cock, but it was nice, and I opened my eyes, just giving in to whatever they wanted to do to me.

François was watching me get buggered. His hand was on his big, thick cock, wanking it slowly up with the big purple head coming half out of his thick foreskin with each tug. I opened my mouth, offering him a suck, eager for the fat, ugly cock to go in me. He obliged, standing and flopping it in my face as I leaned over. I rubbed my cheeks on it, enjoying the way the fat shaft rolled on my face, then took it in my mouth and began to suck.

Percy was buggering me with short, sudden jerks of his hips, each one ramming his erection home in my bulging rectum. His hands were on my tits, moulding them and rubbing my nipples while he used my bumhole and his friend came to erection in my mouth. François was huge erect, his cock a really big, fat one, filling my mouth right to the back, even with a good bit of shaft still sticking out. I was feeling his balls and wanking him in my mouth as Percy found my cunt. A finger slipped up me and his thumb started on my clit and I knew he wasn't going to be content just to use me: he was going to make me come as well.

I was getting eager, urgent in fact. Two dirty old men had spanked me and were using me, one at each end. It didn't matter. I had a cock up my bum and another in my mouth, and soon I was going to come: that was everything. I was bouncing on Percy, revelling in the squashy feeling up my bottom, wanking François hard into my mouth, desperate for his load down my throat.

François said something and Percy laughed. His hand pushed up, raising my bum, easing his erection from the dirty little hole at the centre. It came out with a squelch and François pulled back, depriving me of his lovely thick cock. He sat down, his erection rearing from his lap like a pole. I went, happy to try and take the massive thing, expecting him to fuck me, only to have it pressed to my anus instead, my soggy, gaping bumhole, from which Percy had only just pulled out. It went in – it hurt, but it went, jamming slowly up, filling my dirtbox until I felt I was going to bust, and then his big balls were against my cunt and my thighs were open and I was frigging and squealing and laughing all at once.

A hand was scooped under me and François's big balls had been pushed into my cunt, filling me beautifully. It felt all squashy under my bottom and his cock was sliding in and out of my ring. I felt it clench and I was coming, cunt and bumhole tightening on their loads, and my mouth was open and I was crying out in ecstasy . . .

And Percy was standing and prodding his cock at my face, the cock that had just been up my bottom. My mouth was wide, so were my eyes, in pure shock at what he expected me to do. Even as my brain shrieked at me not to be so utterly, utterly filthy I was leaning forwards, letting it in, closing my mouth and then sucking, sucking on the erection that had been up my bum.

I came, one long, glorious peak, better than anything before, with my holes pulsing and my bum squirming in François's lap, with my breasts squashed tight in his huge hands, with my slapped bottom bruised and throbbing, with my mouth full of a penis that tasted of my own bumhole. It went on and on. François grunted and spunked up in my box and still I was coming. Percy sighed and filled my mouth with his sperm and still I was coming. I finished it with spunk coming from both used holes, squirting from my mouth as Percy fucked it, squelching and oozing from my bumhole as François stuffed himself in to the very hilt.

It was over and I was coming down, dizzy and weak with reaction. François helped me off his lap while Percy sat down to get his breath back. They stripped me nude and cleaned me, hosing me down as I squatted naked over the big drain in François's tractor shed. They were laughing together and talking in French as they did it, but Percy was really considerate and made sure I understood everything, which he had never done before.

I had to wash my panties, but otherwise my clothes were OK, so I dressed and bundled the little wad of soggy white cotton into my bag. Being nude kept me reminded of what I'd done, of how dirty I'd been and how good it had felt. I kissed François goodbye, mouth to mouth, and let Percy hold my arm as we walked down towards Pommard. I didn't even feel bad when we rejoined Mum and Dad, just well pleased for a great sexual experience and smug over my guilty secret.

That night I frigged over what I'd done, stroking my sore bottom after inspecting the bruises in the mirror. Only after I'd come did I start to feel a bit bad, thinking of what my friends would say if I told them. I wouldn't, although that didn't mean I might not let someone give me another spanking in due course. Not Percy, though. It was just too much to handle, letting a dirty old man do it.

What I had to know was whether Mum would really have sent me to him, or if it had just been said to make me behave.

We left Burgundy the next day, driving slowly back across the hills and down the Loire valley. I didn't get a chance to speak to Mum alone until we were on the ferry. Dad had gone to the bar and she and I went out on deck, and as soon as we were out of earshot I asked her.

'Do you . . . I mean, would you really have sent me for a spanking from Percy Ottershaw?'

'Oh, Lydia,' she said after a moment's pause. 'Of course I wouldn't, darling! I'm sorry, I was just cross, and you must admit you were being a bit much. Really, do you honestly think I'd let that old pervert touch my own daughter?'

I couldn't answer. I could only stare out over the sea and think of hands like spades and the taste of a cock that had been in my bumhole.

13

Perfection

I sat back in the armchair, absolutely relaxed, feeling slightly drunk and slightly naughty. Percy's flat was just the place for my mood, too: masculine, snug and secure, a place where I could equally well doze happily or indulge in the very rudest of misbehaviour.

'Coffee, Penny?' Percy enquired as he looked round the kitchen door.

'Please,' I answered.

It had been quite a day, Percy's sixty-fifth birthday party, for which he had hired a substantial hall and invited just about everybody he knew. All day I had been drinking and chatting and trying to remember who was who. Gradually they had begun to drift off, until Percy had invited me back to his flat for a nightcap.

I had had no illusions about his intentions, and I had barely been in the flat ten minutes before I was draped across his lap with my dress up around my waist and my panties pulled well down. He'd spanked me until my bottom was hot and my pussy was ready, then he'd fucked me, kneeling over his armchair with his fat belly resting on my upturned bottom.

Since then we had been sipping a fine wine from his cellar as he went through his life story. It was worth listening to, with two marriages, successes and failures in business and lots and lots of girls, most of them either spanked or with wet panties, which were his two great erotic passions. What made it even more fascinating was having met so many of the people involved that very afternoon.

There was Elaine, his first wife, a kindly, grey-haired woman who had apparently been the one to introduce him to the pleasures of seeing a girl wet her panties, right back in the 1950s. Percy's daughter, Alice, had been with Elaine, and two grandchildren, all of them, supposedly, blissfully unaware of his behaviour.

I'd met his second wife Susan, too, a cheerful woman not much older than me. They had married after he had helped her break the conventions of her upbringing and introduced her to the pleasures of a good spanking. With thirty years between them it hadn't lasted, but I'd noticed he greeted her with a kiss and a squeeze of her well-rounded bottom.

There had been Gabriella, too, now a Grecian matriarch, still beautiful at sixty, once stripped in public and smeared with tar for being a prostitute. She was with her daughter Anna who'd been spanked as one of Percy's waitresses, years later. Also there was Elaine's niece Joanna, who had been with her girlfriend, Tina, since nineteen-seventy. She also knew Anthony Croom, who had been responsible for my own meeting with Percy.

Almost every female there had either been spanked or caned by Percy, excepting only his own daughter and the wine writer, Sophie Carlisle. He had buggered Sophie anyway, so he pretty well had the complete set. Certainly he'd had me, spanked the first time we'd met and several times since. For me he was that rare thing, a dirty old man whom I could respect: a friend most of the time, stern when I needed to be punished, rude when I was ready for dirty sex.

Percy came in with the coffee and we drank it slowly, chatting casually about spanked girls and wet panties. He told me about Tina, who had seemed to really hate

235

Joanna, when all the time what she really wanted was to be her lover, and the submissive partner at that. As Joanna was Elaine's niece, he had never felt it appropriate to have sex with her, but as a teenager her bottom had been simply too magnificent to ignore. He and Elaine had caned her to help her lose weight, despite considering it more loss than gain. As I always reckoned my own bottom was a bit fat for my petite figure I felt I could sympathise with Joanna. Still, I couldn't deny that there was a thrill in making a girl who was embarrassed about the size of her bottom take down her panties for the cane.

Better still was his description of a time with Elaine, shortly after they'd married. They had been in Yorkshire, visiting his old school where they had met. It had made them feel more melancholy than anything, and they'd wanted to do something rude to lift their spirits. That night they'd bought fish and chips in a shop in Settle. In an alley Percy had put the lot down the back of Elaine's panties, cod, chips, mushy peas, all squelching around over her bum and pussy. She'd wet herself in it and he'd had her over a wall, with her panties pulled aside and his cock in the mess.

I was getting turned on, and he knew it, so he described a punishment he'd given Susan. She had a thing about frilly knickers, finding wearing them a deep humiliation. Usually he would just make her wear them under a short skirt, so there was a chance the wind would lift it and people would see them. She'd been like that when they went to a lonely beach in Norfolk and he'd made her strip and go in just her frillies, nothing else, all one afternoon. When she needed the loo he had made her do it in her frillies. They'd fucked like that, on the beach, in broad daylight, with Susan kneeling and the back of her frillies pulled down to show what she'd done.

My own bladder had begun to feel strained, and I was feeling naughty enough to want to come. Knowing how much Percy enjoyed seeing girls wet themselves, the opportunity seemed too good to waste, especially with what I was wearing. This was my most expensive dress, a simple but beautiful red silk affair given to me as a present by a hopeful admirer. It was by some designer, but I couldn't even remember the name although I had been assured it cost more than I earned in a month.

Really I prefer girls, but three types of men excite me, more or less. The powerful, Neanderthal type, with his brain wired straight to his cock, the sort who just want to fuck me because I'm female. Really skilled eroticists, who can handle me to perfection and who understand every nuance of sadomasochistic play. Dirty old men who just want to get my panties down and spank me until I howl.

The man who had given me the dress was none of these, and I shouldn't really have accepted it, especially when he knew full well I was in a cosy lesbian relationship with Amber. Wearing it had made me feel beholden and a bit uncomfortable, and I began to wonder if it might not be fun to just let go and pee in it. Percy was still talking, but I interrupted him, offering to pee for him in the bathroom, or, if he didn't mind, right where I was sitting.

'My dear Penny,' he replied, 'a chair is just a chair, and may be cleaned, even replaced if necessary. The memory of you wetting yourself in a pure silk designer dress will linger with me until my dying day.'

That was all the encouragement I needed. Cocking one leg over the arm of the chair, I pulled up my dress, exposing my legs and then the crotch of my panties and my tummy. Percy smiled and folded his hands over his gut. My bladder felt tight, straining, but I held back, enjoying that blissful moment before doing something really dirty, the moment I could stop but knew I wouldn't.

'Come on, Penny, pee-pee time,' Percy urged.

I just let go, letting it well up out of my pussy, into my panties and down between my bum cheeks. It started to squirt as it got stronger, spraying out of my panty crotch in a little fountain, over my thighs and dress. I tugged my dress high, baring my breasts as a warm, wet pool of pee formed under my bum. It was really coming, spattering on the carpet, soaking the chair and my dress and my panties. The feeling was glorious, abandoned, really dirty, just sitting there and wetting myself in my clothes and all over the floor. My breasts were in my hands, the nipples hard and tight between my fingers. The soggy panties felt tight on my bum, wet with pee, see-through with pee, so that Percy could see the outline of my pussy with the piss spraying out of the centre.

My hands went to my thighs, stroking the wet flesh, then to my pussy, cupping it, feeling the piddle run out through my fingers. It was hot, the temperature of my body, hot and wet and lovely. I pulled my hands up myself, smearing the clear warm liquid on my tummy and over my breasts. My bottom was soaking, my dress ruined, and I was in absolute ecstasy. I held the moment as my pee continued to come, spraying out over me and around me, squirming my wet bum in it as Percy watched.

The gush died to a trickle and stopped, leaving me sodden and happy, with my thighs spread wide. I wanted to come and reached down, intent on pulling my panties aside to show him my pussy as I frigged off, only for him to raise a finger and wag it at me in admonition.

'You are disgusting,' he said. 'You should be spanked immediately, in your wet panties to remind you of your sin.'

'Yes, please. Hard.'

'This really will be rather messy,' he remarked, 'but no matter. Turn over.'

I obeyed, wriggling round in the chair to present Percy with my bum while my tits went in the pee pool.

He stood up and I wiggled for him. I could feel the pee dripping from my panties and on to the floor, while I was picturing how I would look, with my sodden dress clinging to my bum cheeks and the piss-wet panty crotch showing under the hem.

'Dirty, dirty, little girl,' he said as he came to stand over me. 'You need this. You need this badly.'

I looked back and nodded. Percy took my dress and jerked it up, exposing my bum with the cheeks straining out the soaked panty seat. I knew they would be completely see-through, with my cheeks bulging out around the edges, wet and pink, ready for spanking. As I stuck it up hopefully he put a hard slap across it, sending pee droplets spraying out. It stung and tingled afterwards. Spanking always hurts more on wet skin, and what better way to wet it than have the girl pee herself before she's beaten?

Percy gave me two more hard swats across the wet seat of my panties, then took hold of the waistband and pulled them up hard, spilling my cheeks out around the edges and drawing the crotch tight up between my pussy lips. Three more sound smacks landed on my bum, pinking my flesh and drawing little squeals from my lips.

'I think we had better pull these down now, don't you?' Percy asked. 'Then I shall spank you properly.'

'Yes, please,' I sighed. 'Pull my panties down. Spank me well. Punish me.'

Percy took hold of my waistband, lifting it and starting to pull. I savoured the moment as my pee-sodden panties were peeled off my bum, leaving me wet and ready. The pee was trickling down my cheeks as they were laid bare. My bumhole was showing, and my pussy, just as I like it, just as it should be for a punished girl, rude, with no modesty whatever.

He settled my panties around my thighs, inside out, with my pee dripping slowly from the waistband. The spanking started again, sharp, quick fingertip slaps, bringing the heat to my bottom and pussy. I was feeling my tits as he did it, with my eyes shut, focusing on the exquisite pleasure of being spanked into heat while my bum was wet with my own pee.

Percy's slaps became harder, slowly building up in tune with my rising pleasure, the mark of a true expert, a real spanking master, handling me like the little slut I am. The pain began to grow, his hand smacking down on both cheeks at once, firm, admonishing, teaching me my place. His arm went around my waist, taking me in his firm, masculine grip and lifting my bottom. I cocked my legs open, showing off, displaying my wet pussy and the hairy crease of my bum, with the little pink and brown hole in the middle. He smacked me full across both cheeks, then tightened his grip and really started to lay in.

I let my feelings show as I was beaten, kicking and squealing and trying not to giggle too much. In his mind I knew he was punishing a bad little girl, giving me a well-deserved spanking for wetting myself. My fantasy was the same – beaten bare-bottomed for being disgusting – but I was so excited it was hard not to be eager and wanton and as my bottom got hotter the urge to have my pussy filled grew and grew.

It was Percy who gave up in the end, stopping suddenly and grabbing at his fly. I waited, expectant as he fiddled with the buttons, then sighing deeply as he pressed his cock and balls in between my hot, wet buttocks and began to squirm them around against my bumhole. It took him ages to get erect, but I didn't care. I was enjoying it too much, with his genitals between my open cheeks and his belly slapping and squashing against my wet skin. When he was hard he entered me, fucking me with a quick flurry of pushes while he held me by the hips.

I'd known he would do it. He always did if he had the chance. His cock came out of my pussy and he rubbed it on my bumhole. I just sighed, having learned to accept buggery when I was still a virgin. Again and again he dipped his cock in my pussy and slimed my juice on my bumhole, until I was greasy and ready, with my ring relaxed. He put his cock to the middle and pushed. There was no pain at all as my rectum filled, just the lovely, rude feeling of a cock sliding up my bottom-hole, right in, until his belly and thighs were pushed against my sore, wet flesh.

I began to frig as Percy buggered me, slowly, teasing my pussy lips and rubbing his balls on myself each time he pushed in. Again and again I put a finger in my vagina, taking pleasure in its being empty while my bumhole was full of cock. Feeling that my vagina had been abandoned was part of the thrill of being buggered, and I was getting it now, fingering the empty hole while my bottom-hole strained on its load. I knew he wanted me to come first, so my anus would tighten on his prick, but I had other ideas and held off, just enjoying being sodomised in my own piss pool and teasing myself slowly towards climax.

Percy gave in in the end, spunking deep up my bottom as he panted and grunted his pleasure out over me. As his cock left my anus the sperm began to run out, dribbling down over my pussy to mingle with my pee and my juice. I started to frig in earnest, alternately slapping the mess over my pussy and rubbing my clitty. My pussy and bumhole started to pulse and more goo ran out down over my hand. I gripped my panties and twisted them hard, feeling the pee squirt out of the sodden cotton. My mouth was gaping, and if Percy had offered me his cock I'd have sucked it clean for him and come while I did it. He didn't – but he did something better. As my orgasm started I felt something hot splash my thigh and I knew he was pissing on me. I screamed out, begging for it, and the hot stream hit my hand, splashing in my panties and over my bum, then in a high arc to wet my hair and back, adding to the ruination of my dress. More hit me as he aimed lower again, filling my vagina until it ran out from the hole. I screamed and screamed, and as I hit the very highest peak of my ecstasy he did the perfect thing, pissing up my still-open bumhole.

It was truly superb, a high of highs, coming and coming in a mess of pee and spunk while the man who'd had me urinated in my anus. I felt it go in and I felt it squirt out as my muscles spasmed in orgasm, but it was still coming, running in and then spraying out, running in and then spraying out, until finally I could hold the climax no more and sank gasping into the chair. Percy finished off over my bum and into my panties, chuckling to himself as he soiled me and I mumbled my thanks over and over.

It took ages to clear up, and I did most of it, mopping and scrubbing on my knees in the nude while he sipped a brandy and pointed out bits that I'd missed. When I was finally clean and dry I was happy to stay naked, just to enjoy my nudity for its own sake while he stayed fully dressed. I stayed like that for a while, until he suggested that I should put on a pair of white cotton panties, of which he had a large collection. That was fine by me, so I chose a pair with a nice snug fit, only to be told to put on a pair a size smaller. I obeyed, then accepted a brandy and curled up on the floor at his feet, positioned to give him a good view of my panty-clad bottom.

'You love panties, don't you?' I asked, even though it was stating the obvious.

'Knickers, please,' he answered. 'Panties is such an American word. Yes, I do. To me a girl in just her knickers is more erotic by far than a naked girl.'

'I read something by a feminist once who said that men liked panties . . . sorry, knickers, because they were scared of what was underneath.'

'*What?* Nonsense, sheer drivel, a theory that reveals only the ignorance and prejudice of the theorist. No, no, the true joy of knickers is in taking them down. A girl's knickers are like the wrappings on a present. You would never deliver one without them, but ultimately they must come off. Or down, anyway – the analogy is perhaps imperfect.'

'You're right. In fact, I think the same woman said that knickers are only erotic to men, but *I* get a kick out of them so you can be sure that one's rubbish. Knickers are so intimate it's hard not to associate them with sex.'

'I agree, but opinions vary. Elaine adored the whole concept. Gabriella wouldn't wear any if she could help it. Susan felt it was a punishment to be made to wear frilly ones. Each person is ultimately an individual, and those who speak of "women" and "men" as if each were a distinct and homogeneous group deserve nothing but contempt.'

'True,' I agreed. 'Even the colour is important for me. Black or red to vamp in, pretty, pale colours to show off in, white for a girl who's going to get a spanking.'

'Absolutely,' he went on. 'Although there too there is variation. Anna wore plain white knickers because she thought they'd make her bottom less enticing. She was wrong. Elaine wore them because she felt it was proper, and that made peeing in them all the more exciting. Pippa, who wasn't there today, got made to wear them and so came to link them with sex.'

'Who was the rudest?' I asked.

'The rudest?' Percy pondered. 'Hmm, not an easy question. Elaine could be quite filthy at times. Gabriella was worse, and certainly the most promiscuous. Then, she never had any concept of moral values anyway. There was a little nurse called April who delighted in being given an enema, but it got to her – she wasn't truly abandoned. You yourself, after your behaviour in Brittany last summer, might well qualify. Little Natasha, too, has her moments. Sophie has done some extraordinary things with wine, although not with me.

243

No, it is impossible to say. Each girl has her vices, and in each vice there is virtue. Which is the rudest? Who can say?'

'OK, then, what's perfect for you.'

'Perfection? Perfection is a girl, a girl with a full, round, female bottom, presented for a bare-bottom spanking in nothing but her knickers: tight, white, cotton knickers.'

Percy licked his lips as he repeated the words: tight, white, cotton.

NEXUS BACKLIST

This information is correct at time of printing. For up-to-date information, please visit our website at www.nexus-books.co.uk

All books are priced at £6.99 unless another price is given.

ABANDONED ALICE	Adriana Arden 0 352 33969 1	☐
THE ACADEMY	Arabella Knight 0 352 33806 7	☐
ALICE IN CHAINS	Adriana Arden 0 352 33908 X	☐
AMAZON SLAVE	Lisette Ashton 0 352 33916 0	☐
THE ANIMAL HOUSE	Cat Scarlett 0 352 33877 6	☐
THE ART OF CORRECTION	Tara Black 0 352 33895 4	☐
AT THE END OF HER TETHER	G.C Scott 0 352 33857 1	☐
BARE BEHIND	Penny Birch 0 352 33721 4	☐
BELINDA BARES UP	Yolanda Celbridge 0 352 33926 8	☐
BENCH MARKS	Tara Black 0 352 33797 4	☐
THE BLACK GARTER	Lisette Ashton 0 352 33919 5	☐
THE BLACK ROOM	Lisette Ashton 0 352 33914 4	☐
CAGED [£5.99]	Yolanda Celbridge 0 352 33650 1	☐
CHERRI CHASTISED	Yolanda Celbridge 0 352 33707 9	☐
COMPANY OF SLAVES	Christina Shelly 0 352 33887 3	☐

------- ✂ -----------------------------

Please send me the books I have ticked above.

Name   ....

Address   ....

            ....

            ....

            .... Post code ....

Send to: **Virgin Books Cash Sales, Thames Wharf Studios, Rainville Road, London W6 9HA**

US customers: for prices and details of how to order books for delivery by mail, call 1-800-343-4499.

Please enclose a cheque or postal order, made payable to **Nexus Books Ltd**, to the value of the books you have ordered plus postage and packing costs as follows:
   UK and BFPO – £1.00 for the first book, 50p for each subsequent book.
   Overseas (including Republic of Ireland) – £2.00 for the first book, £1.00 for each subsequent book.

If you would prefer to pay by VISA, ACCESS/MASTERCARD, AMEX, DINERS CLUB or SWITCH, please write your card number and expiry date here:

....

Please allow up to 28 days for delivery.

Signature ....

Our privacy policy

We will not disclose information you supply us to any other parties. We will not disclose any information which identifies you personally to any person without your express consent.

From time to time we may send out information about Nexus books and special offers. Please tick here if you do *not* wish to receive Nexus information.   ☐

------- ✂ -----------------------------